MOVING TARGET

Born in Essex in 1964, Ross Kemp worked for the BBC for ten years and ITV for four years as an actor. He then had a change of career and started making documentaries. He has subsequently been nominated for three BAFTAS for his series on Afghanistan, Gangs and Africa. He and his team won the BAFTA for best factual series in 2006. He is a patron of Help for Heroes and has spent time on the front line in Afghanistan with 1 Royal Anglian, 5 Scots, 16 Air Assault and 45 Commando.

Also by Ross Kemp

Devil to Pay
Warriors: British Fighting Heroes
Gangs
Gangs II
Ross Kemp on Afghanistan
Ganglands: Brazil
Pirates
Ganglands: Russia

ROSS
KEMP
MOVING
TARGET

arrow books

First published in Great Britain in 2012 by
Arrow Books
Random House, 20 Vauxhall Bridge Road,
London SW1V 2SA

www.randomhouse.co.uk

Addresses for companies within The Random House Group Limited can be
found at: www.randomhouse.co.uk/offices.htm

The Random House Group Limited Reg. No. 954009

A CIP catalogue record for this book
is available from the British Library

ISBN 9780099550624

The Random House Group Limited supports The Forest Stewardship Council
(FSC®), the leading international forest certification organisation. Our books
carrying the FSC label are printed on FSC® certified paper. FSC is the only
forest certification scheme endorsed by the leading environmental
organisations, including Greenpeace. Our paper procurement policy
can be found at: www.randomhouse.co.uk/environment

Typeset by SX Composing DTP, Rayleigh, Essex
Printed and bound in Great Britain by
CPI Group (UK) Ltd, Croydon, CR0 4YY

No one knows who they are selling drugs for, who they are killing, or for which cartel.

Antonio Brijones, former member of the Juarez
Calle Jon gang, Mexico

The crackdown against cross-border traffic [between Mexico and the US] [is] forcing Mexican cartels to shift their attentions and potentially their operations, and focus more closely on Europe.

Ed Vulliamy, *Amexica: War Along the Borderline*,
2010, quoting Eduardo Medina Mora, Mexican
Attorney General

Chapter 1

'Nick. It's Andy here. Andy Lyons.'

I know something's up straight away – I can hear the tension in his voice. I haven't heard from Andy in ten years. He was a raw squaddie of seventeen when I was doing my last couple of years in the Royal Anglian Regiment. I sort of took him under my wing. He was an Essex boy like me, came from a pretty rough background, and last time I saw him we were both still in the army.

I might have kept in contact more, but a life in special forces, particularly a regiment as secretive as 14 Company – 'the Det' to friends – doesn't really encourage you to keep up with old acquaintances. Too many questions, really. Andy knows nothing about that side of my life, or at least I thought he didn't.

'Andy. Good to hear from you. How did you get my number?'

'Your wife gave it to me. I got hold of her through Facebook.'

'How did you find her on that?' I always told my

1

ex-wife Rachel never to use our married name in anything she did.

'Friends of friends. I just asked if anyone knew where you'd gone and someone had her contact. Look, I'm in a spot of bother.'

Andy was always the king of understatement, and I've already guessed he isn't calling me up because he couldn't find a golf partner.

'Yeah?'

'Yeah. Look, can we have a chat?'

'What's on your mind?'

'I'd rather talk face to face if that's OK.'

In the background I can hear a kid's voice – sounds like a little girl – asking him who he's talking to.

'Give me five minutes, precious,' he says.

'More kids?'

'Four now.'

'You only had one when I last saw you. How old is she now?'

'Sixteen.'

'Christ. That went quick.'

'Yeah. Look, can I come down and see you?'

'Sounds like you've got your hands full. I'll come up and see you.'

'No, don't do that. I don't want to trouble you.'

'You won't be troubling me. I'll be troubling you for a few beers and a curry, as well as a bed for the night.'

'That'd be great, mate, no problem.'

Truth is that I feel like a bit of a break. It's early November, wet and grey, and I've spent a hard summer working out of Southampton on a little sailing boat – corporate trips, stag nights, hen nights if I'm lucky. And though I like the work, there's only so much fascination to be had from watching Derek from Sales failing to grasp what you've told him for the nineteenth time. I'm missing the company of my old soldier mates.

I drive up from Southampton in my knackered old Mondeo. I'd like a nicer car, but it's a lifestyle choice really. I love sailing, so I do something interesting that I get paid peanuts for, thereby being forced to drive a fourth-hand car. For me that's better than being paid more but being stuck indoors.

Andy has moved up in the world – a big modern house to the north of Cambridge on a new estate, double garage, four bedrooms, smart car on the drive. Very nice – apart from BT tearing up the street as I arrive.

He meets me at the door. Some people change a little over the years, some a lot. Andy's changed a lot. He's gone completely grey since the last time I saw him, and his face is showing the wear of his forty-a-day habit. He doesn't look fit any more either – belly on him, and an extra chin.

'Come in,' he says, above the sound of a pneumatic drill.

'Are we going to be able to talk with that banging away?'

'Sod's law,' he says. 'They dug a hole a week ago, left it and now they've started again.'

As he speaks, the drill stops.

'Knew it couldn't last long,' he says. 'I bet that hole's still there in thirty years' time. Look on the bright side, though: they'll be able to bury me in it.'

He laughs and so do I. We go in. It's a nice set-up:

a clean, modern room with a big basket of toys at one end, a deep pale carpet – which is brave with a six-year-old in the house – one of those big corner sofa units in deep brown. We talk some crap for a while, crack a couple of beers. As he drinks, I can see that his hands are shaking.

'What's up?'

'It's my job. I work for the Borders Agency at Cambridge Airport. I'm the operations director there.'

'Congratulations.'

'Yeah. Thanks. Only, well, I . . . I got given this the other day.'

He goes out of the room for a bit and comes back with what used to be called an attaché case – combination-number job. He puts it on the dining table and clicks it open. I've been in enough sting operations to be quite good at evaluating amounts of cash. I'd say there was about fifty grand in fifty-pound notes in there.

Then he takes something out of his pocket and puts that on the table. It's a bullet – a 7.62 rifle cartridge. If the world has a favourite bullet, that's it. It's what an AK-47 takes. You don't often see them in England.

'Who gave you them?'

'Some new bloke at work. Me and a few of the boys go for a drink on a Friday night at a pub near the airport. I only ever have a pint and then walk home over the common. That's when this geezer comes up to me, Spanish I reckon and sticks that case in my hand. Says I've got a new employer.'

'What did you say?'

'I told him to fuck off. Then he opens his coat and shows me a gun.'

'What sort of gun?'

He's toying with his bottle of Beck's, rolling it around in his hands. I've never seen him so nervous.

'Snub-nosed revolver of some sort. To be honest, I was a bit too panicked to really concentrate.'

That's potentially bad news. The .38 is what I might carry if I wanted to hit someone. Light, small, five shots, doesn't jam. Most British gangsters don't have the contacts to get something like that and arse around with converted starting pistols. So we know this guy is serious. Or at least, he's got a serious gun.

'So you reported it straight away?'

Andy looks at the floor.

'No.'

'Why not?'

'He said, "Say hello to Shelley and the kids for me."'

'When did this happen?'

'Two days ago.'

'Anything else?'

'I got a call on my mobile. Flight A231 from Valladolid on Friday will have its cargo sent through without inspection.'

Well, there'll be nothing in that cargo, that's for sure. Whoever's doing this will want to make certain Andy is on side before risking any valuable merchandise.

'You should inform your bosses,' I say.

Andy's eyes go to the bullet.

'It's a game-changer, Andy. You're thinking about this all wrong. You're thinking, "How do I hang on

to this lovely life I've worked out for myself here?"
Answer is that you don't. This is going to need police
protection, real investigation and these guys inside
before you'll be safe. Your job at Cambridge is over
– at least for the meanwhile – and you'll have to go
somewhere else. You've got a choice. Prison,' I tap
the money, 'the local crem,' I tap the bullet, 'or you
get protection, get moved in your job and start again
somewhere else. Best case, they're a bunch of plastic
gangsters chancing their arm, they get nicked, it's all
over.'

'Do plastic gangsters have fifty K to throw at
people?'

I don't bother answering his question, because he
knows what the truth is. Of course they don't. They'd
come in with just the threat, I'm sure. So what is the
truth? Who knows?

'You need the police. Just by having me here
you've made your decision. If they know about
Shelley, they might have some sort of bug in the
house, have you under surveillance.' Paranoid?
Maybe, but I'd rather be paranoid and alive than
chilled out and dead.

'I hadn't thought about a bug. Jesus.'

'As soon as you tell your boss, you're useless to
them. Completely useless. So then they've got to
come after you out of revenge. Which they could do
but it doesn't make good business, does it? They've
already staked fifty grand on you. Why would they
want to risk prison by killing someone for no profit?'

'I hope they're listening to that,' says Andy.

We both laugh a bit.

'Why did you call me, Andy?'

'We always got on. I was trying to think of someone who might be able to advise me, and you were the only bloke I thought might have a clue. You always seemed to know what you were doing when we were in the Battalion.'

'That it?'

'I know you did some stuff after.'

'How do you know that?'

'I saw you. I was on foot patrol in Northern Ireland and I saw you sitting in a car. I guessed, you know, you weren't there on your holidays.'

I'd told my commanding officer it wasn't a good idea deploying me at the same time as my old regiment. He'd told me to shut up and do my job. Seems I was right to consider it a risk.

'Let's go for a drive,' I say, passing him my phone.

We leave the house and get into my car. I've had half a can of beer and normally wouldn't like to drive – particularly in these circumstances. You'd be amazed how much even that amount can affect you. It might not matter too much if you're just bimbling down the shops, but if you're called upon to do something a bit more demanding, it can make a difference.

Still, the advantage of the car is that, if we are under surveillance, it's much harder for anyone to listen to what we're saying. I'm not anticipating having to get lively behind the wheel, but you never know.

I start to drive into Cambridge. I check the mirror. No one following straight away.

'Call your boss,' I say. 'Your wife's gone away with the kids?'

'Yeah.'

'They're going to need protection too. I'll lose any tail and then I'll drive to whatever cop shop we need to go to.'

Andy looks white as a sheet, but he makes a call to his supervisor. Luckily this is the sort of thing the Border Agency plan for and he has an idea of what to do. We're to meet him at a hotel in central Cambridge and he'll have the cops with him. Andy gives him the address of his wife and kids, which is reassuringly up in Cumbria at her mum's.

We pull in to the University Arms hotel – a big, imposing Victorian building with a weird modern basement car park stuck on the front – and I'm immediately relieved to see a man Andy appears to know in the foyer. It's his boss, a man called Philip Patterson. He wants to know who I am, and Andy explains that I'm a mate of his who he's asked to come over and look after him until he gets to the police.

'Well you can go now,' says Patterson. 'We've got a room upstairs to interview Andy, and there are two armed coppers here.' He nods to a couple of blokes behind him who are leafing through some flyers on the reception desk, trying to look inconspicuous.

'Thanks,' says Andy.

'Sure,' I say. I shake his hand. 'You've done the right thing, mate.'

'Where are you going to stay?'

'I haven't really thought about it.' I'd sort of assumed I'd crash at his house, but clearly that's off the agenda now.

'Look, let me put you up here, it's the least I can do.'

I tell him I'll be all right at a service station hotel, but he insists on checking me in.

'Well, cheers,' I say.

'Yeah, we'll meet up for a beer when this is all over. And here, I owe you your petrol as well.' He takes out his wallet.

'Forget it. Just stay safe.'

'I will.' We briefly embrace. As I turn towards the car park to collect my bag from the car, I have no idea that that's the last time I'll see Andy alive.

Chapter 2

Cambridge is a nice town. The day is bright blue, cold and lovely, and I think that I'll have a look around the place. To be honest, I've always fancied a go on one of those punts, but it's not the sort of thing you do on your own. I walk around for a bit, marvelling at the architecture of the university. Some of this stuff goes back to the fourteenth century. The city's like something out of a film – one of those ones about an England you don't think exists if you come from a council estate in Southend: tall spires everywhere, girls with scarves flying behind them riding bikes with baskets on, loads of public schoolboys – a few of whom will doubtless end up as army officers within not too long a time.

I'm thinking about Andy and hoping he's going to be OK. Well, I know he's going to be OK now, because he's in police protection. Who's behind this? Whoever it is has got some nuts and doesn't mind taking a fifty-thousand-pound punt. Really, it doesn't make sense. I know drug dealers sometimes use this tactic in South America and South Africa, even in the States. But it depends on a corrupt system. This is why it works in places like Colombia and Mexico, where – let's be honest – corruption among the police has got to be widespread. If you can't rely on the police to protect you, then the choice between cash and a bullet – the silver or the lead, they call it – becomes pretty unavoidable. Here, though, while police corruption isn't unheard of, it is rare. And they're not going to stand by while some drug dealer murders you and your family. Or worse, as is the case in some parts of the world, do it themselves. So, like I say, it doesn't make sense. The drug dealers would need more clout to be able to make their threats real.

I decide to sit down and have a cigarette at a big pub near the river, a swift coffee under the patio heaters of its concrete plaza before the drive back to Southampton. It does make me laugh when I consider that in a city of lovely little old boozers, all nooks and crannies, real ale and history, I've picked the only one that looks like an Essex supermarket, but hey, you go with what you know.

I draw in the smoke and start to think. Maybe I'm jumping to conclusions in thinking it's drugs. Andy said it was a Spanish bloke who approached him. I know there's an awful lot of drug money there, and it's a favoured point of access to Europe for the South American drug gangs. It helps if you share a language with the people you're dealing with. You also understand them culturally a bit better, know how they're going to react if you squeeze them in certain ways. Terrorism's caught up in narco money, so I do know a bit about this. The 500-euro note – the money launderer's friend, because large amounts of cash can be shifted about using relatively few notes – crops up more in Spain than it does anywhere else in Europe. Like, seriously more. A quarter of all bills in circulation are in Spain – far more than you'd expect. On the positive side, they're useful to the police because they use them to track money laundering.

All this is in my head when I notice a flash of sunlight from up on the bridge. I don't think anything of it, but it takes my eye. It's then that I notice a person with a camera turning away slightly and realise that he's got a big zoom lens on it. Now, I have spent long enough doing surveillance and long enough in the holiday business to know the difference between the cameras you need for each. In the Det – and the Special Reconnaissance Regiment, as it became – we had extensive training in photography. So I know you don't need a 500mm telephoto lens when you're out and about snapping the architecture – not unless you're doing some serious detail. I watch as he pans around. The camera pauses on the balcony of the restaurant across the road, then moves to the street that leads up to the bridge before lingering on me. He's using completely the wrong lens for the job he seems to be doing – taking photos of street scenes. Now, if this bloke was directing his camera up at some gargoyle on one of the churches, I'd regard it as completely normal to be using a lens like that. However, he isn't. He's pointing it at me sitting outside a pub that looks like a 1980s Sainsbury's. So why would you want a photo of an ex-squaddie smoking in front of a pig's ear of a building when you can go and snap some fit student bird outside a five-hundred-year-old architectural masterpiece? I know this sort of slice-of-life stuff appeals to some art students, but there's got to be a limit, hasn't there?

Am I paranoid? Maybe. He could just be a bad photographer with more money than sense to spend on flashy lenses. But it won't hurt to go and have a quiet word with him.

I get up and walk towards the bridge, pausing a moment as if looking out over the water. From the corner of my eye I see him starting to walk away. He's wearing boating shoes, blue jeans, a red checked shirt, one of those padded gilets and a Ferrari baseball cap. He's around thirty-three, six foot one, dark hair, pale complexion. He's carrying a big blue camera bag over his shoulder, so, as I suspected, he has a few more lenses to choose from.

I walk along after him, not too quick at first, but before long he starts to run.

Seems the pretence is over. The thing is, he's got a big bag weighing him down and a camera round his neck. He runs about two hundred yards up the street of half-timbered houses and shops till he reaches a main road which is temporarily too busy to cross. That's when I catch up with him. Whoever this bloke is, he isn't a major-league drug gangster. He looks about fit to faint.

He turns sharply left and runs down the main road towards a traffic island. There are some big gates to a park there. This is ideal. We can find a shady nook and have a little chat.

I catch up with him and take him by the elbow.

'Do you know who I am?'

'No.'

'Well, if you don't want to find out, I suggest you come with me.'

'I don't know anything about this.' His voice is not as middle class as his look.

'About what?'

He starts to stammer and I walk him into the park. There's a bench and I tell him to sit on it.

'You've got no right to question me.'

'And you've got no right to photograph me and I've got no right to ram that camera up your arse. I should sit down if I were you.' He catches my look that tells him he'd better do as I say for his own good.

He sits down.

'Who are you?'

'Kevin.'

'Kevin what?'

'Kevin Barstow.'

'And why's a nice boy like you taking photos of a nasty man like me?'

'I wasn't, I . . .'

I take the camera off his neck, turn it on and scroll through the memory. There's photos of me at the pub, and also some of me and Andy going into the hotel the night before. Really disturbingly, there are about ten of Andy picking his kids up from school.

'You want to explain?'

'There's nothing *to* explain.'

'I'm losing my patience here, Kevin.'

He swallows hard. 'I'm a private investigator. I've been hired to follow that man who was with you last night and build up a picture of who he is and where he goes. The ones by the school are old photos. I just haven't deleted them.'

'You've sent these off to someone?'

'Yeah.'

'Who?'

'I can't say, client confidentiality.'

'Believe me, Kev, you can say and you will.'

'I don't know. I was given a payment and an email address to send them to, that's all.'

'So you don't know who you're working for?'

'No. I—'

'Yeah?' I don't let him finish. This idiot hasn't bothered to check out his client, meaning he's aided and abetted intimidation at the very least, potentially far worse.

'If you hurt me, I'll go straight to the police,' says Kevin.

'No you won't,' I say. 'I will.' I take out my phone and dial Andy's number. No reply.

I don't really know what else to do, so I call 999, explain that I've detained someone who might pertain to an important investigation. Ten minutes later a police car pulls up, and there's a bit of arguing because the cops haven't heard about the threat to Andy.

Still, they listen to what I have to say, look at the photos and try to check out my story. Eventually they manage to get through to CID, who confirm what I say. They nick the private eye and ask me to attend the station to make a statement, which they say might take a while because they'll have to decide who's going to interview me and who I'm going to make my statement to.

You would imagine that there's lots of inter-agency co-operation between the Border Agency and the police, the police and the intelligence services, the intelligence services and the army. Sometimes there is and it works well. Other times, particularly at the start of an investigation, the channels of communication aren't there.

I expect it's going to take a bit of time to sort all this out, so I relax. To be honest, I'm feeling good that I've provided the cops with something to go on. The thing I'm worrying about most is whether the hotel are going to charge me for overstaying my parking permit.

The private eye is taken down to a cell and I'm left to mooch about drinking coffee by the custody desk, watching the various lowlifes being brought in, processed and released. I've been there about five hours and have virtually read the print off the posters on the wall when there's a big buzz and lots of cops running about. Some sort of emergency. No one tells me anything, though. All that happens is that I'm moved out of the main area into a blank little interview room where the only entertainment is counting the wiggles on the polystyrene tiles on the ceiling. I've been there another couple of hours when a big plain-clothes copper comes in.

'Mr Kane?'

'Yeah.'

'Detective Inspector Peters.'

Behind him are three other blokes – also plain-clothes coppers as it turns out. They introduce themselves. Peters is Cambridgeshire CID, there's a Brightson from the Border Agency, a Philips from SOCA – the Serious Organised Crime Agency – and a Davies from the Met CID.

This is the first time that I get an inkling something's up.

'Can you describe your relationship with Mr Lyons?' says Peters.

'We're old army friends.'

'And you happened to be visiting?'

'No, he called me up and asked me for advice, so I came up to see him.'

'What sort of advice?'

'He said he'd been threatened at work.'

'And what did you advise him.'

'To report the matter immediately. What's happened?'

He ignores my question. 'Are you aware of Mr Lyons being caught up in any criminal activity?'

'Depends what you mean by caught up. I'd say someone threatening your life unless you accept a bribe is fairly caught up.'

'He hadn't, to your knowledge, had any involvement with organised crime before?'

'No. I'd be very surprised if he had.'

Peters nods.

He then has me run through my entire association with Andy, my whole military career. He gets the hump when I tell him there's lots I can't discuss, but there's no way round that. I've signed the Official Secrets Act and I'd be breaking the law by telling him.

The 'This is Your Life' interview goes on for about an hour before Peters sits up straight and says:

'You need to know that Andy Lyons was killed at about six thirty this evening.'

I'm reeling, shocked. 'How? He was under your protection!'

'The policemen protecting him were killed too. We're still establishing the details, but there was some sort of explosion.'

I can hardly speak. No one has ever used that sort of method in England in anger. An explosion is bold; it might even suggest some sort of military connection.

'I told him he'd be all right,' I say. 'I mean, there's no point in killing him once he's gone to the police, is there? The logic doesn't add up.'

'No,' says Peters, 'it doesn't. Which is why we were hoping you might shed some light on the matter.'

'I've brought you the private detective,' I say. 'Beyond that I can't help. Did you find any listening devices in his house?' Jesus, poor Andy.

'No.'

'Did you look?'

'Yes. Or, rather, we were looking when it was attacked.'

'Is there CCTV on that estate?'

'No, but we'll check the neighbours. People sometimes have it for home security, and you never know what you can pick up.'

'More than check them,' I say. 'If there's no bug in the house, then he might have been watched from across the street. If there's an empty house there, that might be it.'

Suddenly it hits me.

'BT were digging up the street when I arrived. He said they'd done nothing on it for a week. You should check that out and make sure it really was them.'

'We'll do that.'

'Have you moved his wife and kids?'

'Yes. Look, I'm sorry, it's about assessing the nature of the threat. Normally an armed policeman on the premises is enough to deter people. Moving him to a safe house seemed a little over the top.'

I can't argue. If I'd been assessing him as a close protection subject I might have moved him, but I might not. There was no history to suggest the response was going to be this violent.

Almost without thinking, I say what's on my mind.

'This is something new, isn't it?'

'Yeah,' says Peters. 'I think it is.'

Chapter 3

It doesn't occur to me that I might become a target myself. I was an old friend of Andy's but my association with him wasn't a strong one. I've hung around in Cambridge because the cops asked me to stay for a few days and because I want time to think, free of distraction.

It must be habit that makes me move to a motorway service station hotel at Birchanger Green. It's cheap and it allows me to nip down and see a few mates in Essex, but – although I don't think about it at the time – it also makes me quite difficult to get to. Motorways are full of CCTV, as are service stations. It would be hard for someone to come for me there without getting caught on camera.

As it is, I don't much feel like catching up with old friends and need something to take my mind off the whole thing. I decide to go to the pictures in Braintree.

In retrospect this seems like a very stupid idea. But at the time, when you don't think you're a target, why would you bother taking precautions? Yeah, I was in the private eye's snaps, but he was just gathering information on Andy's associates. I mean, the threat was to Andy and his family, not his network of friends. Wrong.

I choose a comedy to watch but I'm not in the mood. To be honest, I'm not in the mood for anything. About halfway through, I finish my popcorn and decide to head back and try to get some shut-eye.

I make my way back to the car park. It's half full. Ingrained habit makes me take a quick look beneath the car – too long in Ireland to feel easy if I haven't done that. As I stand, I notice a big Merc with people in it. Four blokes. The engine's not running and I tell myself I'm being paranoid. Even if I'm not, what am I going to do about it? Running off and leaving my car seems a little over the top, confronting four blokes is a big ask and I'm going to look like a nutter if I go up and start questioning them and they've got nothing to do with this. And if they are the people who did Andy, then I'm putting myself in danger by approaching them.

Best thing is to calm down, breathe deeply, get in the car and head for the exit. So I do.

It's then that the lights on the Merc come on and it starts to follow me.

I check the mirror. Can't see anything because it has its headlights on full beam.

We make it to the barrier of the car park and I've got my window down, ready to put the ticket in. It's then that I hear the doors of the Merc open. Paranoid or not, I'm out of there. The barrier's only half way up as I gas it. It scrapes up and over the roof as the

Mondeo lurches forward. I feel a massive impact from the back and I realise the Merc has rammed me. All right, game on.

The Mondeo slews across the street with a sick squeal, hits the kerb and I know even before I try to drive forward that I'm not getting far in it.

One thing they hadn't counted on – which makes me suspect that I'm not dealing with professionals – is that all the Merc's airbags have popped, making it briefly impossible for them to see.

One thing's certain, I can't stay here. Almost before I know it, I'm out of the car and sprinting for the multi-storey.

I make it over a wall into the car park as rounds start snicking into the concrete all around me. Silenced rounds. That shouldn't make too much difference to someone reporting this. If I can stay alive, these goons haven't got long. Braintree's dead on a Sunday night, but nowhere's that dead. The police will have to be here soon. The metal jackets are whizzing past my head, slamming into cars, setting off alarms. I run in a zigzag and duck into a stairwell. Six floors. Excellent – they can't get a clear shot at me here. Once up there, however, there's no way down. Not so excellent.

I hammer up the stairs, can't even take the time to get my mobile out. As I climb, I can hear the goons slamming through the bottom floor and sounds of squealing wheels. They've got the Merc back in and are driving up the ramps to block that way of escape.

At the top, I come out into the murky Essex night, planes taking off and landing at Stansted flashing their lights in the distance. There is one bloody car parked up here. Luckily it's an old Volvo. I always carry a Leatherman. It's got a decent blade on it – which I suspect isn't strictly legal – and a host of other stuff which I've found pretty useful over the years.

Now I just use it to smash the Volvo's window. I pop the lock, get in and curl up low behind the steering wheel, almost crouching on the floor as I work the ignition. I have done this so many times in training, it's second nature. I'll have a few seconds before they realise I'm in the car – the pile of smashed glass will give it away – but it's seconds I'll need. I still haven't had time to call 999 but I'm hoping the amount of noise will alert someone. No sirens yet, though.

I hear the first goon come out of the stairwell, calling to his mate. The door goes again. The second man must be on the roof too.

One of them sticks two rounds into the car, though I'm convinced he can't see me. The windscreen shatters. He's aiming high, though I don't know what damage he expects to do firing through a Volvo's engine block.

I have the wires in my hand, my foot on the clutch and the car in first gear, ready to go. I count to ten. I want to give them time to come closer. I squeeze the wires together, the engine jumps into life and I bang the accelerator and slip the clutch, sitting up only as far as I need to see where I'm going. No need to steer, the idiot's right in front of me, with his gun up at the side of his face pointing into the clouds like Bruce Willis in *Die Hard*. Well he should have it pointed at me, because the clouds aren't going to run him over.

He's got a balaclava on, but I can see the surprise in his eyes as the car hits him. His body slams into the bonnet, his head coming through the shattered windscreen before he rolls off. I can just see his mate behind him running for the stairwell as if in slow motion. At the last second he dives aside, but I've clipped him, hit him in the leg. The Volvo slams straight into the stairwell and my face bounces off the steering wheel, breaking my nose, but the airbag saves any worse damage.

No time to worry about that. I jump out of the car. Goon two is on the floor holding his leg and screaming. His gun's been knocked from his hand and it's about ten feet away from him. He tries to crawl forward to get it but the pain's too much for him. The Merc is squealing up the ramps, must be nearly on top of us by now. I could hoof it down the stairwell, but I don't want this lot scraping their boys off the floor and running away.

I run over and pick up the revolver. It's a First World War Webley – very much a UK criminal's weapon. Probably been gathering dust in someone's grandad's loft for eighty years before getting sold off to these idiots.

I quickly check the shells. Three left.

The bloke on the floor's screaming like a little girl. I take that back. My daughter got a greenstick fracture aged nine falling off her bike and made less noise. Good, I'm glad he's in pain and I'm glad he's attracting attention.

Here comes the Merc, slewing around the corner like something out of *2 Fast 2 Furious*. I jump into the doorway and pretty much fall down the first flight of stairs. I'm now protected by the bulk of the Volvo and the brick of the top of the stairs.

A click and a dull thump. I'd know that sound anywhere – it's a tear gas canister. Sure enough, it comes rattling down the stairs towards me. Great. I can't pick it up because it's going to be red hot if it's been fired from a gun. I kick it away from me as far as I can, scrunching up my eyes in an effort to protect them. No way of running now. I get flat on the stairs and point the gun upwards. My eyes are streaming and my vision is blurred but I'm trained to resist the panic this causes. Furthermore, this stuff isn't as bad as the stuff I trained with. A bizarre thought goes through my head – I bet it's US tear gas. That's five times more dilute than the kind we use over here. It's not pleasant but, through training with it so much over the years, I've developed some resistance.

The goon comes over the top of the Volvo and peers in. He hasn't got a gas mask, which is a bit of an oversight and means he's going to have difficulty seeing me.

I see the gun come up and I fire blindly, two rounds. He disappears, and his gun comes crashing down the stairs. I'll have that. Upstairs I hear two more shots. The screaming stops and I hear the Merc pulling away. I have to get out of this stairwell – the gas is making it unbearable. I feel my way down the stairs to the floor below, get out into the car park and roll behind the nearest car. I hear the Merc going down the ramps. I also hear another car. Police? I hope so. Maybe not, though. I feel for my phone and dial 999 blind. I get through, and five minutes later I hear the sweet sound of sirens and the call 'Armed police!'

I throw out my gun. Never in my life have I been more pleased to be nicked.

Chapter 4

This time I'm taken to a police station in Essex. Not ideal, but I'm quite relaxed about it. If I stick to the facts then I should have nothing to fear. Still, I use my phone call to give John Fardy a shout. John's my old mate from back in the Det. He came from the Pay Corps, which might surprise a few people, but the Det has always been more concerned with what you can do rather than where you come from in the army. Engineers, Royal Logistics Corps, infantry regiments, tanks – you can come from anywhere. It's the only special forces regiment that's open to women. John's now a forensic accountant for SOCA – the Serious Organised Crime Agency. He finds criminals' money and tries to take it off them.

I don't have time to go into all the details, but he says he'll start some balls rolling – get me a solicitor and rattle a few cages at SOCA, see who they're thinking might be behind all this.

This makes me feel a bit better, because with John on the case, I'm sure I've got a good chance of having my story believed.

What I'm more concerned about is what happens when I get out. Andy's dead, his family are in hiding and these heavies are coming for me. And they *are* heavies, or at least one of them is, as it turns out in the police interview, which goes badly right from the off. I run them through my account of events, from coming up to Cambridge, what Andy told me, the meeting at the hotel, Andy's death, down to when I threw the gun out from behind the car.

'So you're attacked by four armed men in a deserted location, somehow you escape unharmed and yet you say the gun wasn't yours.' The copper is Richardson, an Essex CID boy, big but soft-looking. Doesn't look like a copper. His mate sitting next to him is more like what you'd expect – a hard-faced little Cockney in a nylon suit. His name is Bates.

'That's correct.'

'So what about the bullet wounds in the men we found?' asks Bates.

'I doubt any of them were me.'

'Who do you think it was then?'

'I don't know, but I'd guess the bloke in the Merc. Have you recovered that?'

He ignores my question.

'You used a gun you say you took from the body of the man you ran over and killed.'

'No. He lost the gun when I ran him over. He was still alive when I left him.'

'You're seeing why I find it difficult to believe you're an innocent party in all this. If your story was true, I'd expect you to be dead by now,' says Richardson.

'Why?'

'Because only someone very well versed in violent confrontation would have been able to defend themselves as you say you did.'

'I *am* well versed in violent confrontation.'

They both take on a look of surprise.

'I was in the army.'

'Which regiment?' asks Bates.

'The Royal Anglian with Andy. After that, I've signed the Official Secrets Act so I'd be breaking the law if I told you.'

'If I had a quid for every criminal I've met who's claimed to have been in the SAS, then I'd have enough for a very nice holiday. Every doorman in the town makes up bullshit like that,' says Bates.

'I haven't said I was in the SAS.'

'Were you?'

I just look at him. I've told him everything I'm going to on that score so there's no point wasting my breath. I could do with a smoke. I must cut that out, I think. It's a weakness and it stops me thinking straight. It's got to go, but I've been telling myself that for years.

'I suppose the army taught you how to hot-wire cars?' says Bates.

Standard training in 14 Company and the Special Reconnaissance Regiment. Not that I can tell him that, so I keep quiet.

'There's more to this than you're telling me.'

'My story is true. I've told you exactly how it happened.'

'I don't have an argument with what happened – what you say sounds plausible given the evidence. I have an argument with *why* it happened. And I don't believe you were unarmed,' says Richardson.

'But you believe that three of the guys in the car were armed with very similar weapons, and one wasn't. And I happen to have brought along my own old gun – an antique revolver just like theirs.'

'You know a lot about guns, Mr Kane?'

'A fair bit. Like I said, I was in the army.

'Are any of these men known to you?'

He takes out a folder from the briefcase at his feet. In it is a series of mug shots – shaved heads, thick necks, the Steroids R Us look.

'They're the men who were in the car.'

'And you've never met them before?'

'No.'

'Do you want me to tell you who they are?' says Richardson.

'I'd be interested, since they were trying to kill me.'

'The first one, the one you ran over, is a local boy, Andrew Mortimer – owns a gym in Braintree and runs security on eight nightclubs in Essex. Previous convictions for drug possession, GBH and making threats to kill. The second one, also a local boy, is David Mercer, only twenty-two. A series of convictions for car theft and minor drug dealing as a kid. The third is Ashley Campbell. Now he is a naughty boy. Thirty-eight years old, never been nicked for anything substantial, but people who fall out with him have a habit of disappearing, and we find a great deal of difficulty ever getting any witnesses in cases involving him. Former rated cage fighter and later power lifter. Works as a "tax man" – basically robbing drug dealers. If I was a more cynical man, I'd say that thanks to you, Mr Kane, our serious crime figures have probably been reduced by about eighty per cent in one evening. That would be the case if you weren't also contributing to those figures yourself.'

I almost have to laugh at this. 'Have you seen my car? You telling me that's the ride of a major gangster? And ask yourself another question. If I turned up there to kill those men, why did I do it on my own in a car that's registered to my name, driving through the centre of a major town full of CCTV cameras, not wearing any sort of body armour or protection? Why did I let those men get behind me in the car park?'

'You tell me,' says Bates.

'Look, someone was leaning on Andy Lyons. They killed him. They couldn't get to his family, so presumably they're now going for me. Why, I don't know.'

'They have got to his family,' says Bates.

'What?'

'His wife's mother and father's house in Cumbria was hit today.'

I put my head into my hands.

'Anyone killed?'

'The family had been moved and luckily no one was hurt.'

'Thank God for that.'

'So you're still maintaining you're just an innocent passer-by in all this?' says Richardson.

'That's what I am.'

'I think it's too much of a coincidence that someone like you – who's clearly a trained killer – happens to be caught up in it. You're working for someone, Kane, and we will find out who. As you can imagine, this is beyond CID now – it's potentially a terrorist issue, serious organised crime. Everyone from MI5 to Special Branch is going to be looking into it. Whatever you're hiding will come out.'

'I'm not hiding anything. I've told you what I know.'

'I don't believe that to be the case. The way I'm looking at this, we have enough to charge you with murder. You admit pulling the trigger, though you argue about why. You might be telling the truth, you might be lying. I think we just present the evidence and see what the court has to say.'

This isn't what I want to hear. I'm still certain I'd be acquitted, but do I want three months in nick or however long it takes to get the case together?

I shrug.

'Look, I've talked to you without a solicitor and in all openness. If that's the way you want to go then that's the way you're going to go. Take me back to my cell, I'll wait for my brief and we'll take it from there, shall we?'

The two cops look at each other.

'Sounds like a plan,' says Bates.

I'm alone in the cell, just looking at the walls, kicking all this around in my head, when it hits me – what's going on here.

Whoever made the offer to Andy was in a no-lose situation. If Andy had taken the fifty grand, they had an in at a British airport – doubtless the way they'd have liked to have done it. But if he didn't, if he took the lead rather than the silver, they won anyway – as long as they could prove the police couldn't protect him. In fact, Andy's refusal of the money and going to the police was an opportunity for these people.

They came after him with terrible and overwhelming force, taking huge risks to get at him, happy to kill not just him but his family and the man he turned to for help.

Next time an airport worker gets the cash-or-death offer, he's going to know which one to take.

But this just isn't the UK gangsters' style – even though it's UK gangsters that were trying to kill me. It's more ambitious, more violent, with access to better weaponry than most of the home-grown boys could dream about. The fact that they're targeting an airport means there are some genuine international connections here. So an international force using local help? Maybe. What are they looking to smuggle, though? Drugs? Maybe. Weapons? Well, whoever it is has access to some serious kit. But the guys who came for me didn't have anything nearly as sophisticated. And Andy said he'd been approached by a foreigner. That makes me think we have two groups of people here – the outsiders, and the local muscle they're hiring in. They're laying down a marker, raising the game in terms of violence and asking who wants to stay with them.

I look at the graffiti on the wall of the cell, breathe in the smell of disinfectant and piss, and realise that this may be the safest place I'm going to be for a very long time.

Chapter 5

I'm ninety-six hours in the cell – despite the best efforts of the brief John has sorted out for me. In that time I get all sorts of visitors – SOCA, Special Branch and even a couple of blokes from MI5. I stick to my story, and when the CCTV starts rolling in, it turns out that what I'm saying makes sense.

The cameras in the multi-storey show nothing – they just cover the entrance, and the Merc – stolen, natch – is seen coming in about ten minutes after I did. Which means someone has been following me and called in the gunmen. I can't believe I've let myself be so stupid as to be tailed. That's not going to happen again.

The cops say I'm on CCTV at the cinema, and being rammed by the Merc as I try to put my ticket into the machine. There's just enough coverage out on the street to see me running for the stairwell and them – both balaclavaed up – chasing me. The Merc is picked up again going back into the car park and coming out later. It's been found abandoned just by the entrance, and CCTV from the rest of the town makes a BMW 3 series favourite as the car the remaining shooter left in.

The bullets in the body of Dave Mercer don't match the ones from the gun I was using. They don't tell me what sort of gun that was, but I have a feeling it might be a .38 revolver.

An additional slice of good luck is that Ashley Campbell's prints are on the barrel of the gun I threw out. That is majorly sloppy of old Ash, but there again, he didn't expect that with four against one, the one would be getting the gun off him, did he?

Plus – the real clincher – photos of me and Andy Lyons at the hotel have been found in the Merc, along with three more tear gas grenades. It's plain as day that these guys were trying to hit me.

My brief – who tells me proudly that his nickname is Dumbledore – works his magic and the CPS decide that I'm telling the truth, or at least that my story holds up enough to make my acquittal quite likely.

I pick up my stuff and I'm quite surprised to see they give me the Leatherman back. Bates gives me a warning before I go.

'Fuck off out of Essex,' he says. 'I don't want this nonsense on my patch. Consider your card marked.'

'Has it occurred to you that I might be telling the truth?'

'Even if you are, you're trouble and I don't want you here. Go back to Southampton and stay there.'

There's no point in any further conversation.

My car has been impounded for evidence and there's no way I can drive it in that state anyway. Luckily I turned the mobile off when they confiscated it at the custody desk, so I call John.

'You out?'

'Yeah.'

'Wanna meet?'

'Yeah.'

'Where?'

'Usual?'

'Yeah. What time?'

'Six?'

It's four now and I'm in Braintree. Should be doable if I'm lucky with transport.

'See you there.'

I'm not going to be talking over a mobile again. I need to get moving and fast. I run out of the nick and across the road to a newsagent's, where I buy a pen – one of those with a decent softish tube on it.

I don't like what I'm about to do, but I can't be allowing anyone to get on my tail easily. In fact, let's rephrase that. I hate what I'm about to do – I can't stand thieves – but, as I've seen, my life is on the line here.

I jog out of the shop and into the city centre. I know what I'm looking for – the main office area. There it is – among all the commuter motorbikes in an office block car park, under a little shelter they've built for bikes and motorbikes. That'll protect me slightly from anyone seeing me from the building. The bike is a six-year-old GSXR 750 – 140 mph plus, with acceleration like the Starship *Enterprise*. It has exactly what I'm looking for – a D lock with its helmet attached. I pull the pen to bits and insert the barrel firmly into the lock. A bit of shoving and turning later and it comes free. This is an old Det trick – the round sort of lock is very vulnerable because these semi-soft plastic pens deform, once they're shoved into the barrel, to the shape of the key. Thirty seconds later I've got the bike, have the helmet on and am out of there. Now if someone wants to follow me, they better be on something similar or they've got no chance.

Downside is that it's freezing – no gloves, only my jumper and leather jacket for protection against the November wind. Never mind. I'd be a lot colder dead. I hit the M11 and give it some – 100 mph on this thing feels like you're standing still, and once I'm carving through the traffic, there's no way anyone in a car could possibly follow me.

I turn on to the M25 and stay there all the way around to the M40, where I peel off for Hammersmith. By five o'clock I'm there and sit down in the golden light of the pub to wait for John, delighted to be out of the wind as the feeling slowly comes back into my fingers.

John and I had a bit of bother a while back and this is where we met. No one apart from me and him would know that, so I'm safe here. It's the Andover Arms in Hammersmith – an old-fashioned boozer down by the river. I'd like a pint but I still think I need to stay sharp, so it's a Coke for me.

John's there at six on the dot. Someone holds the door for him as he comes in. John's in a wheelchair after he left both legs in Afghanistan. Remarkably, he hasn't really put on any weight. He still looks fit and his arms are like King Kong's.

I get him a drink and he passes me an A4 folder.

'I got these,' he says. There in the little see-through pockets are a series of photographs from Heathrow

Airport CCTV. There's a man at the immigration desk. He's about five foot six but with a stocky boxer's build. He's very dark in his complexion, as is his hair. He's dressed smartly in a business suit and tie.

'Who's this?'

'Alberto Soto, we think. Travelling under an alias and on a false passport, but we're sure it's him.'

'Criminal?'

'Not wanted here. But yeah. Big style.'

'Name means nothing to me.'

'No, it wouldn't. No criminal convictions, no international profile. He's number four in La Frontera cartel out of Mexico, we think. Whatever his position in the pecking order, he's the enforcer. Nickname's Mr Death and he does what it says on the tin. Turn the page.'

I do. It's more CCTV – this time from Andy's common in Cambridge.

'There's a camera on the bridge. This is from the night Andy Lyons says he was approached.'

The picture shows a blurry image. It could be Soto, definitely, or it could be any other short, dark man.

'I've got facial recognition to run a profile on it. It's eighty per cent certain it's him.'

I think for a minute. It's a big coincidence if this thug just happened to be on the common the same night Andy was threatened.

'This is unusual,' says John. 'Most coke and dope coming into Europe comes via Spain. It is flown into Britain, but normally in much smaller quantities.'

'So why's he here?'

'Things are hotting up for the cartels over here.

There's big usage in Britain – Italy's the only other EU country that comes close. But the price is falling so their margins are worse. And the further they have to bring it, the worse those margins get. If they could fly big loads directly in, things would look a lot rosier for them – they could cut a whole level out of the supply chain.'

This is beginning to make sense. I know a little bit about the drugs trade through Afghanistan because before we went out there we received a big briefing on it; and a lot of that briefing was about Mexico.

The Mexican drug gangs are very interesting. They grow dope in large quantities, but virtually all their hard drugs come from outside. They realised a long time ago that their main asset wasn't growing the product but their two-thousand-mile border with the USA, the hungriest drug market on the planet.

They've got the clout, the money and the guns to buy or threaten their way into influence in government and to gain virtual control over the police in some areas. So coke comes into Mexico very easily. From there it goes up to the USA, where the price is much higher, to be snorted by Westerners who don't know or don't care about the trail of those killed and tortured – men, women, children – it leaves behind.

When you play by Mexican rules, it means there are no rules. The gangsters target each other's families, girlfriends, priests, villages, anything they can get their hands on. I read a story about a guy who was caught with his fingers in the till by a drug lord. He was ordered to turn up to be executed at a place in the desert a week later. The man turned up. He knew that if he didn't, his whole family would be killed in the most horrific way. They cut off his fingers, made him swallow them and then peeled his face to kill him. This is common practice over there, very common. If a gangster finds out a rival is at a disco, he just sends in his guys with grenades and machine guns, starts blasting and doesn't stop until he gets the man he's looking for. Whole communities live in fear with no protection from the police, who are in the pockets of the drug lords. If you're looking for serious organised crime, it comes no more serious, no more vicious and no more deadly.

'This guy is here?'

John turns another leaf. More CCTV. It's Soto in a shop. He's buying some perfume.

'That's the morning after you were attacked,' says John. 'Guess where?'

'Go on.'

'The Arndale shopping centre, Manchester.'

'Jesus. All circumstantial so far.'

'This isn't,' says John.

He flips again. CCTV once more – Soto, this time clearly pictured in the driver's seat of a white van.

'That van was found burned out five hundred metres from Andy Lyons's in-laws' house. A stolen Audi picked him up.'

'Is this enough to convict him?'

'It will be when the cops have had a bit more time. As you can imagine, not everyone's falling over themselves to volunteer information.'

'Do they have any idea where he's gone?'

'They know exactly where he's gone.'

'Where?'

'Mexico,' says John. 'He left two days ago.'

'How?'

'New passport, flew to Spain by light aircraft, from there to Juarez.'

'Are there grounds for extradition?'

'Yeah.'

'So what are they waiting for?'

'The Good Fairy to wave her wand and everything to be OK. He's a leader of one of the biggest cartels in the country. You'd have a better chance of extraditing Acapulco beach.'

'This is an international incident. People have been shooting up the UK mainland. Are we so toothless we can't do anything?'

'We can put pressure on through the Americans, but there's only so much they can do. They have nothing on this guy officially, although they know he's up to his ears in blood. If the Americans had any real influence, they'd stop the drug war.'

'So this guy marches in, puts the fear of God into people, pulls out and . . .'

'Others come in behind, more subtly, in his wake. They've set their stall out, they'll get their in, if not at an airport then a port, through bribery or threats. Everyone's got to take them seriously now. It's their tried and trusted method of operation. *Plata o plomo*. The silver or the lead.'

'He killed my mate,' I say, 'and he tried to kill me.'

'May still be trying,' says John. 'Your picture's out there. You've got a price on your head. They're looking to make a point.'

'What about the private detective?'

'Soto flew out of Stansted.'

'So?'

'He took a detour to Cambridge before he left. He was out of the country by the time they found the detective's body.'

'He killed that PI? Jesus.'

'Yeah. There's more CCTV on that too – the PI had his own system at his flat. He got caught on it.'

'Why is he so sloppy?'

'He's not being sloppy. At first I thought it was just a cultural thing – you know, he doesn't realise just how much CCTV there is in this country. But I don't think it's that. I think he wanted to be seen. He was confident he could get out on time, confident we couldn't get him once he was in Mexico. So he has a couple of weeks' holiday over here tearing up the place, making an impression. He wants people to know – Alberto Soto, Mr Death, is here and so are La Frontera cartel, and they don't care who you are or how you're protected, if they want you dead, you're dead.'

'Why the private detective?'

'Why not. He made a mistake, he got caught by you. The way these people think, it doesn't hurt to kill him. More bad rep, more fear. That's what La Frontera do to a private investigator who doesn't even know enough to harm them. Imagine what they'll do to you if you cross them.'

'He hasn't got the manpower here, though.'

'Not yet. But he will have. He'll hire in in the short term. In the long term you'll notice a few more Mexican restaurants in Cambridge, or Bristol or Glasgow – wherever they turn a customs guy and get their in. This is new, Nick. The Mexicans are coming and the Kurds, the Turks, the local English boys and the Chinese are in trouble. Not as much trouble as the general public when the coke starts flowing in like a river, but still, a lot of trouble.'

'They can't put that many people on the ground. This isn't San Diego.'

'They don't need to. Their business model works on twelve per cent. They're scarier than the local gangsters, and they're cheaper too. If you deal with them, you get to keep much more of your money, and they don't tell you what to do. As long as you pay them for the coke, everything's sweet. When you don't . . .'

'Sour.'

'Very bloody sour.'

'Sounds like you've got your work cut out,' I say.

'Yeah, we will have.'

'Would it make it easier if you could get Soto?'

'It would certainly show that they're vulnerable. Their whole aura of fear rests on them being untouchable. *Intocable*, as they say.'

'Right,' I say. 'Have you got any contacts in the states? DEA or anyone?'

'Why?'

'Because,' I say, 'he killed my mate. And I'm going to go over there and bring him back.'

Chapter 6

I'm flying into one of the safest cities on earth, but as the plane wheels round in the sky, I've got a pretty good view of perhaps the most dangerous one too. Funny thing is, from here in the plane you can't tell them apart. Juarez and El Paso sit either side of the Rio Grande river, the great red mountain of Juarez looming out of the Mexican side, the familiar office names of AT&T, Citibank and Shell Oil lighting up the skyscrapers on the other.

It all looks like one big city, but El Paso is in the US – on the right side of the Rio Grande if you're interested in such luxuries as not getting shot, carjacked, kidnapped or raped. It's the second safest city in the US, and no surprise. This is Narco-Cop Central. There are so many law enforcement agencies here you'd be forgiven for thinking that police officers of various sorts outnumber the ordinary citizens. This is where the war on drugs is run from and where, largely, it's spectacularly lost.

On the other side of the Rio Grande sits Juarez. It is statistically the most violent city on earth. Now arguably this is because the Mexican cops actually do bother to keep statistics, whereas those in Liberia or Sierra Leone don't, but this place makes the roughest parts of British inner cities look desirable in comparison.

The flight has cost me a fortune, and I've had to lie low for a few days – crashing down at John's house. Things have been hotting up in Britain since I left. Three major English gangsters have been found dangling from straps on a forklift in a warehouse in Liverpool. Each one had been tortured and mutilated. A message was daubed on a big sheet that had been wrapped around them.

You have two choices. This is one of them.

Another very interesting thing too. The decapitated body of a Mexican has been found in the Thames near the Isle of Dogs. His head was left in a locker in a major steroid-infested gym in Millwall.

More remarkably, a YouTube video of both killings appeared for about an hour before the site took it down. The Liverpool killing was accompanied by another message – a warning to English gangsters that La Frontera is coming. The killing of the Mexican – which was protracted, gruesome and inventive – bore a message in Spanish saying: *The Spider dies in England. La Frontera washes it away.*

This brazen approach would be enough to mark out the killers as Mexican, even without the name. But La Frontera is a notorious drug cartel working out of Juarez, and the Spider – Araña – is a rival cartel from the same area. They used to be allies until La Frontera – who have massively infiltrated the army and the Mexican police – split away. This, combined with the fact that the Mexican government has launched a huge crackdown against the cartels, has turned the border area into a war zone. That's not an exaggeration. According to John, La Frontera has four thousand men at its disposal, many of them police- or army-trained and Araña not far off the same.

John – and the police – think it's likely that Soto came over to set up a branch of La Frontera in Britain. If so, this is really worrying. But why would these guys target Britain when they have a two-thousand-mile border with the USA to work? Because, says John, things are getting tough at home. There's a full-on war happening between the gangs on the Mexican border – one that has become so chaotic that it's threatening La Frontera's ability to make money, or at least making conditions hard for them. They're looking for alternative streams of income, and Britain, with its big cokehead and stoner population, is a major new market for them.

I can't worry about that – that's a job for the police. My focus is on what they can't do – bringing this scumbag who killed my mate to justice.

The break has given me a good chance to scan the Internet and find out about where I'm going. It hasn't put me off, but it certainly brings home the need for extreme caution here. Juarez is a scary place.

Three thousand women have gone missing here in the last twenty years – largely factory girls abducted by the psychos of the drugs gangs, raped, murdered and dumped. The police force is a bare minimum and people say many – if not most – of them are in the pay of the drug cartels. In response to this, the federal police have put 7,500 men in the city. There's been no let-up in the violence – again, the word is that the Federales just work for a different drugs cartel to the local boys.

Gun battles in broad daylight are a regular feature here – murders run at around twenty a day, sometimes more in a city about half the size of Manchester. This means the murder rate is getting on for a hundred times greater than it is in the UK. Ninety five per cent go unsolved.

So there you have it, as the dawn sun lights up poor little Juarez and – wittingly or not – the cause of all its troubles, the drug-hungry USA, which also happens to be the world's biggest firearms supermarket. Guns are actually difficult to get legally in Mexico – there's only one legitimate outlet and it's in Mexico City, controlled by the army. But all people have to do is nip across the border and they can get all the guns they need – provided they can smuggle them back. Combine this with the fact that about an eighth of the Mexican army deserts each year, taking all manner of military-grade hardware with it, and you can see why the drug cartels have more in common with private armies than they do with UK drugs gangs. Oh, and by the way, this is a $48 billion dollar a year trade, which – were it all to go into arms – would make it the fourth biggest spender in NATO. Obviously it doesn't all go that way, but this lot are kitted out with a lot more than Saturday-night specials. Landmines are common - place and even home-made tanks are not unknown. Some of the cartels run fleets of airliners.

There's a saying there – Juarez is the city of God, because the devil is too scared to come here.

John has put me in contact over the phone with someone he knows who used to be involved in the US Drug Enforcement Administration in El Paso. They're not going to help me directly, but they will fill me in on the local scene. He's told them I'm a journalist who's doing an article about the Mexican link to the murders in the UK, and that I'm particularly interested in Soto.

They've warned him that if I – a gringo and, to them, a Yanqui – go asking questions about Soto in Juarez, I'm very likely to find him, which won't be good for my health.

Crucially, though, it's got me an interview with the DEA and with the local sheriff. I want to go about gathering intelligence as best I can. I've sorted out a UK press card through John, who's called in a favour from a bloke at the BBC. It means absolutely nothing in the US, but it's something to show if I'm stopped. To that end, I've kitted up with a voice recorder, notepad and camera. I've also been listening to one of those 'crash course Spanish' recordings on my iPod. I'm not going to be conversing with anyone at all well, but if I can pick up a few words, it'll be better than nothing. In my experience, there's nothing like being in a country and under pressure to help you learn. I did get by with a little Arabic in Iraq, though I'm not sure I'd be able to speak any now.

So I find myself in downtown El Paso at the offices of EPIC – the El Paso Intelligence Centre. It's home to a bewildering number of anti-drug agencies, including the DEA and the office of the sheriff, who I'm here to see.

I'm buzzed in. A trooper pats me down and runs a

metal detector over my body. Then my ID is checked and I'm let through to a reception area with a view of the palm trees and concrete of the street outside. I end up waiting so long for my first appointment – three hours – that my second one becomes due. This is answered more timely and I'm buzzed up to see Sheriff Doug Macmillan. His office is kitted out in grand style – wood panelling, leather chairs – and he looks exactly like Boss Hogg off *The Dukes of Hazzard*, right down to the cowboy hat and two pistols at his belt.

He's welcoming and friendly, with a big made-in-Arizona smile. He asks me to sit and offers me a drink from the glass-fronted fridge he keeps behind the desk. I have a Coke.

'So you're going to interview Soto?' he says.

'That's right – if I can.'

'I got a better idea. Why don't I lend you my gun and you can shoot yourself right here – cut out the middle man.'

'It's a kind offer, but I think I'll pass.'

'Suit yourself. Be quicker and a lot less painful than what's going to happen to you.'

'He can always decline my request for an interview.'

'The thing is, Alberto tends to decline things with a goat's horn to the head.'

'A what?'

'An AK-47. I've got to tell you, sir, you go across that border looking for Soto, and you won't be coming back. That's a gold-plated, underwritten and fully insured guarantee.'

'What can you tell me about him?'

'He's a grade-A asshole. Stone killer.'

'But he's never been convicted.'

'Yeah, we have a whole lot of difficulty getting the dead to testify. If you in England have a way of doing it, we'd sure love to hear it.'

'But why does he concern you? Your jurisdiction's over here.'

'Which is where he sends a lot of his drugs, where he organises hits, where he buys his guns and contributes so handsomely to our local economy.'

'I don't understand.'

'There are three gun dealers every mile for fifty miles on the border around here. There are ten in El Paso alone, that's before you start counting arms fairs. Eight hundred thousand people in El Paso, ten gun dealers but they only need three McDonald's. Illegal arms are worth a billion dollars a year to this country. That's discounting all the shit the narco boys buy in the malls.'

'So I'd like to ask you . . .'

He looks at his watch.

'Interview's over,' he says. 'I just wanted to have a friendly word with you, see your face and try to keep you alive.'

He doesn't look like a man who does a lot of changing his mind, so I get up, shake his hand and a trooper leads me out into the foyer. At the reception desk I'm called over.

'Mr Kane?'

'Yes.'

'Agent Cardoza will see you now.'

I'm shown to the lifts and led up to the third floor, to the offices of the DEA. The people here look different – more academic and middle class than the sheriff and his troopers. Not that that's difficult.

The door's open and I'm greeted by a petite Latina woman – dark hair, big eyes, very pretty, a Glock 9 on her hip. It seems that everyone walks around armed indoors here.

'Maria Cardoza,' she says, extending her hand.

I'm led through to a modern office, slightly shabby, with an American flag in one corner and a picture of Obama beaming down from the wall.

She pulls over a swivel chair from one of the desks and gestures for me to sit. Then she goes back behind her own desk.

'What can I do for you?'

'I just wanted any intelligence at all you had on Alberto Soto.'

She nods slowly.

'Why?'

'It's suspected he was implicated in quite a lot of violence last month in the UK. I'd like to do a story on that.'

'For who?'

'*The Times*. The London *Times*.'

'You've changed career, then.'

I feel my mouth go dry.

She opens a file.

'Nick Kane, soldier, formerly of 14 Intelligence and Special Reconnaissance Regiment. Served in Northern Ireland, the former Yugoslavia, Iraq and Afghanistan. Recently served as a contractor in Afghanistan. No byline has ever appeared in the London *Times*. Or any other newspaper, for that matter.'

That is a bit disturbing. Somehow she's got access to my service record. That's classified Top Secret.

'Well I'm hoping to break into that market. This should be a big story.'

'Goodbye.'

'Sorry?'

'If you're going to treat me like an asshole, I have nothing to say to you. Do you want to tell me why you're really here? Are you MI6?'

'I don't think you'd have got that information quite so easily if I was.'

Presumably someone like MI6 must have handed it over.

'Are you a hit man?'

'No.'

I see there's no point in bullshitting her now, so I come clean.

'Soto threatened my friend, and when my friend didn't give in to those threats, he killed him.'

'*Plata o plomo.*'

'Ah yes.'

'The silver or the lead. It's the cartels' basic business model.'

I think about that. It was exactly the choice Andy was offered.

'Yeah. Well I've decided to come over here and bring Soto back.'

She bursts out laughing.

'How, exactly?'

'Well, perhaps you can tell me.'

'In a coffin. There's no other way.'

'I'm not going to do that. I want to bring him back here so he can be extradited to face trial in the UK.'

'Have you any idea what you're up against?'

'The La Frontera cartel.'

'No. Let me fill you in about Juarez. You think it's scary that two cartels are warring it out on the streets with the army fighting either or both of them depending on the bravery of its officers or who's paying them? That's not what's scary. If that was all it was, there would be a solution, police and army complicity or not. There would be a head we could arrest, deputies, a structure we could map. What's scary is that this is new-model capitalism going on out there. The killers are franchisees. No one is in overall control. The cartels have influence, but that's very far from being in command. Most of the time the guys carrying out the hits don't even know who they're carrying them out for.'

'So there's no one to lead me to Soto?'

'As soon as you ask, it will get back to him. In fact, he probably already knows.'

'How? I've only had contact with you and the sheriff's office.'

She raises an eyebrow.

'Are you so naïve? Someone here will have passed on the message. Do you think corruption stops at the Mexican border? It goes wherever money can go, which is everywhere. Remember that anyone you talk to, you might be talking almost directly to Soto. Anyone.'

'You?'

'No. But could you be sure? And remember: this is a safe city, but he can reach you here. There are thousands of workers who come in over the bridges from Mexico every day. Any one of them can pick up a gun from a contact here.'

'But if he thinks I'm doing a story . . .'

'He will kill you on the slightest chance that you're a narc, they hate a man who cannot keep his mouth shut. He will kill you because you've mentioned his name. He will kill you because he can't think of a reason not to kill you.'

Now this is intimidating, but I figure the very unlikelihood of me getting to Soto is enough to make him feel safe. And when you feel safe, you're in danger if you're a man in his position.

'Are you still determined to go?'

'Yes.'

'Then come with me.'

'Where are we going?'

'The Sheraton Hotel. There's a three-day gun show on now. You'll get a chance to see what you're up against.'

'Nice of you to accompany me.'

'Don't mention it.'

It occurs to me for a second that she might fancy me, which I admit is a typical big-egoed bloke thing to think. But no. She's very pretty, small, trim, clever. One thing Latin culture doesn't lack is good-looking men. Keep your mind on the job, Nick. Besides, she's got a wedding ring on.

She asks me to wait a minute, heads off and returns in jeans and an El Paso University sweatshirt. She hasn't got the Glock 9 any more, but tucks a Glock 23 into a waistband holster that she covers with the baggy sweatshirt.

She drives me out in an unmarked car to the hotel. There are a fair few people there who look, to my eyes, like gang members. They're exactly like you'd expect them to look – tattooed up to the eyeballs, literally, big gang symbols all over their faces and shaved heads, baggy trousers, trainers, designer T-shirts. We get the evil eye but nothing more before we head into a large conference room that's overflowing with weaponry.

As you can imagine, I've seen a few guns in my time, but this place is better equipped than many military bases I've been in. There are racks of M4 carbines for sale – the weapon of choice for a lot of the US military, a serious assault rifle – top-model Kalashnikovs, even a Benelli Super 90 shotgun. These aren't self-defence weapons, they're not hunting weapons, they're the sort of thing you'd want if you were, say, thinking of starting a small war. Or a big one.

There's even a rare old piece, known as the Arctic Warfare Super Magnum, a British-made sniper rifle. A Household Cavalry sniper used one of those back in 2008 to kill two Taliban at the same time, at a range of about a mile and a half.

The crowd is remarkable – young mums, dads, grandparents and kids, along with the thuggish-looking guys with the Latin gang tattoos.

'What are most people buying for?' I say to Maria.

'Hunting,' she says with a raise of the eyebrows that shows she doesn't quite believe it.

'The deer round here drive armoured cars, do they?' Some of the kit here, particularly the .50 cal stuff, is actually powerful enough to pierce the skin of a light tank. It's also heavy enough to require three blokes to use it.

While browsing the stalls, I see an ammunition pouch with an unusual design on it.

It's like the Virgin Mary, but instead of a face she has a skull, and she's carrying a scythe in one hand and a globe in the other. I pick it up.

'Santa Muerte,' says Maria. 'St Death. The cartel guys like to pray to her.'

Seems fairly clear what market these sellers expect their stuff to be going to. I can't quite believe it's all so brazen, but US citizens have the right to buy these weapons, there's no register of buyers and so much of it is changing hands that the police can't possibly follow it all. Nor, under the constitution, do they really even have the right to.

Then my eyes light up. There's a stall run by the Bulwark conglomerate. Bulwark are a huge firm whose interests take in arms, contracting of private armies, industry and, as I saw in Afghanistan, murder in defence of their shady business dealings.

I wander over and look at the stall. There's a whole lot of stuff for sale in their catalogue – from grenade launchers to body armour, night-vision sights and even some 'Street Sweeper' shotguns – like the Striker 12, which looks like a space-age version of the old classic gangster's machine gun. This is in theory a semi-automatic gun; it needs one squeeze of the trigger for every shot, but it's designed so you can pull the trigger so fast that it can lay down a terrifying rate of fire. Again, this is an urban warfare weapon. In fact, it's a favourite of oppressive police forces and, as the name suggests, will shift people off a street sharpish.

I thought they were illegal in the USA but Maria says not, under certain conditions.

The man on the stall smiles at me.

'Buying for yourself?'

'Yeah.'

He has a look in his eyes like this is a mild disappointment but remains friendly and polite.

'What you after?'

Part of me wants to tell him to stick his body armour where it won't fit, but another part finds it quite amusing to be buying stuff off a firm whose operations I did so much to mess up in Afghanistan.

'You after a gun?'

'I'm not a US citizen.'

'No, where you from?'

'England.'

'I'm getting a coffee in ten minutes. If you'd like to join me, maybe we could discuss your options.'

This bloke has just offered to sell me some guns illegally, I think. And not like it's a big deal. He looks about as morally compromised as someone trying to sell you a dodgy DVD in a pub.

'I'm travelling around Mexico.'

'Well, you'll need some protection for that. Here.'

He passes me a card.

It's a proper printed business card, with a number and a name on it – Juan.

'He won't be able to supply you with anything because that's illegal, but he's a good guy to know.' Of course, that statement isn't meant to be taken at face value.

Again, I'm gobsmacked. A representative of a major corporation has just passed me a dodgy arms dealer's number in broad daylight. Can it be that brazen?

I thank him and move on.

'Aren't they afraid of getting nicked?'

'What? *Nicked?*' She says it as if I've started speaking Klingon.

'Getting arrested.'

'There's a big anti-gun-running operation on right now. Americans tend not to get prosecuted. It's kind of political, especially when the company you work for has big contacts in the US government.'

My plastic takes a bashing as I lash out on some Dragon Skin concealable body armour. I have a feeling it would be safer to go for the full military option, but that's not going to be practical. I could do with a night-vision scope, but Maria tells me not to worry about that. She can provide it.

'You're willing to do that?'

'Yes. I can sign a certain amount out from the office. I also have a file on Soto, if you'd like to see it. Though, naturally, you didn't get it from me.'

'Yeah, I would. You're being really helpful. This is much more than I expected.'

'I think you're going to die and die quickly,' she says. 'But your record would suggest you know what you're doing. So on the fraction of one per cent chance you will get Soto, I will help you.'

'Why take the risk?'

'I haven't been given the authority to do what I'd really like to do and put together a team to hit him.'

'You'd assassinate him?'

'Not ourselves – that would cause an international incident. But you could see the attraction for certain sections of US law enforcement in directing a little money towards getting their top targets killed. There are rumours that some agents have taken a risk and found money for local help, let's say.'

'I'm not intending to kill Soto. I'm going to get him back here.'

'We should discuss how you might do that. I have some people you could talk to there. And here, there's someone you should meet.'

'Who?'

'Soto's boss, Miguel Perez,' she says.

She registers my surprise.

'He's in prison.'

'Where?'

'The ultramax at Deming.'

'I can get to see him?'

'Yeah, I can do that. You've got press accreditation, right? I'd need to see that.'

I show her my card.

'Great. That looks in order. I'll get you there.'

'Why are you helping me?'

'I've worked with SOCA for a long time. I trust them and you come with their recommendation.'

I can see, though, that it's more than that. Her voice has cracked slightly, and she seems almost as if she's on the verge of tears.

'I was born in the US, but I grew up in Juarez,' she says. 'Soto killed my husband.

Chapter 7

The ultramax at Deming is a lot smaller than I thought it was going to be. I'd imagined one of those massive places you see on TV – miles of wire, lots of big towers, a solid block of a building.

It's certainly not welcoming, though, set well out in the desert; it looks like no more than two warehouses stuck in the middle of nowhere. There are four towers there, and also razor wire and dog patrols, but it looks more like a medium-sized military research institute than a prison.

Maria drives me, and as I come through the entrance checkpoint, I start to get the shivers. I'm someone at home in the outdoors, always was. I like wildernesses, oceans, those sorts of places. This is like looking at a couple of big coffins full of living people.

I'm searched and my accreditation is checked. Then I'm led through an extraordinary number of doors into the main building. There are cages within cages here. We go through five separate steel-mesh doors before we're led into a small room, also heavily locked. I wouldn't want to be in here if there were a

fire. There are four CCTV cameras in the room –
which strikes me as a bit over the top.

Maria sees me looking at them.

'Remember when you meet Perez,' she says, 'that
his nickname is El Carnicero. The Butcher. We think
he's directly or indirectly responsible for the murder
of about five thousand people. He's probably killed
about two hundred of those himself. He's also
invaded three towns and cleared them entirely of
their lawful inhabitants.'

'Towns?'

'Two or three thousand people. They get a month
to leave.'

'That's generous. What's he like?'

'Personally, very pleasant. His family wanted him
to be a doctor before he got caught up in the drugs
cartels. He was running La Frontera within ten years
of joining them. People who stood in his way had a
habit of ending up as pink soup.'

'What's that?'

'He dissolved them in vats of acid. The lucky ones
were dead before they were shoved into the tank.'

'How did you get him?'

'We followed the money. People informed on him.
We built a case. Then we tricked him into coming to
the US.'

'How?'

'His mother was ill and was here for treatment. We
got a message to him saying she was dying. It's been
used before and it'll be used again. These boys have a
strong sense of family. He had himself smuggled into
the country and we were waiting for him at the
hospital.'

'Has he given anyone else up?'

'No one. He's old school.'

'So why will he talk to us?'

'Like I say, he's old school. He'll understand you.'

My eyes go to the cameras.

'Turned off. DEA-privileged information.'

'With a journalist?'

She shrugs. 'Deep background. The prison authorities look at the paperwork. You're not dealing with thinkers here.'

'Good job.'

The door is unlocked and a man is led in. He looks almost comic. He is actually wearing a suit with stripes on it, like a prisoner in a silent film. He's cuffed and his feet are shackled. He is about five foot four tall, around seventy and clearly not in the best of health. This is a man who would have difficulty escaping from a wet paper bag, let alone a prison.

He shuffles to a chair and sits down at the table opposite us. He smiles.

'I have not spoken to anyone in a year. Excuse me if my voice is rough.'

Solitary confinement means solitary confinement in these places – no books, no TV, no exercise, no human interaction. Do I feel sorry for him? For a second, and then I think about the pink soup.

The guard, a shaven-headed meathead, salutes and leaves us.

Thanks for seeing us,' says Maria to Perez.

'It is a pleasure. How is your boss?'

'Still alive, despite your best efforts.'

'I bear him no ill will. He was doing his job.'

'You still have a contract out on him.'

'I am a practical man. A man like me cannot let his enemies walk free.'

Jesus – taking a contract out on someone is his idea of bearing someone no ill will.

'We want to talk about Soto.'

A flicker of anger goes across his face.

'Is he still alive?'

'Yes. He prospers.'

Perez nods and smiles, but his eyes are full of menace.

'We need to get to him.'

'We do not see eye-to-eye, but I will not give him up to law enforcement.'

Maria gestures to me.

'This is Nick Kane. He's a journalist. But he's also ex British Special Forces. Soto killed his friend. He'd like to speak to him about that.'

Perez's eyes flick between me and Maria.

Then he smiles and laughs. 'What do you want?'

'Money,' says Maria, 'and help as and when we need it.'

She takes out a pen and paper and slides them across to him.

He studies them.

'And for me?'

'Books in your cell. I could see about a radio.'

'How much money?'

'Ten thousand dollars now. More when we need it. Use of resources.'

'What resources?'

'We'll see nearer the time.'

'And for these "resources"? What do I get?'

'We'll see nearer the time.'

He thinks for a second. Then he writes down a series of numbers and a password.

He looks hard at me.

'Soto is an ambitious man,' he says. 'He has ambitions beyond Mexico and the US. Beyond the drugs business. He is a hard man too, and difficult to kill. I have tried. He will be expecting you. He would kill you if he thought you were trying to interview him. If he suspects anything more – as he might, because nothing is secret from La Frontera – he will kill you as you cross the bridge into Mexico. So be very careful. And when you get your chance, take it.'

'What was he doing in Britain?'

'I am not a *soplón*,' he says. I guess that must be Spanish for 'grass', or 'snitch' as I understand they're calling it nowadays.

He sits back in his chair.

'Thank you for your time,' says Maria.

He smiles. 'Don't worry, I got plenty.'

Chapter 8

I take the tourist bus into Juarez. One of the surprising things about a lot of dangerous places, when you visit them, is how normal they appear. I'm rattling into Murder Central on a big red bus that's going to drop me at silver markets, pharmacies and restaurants. I have to say, it's the oddest transport I've ever taken on a mission.

As the bus makes its way over the bridge into Mexico, we are stopped, but the American guard only pokes his head into the bus and the Mexican guys couldn't seem less interested.

I have nothing illegal in my bag, but still I'm nervous as we file off the bus at the bridge to walk through the pedestrian screening from the US border – full X-ray. I'm wearing a ballistic vest under my Harrington, but I'm not worried about any questions to do with that – it just makes me an overcautious tourist. I haven't bothered with a gun, though I've no doubt I'll need one: the vetting procedure is a bit slack – it kind of has to be; the Mexican border is the busiest in the world – and I get waved through despite the vest.

Maria has given me a number to call when I get to the city, along with a mobile to call it on. It's there that I'll pick up the night sight, which will have been delivered by a DEA agent.

We're up over the Rio Grande, which here looks more like the Rio Small. Most of the riverbed is dry, and both banks are sealed by a chain-link fence. Into Juarez itself, the place is a surprise. It's pleasant. There are little plazas full of palm trees, lawns, open-air cafés, fountains. OK, it's a little run-down, but I didn't expect to see the signs of major corporations on buildings here.

The thing is, it's not just the US hunger for drugs that this place caters for. There are hundreds of sweatshop factories for major electronics, pharmaceutical and car firms here too.

So much of the stuff we pass could be in Dallas or El Paso itself. The office blocks look no different. The sun's shining and everything looks lovely. OK, there are cops on the street – a lot of them, driving around in the back of pick-ups, dressed in black, balaclavaed and carrying assault rifles. These are the Federales – the national troops. The military, but acting as a peacekeeping force. They're everywhere, columns of nine or ten vehicles sweeping around the roads, honking the traffic out of the way. It's a wonder anyone ever gets to drop litter without being shot. The police are even more conspicuous than in El Paso.

I've been in the city twenty minutes, crawling through the heavy traffic, and I've come across my first murder scene. A man, a boy really, of about sixteen is dead, handcuffed to a chain-link fence next to a basketball court. There's a sign above his head, but my crash course Spanish isn't up to reading it. He's clearly only recently been discovered, because an ambulance has just arrived and the cops are still walking around, many in masks to conceal their identities. So someone has hung his body up there in broad daylight and put a sign above his head. Maybe they even killed him there. All while the cop cars cruise and the military jeeps sweep by.

The really shocking thing is that no one actually seems that bothered. No big crowd has formed to gawp, there's no one pointing or crying or crossing themselves. It's just business as usual.

The bus pulls up at a smart modern shopping mall. My hotel is a short walk from here. As soon as I get out, I call the number Maria has given me.

'*Si*,' a voice answers.

'It's Maria's friend.'

'OK. Where do you want to meet?'

I don't want this guy knowing where I'm staying, so I look up at the mall. There's a big sign there.

'Outside the Paradiso shopping mall.'

'Sure. I'll be in a silver Toyota Camry. I'll flash the lights to let you know it's me.'

'OK. If you don't see me, don't worry. Flash the lights anyway. What time?'

'An hour.'

'OK.'

I walk to the hotel I'm staying at – the not too promisingly named Micro Hotel.

Despite the heat, I keep the hood of my top up to cover my face; a lone gringo might draw interest.

Five minutes later, and I'm there – it's cheap, clean

and it has a fire escape should I wish to get out in a hurry.

I dump my bag, make myself a coffee and head back out to the mall.

I soon realise that I'm perhaps not as conspicuous as I thought in a town like this. Not everyone is particularly dark-skinned or even dark-haired. You imagine that these places are full of blokes in ponchos with droopy moustaches, but that's like thinking everyone in England goes round in a bowler hat. Even my clothes don't mark me out too much – cargo pants, dark green T-shirt and Harrington jacket. There are a few locals dressed similarly.

I've got quarter of an hour to spare, so I check out the mall – fire exits and other doors mainly. If I have to get away, then I want to know where I'm going. There's no reason to think this deal will go wrong, but you have to plan for every contingency. After I've established exactly how I could get away – through a fire exit at the back – I go up to the front of the mall and pretend to window-shop.

One o'clock exactly, and a silver Toyota Camry pulls up and flashes its lights.

I've begun making my way down the outside steps of the mall when I notice two things. The Camry hasn't got any licence plates on. Secondly, there's another Toyota Camry – a white one – pulling in from the other direction. It too is missing its licence plates and it too flashes its lights. What?

My phone goes. It's the number of the gun dealer. I answer it.

'Get out of there.'

'Which car are you in?'

68

'Get out!'

I turn and start walking up the stairs, but it's too late: they've seen me. Four gunmen are spilling out of the silver Camry, four out of the white. There's a selection of weapons – AKs and pistols. One has a shotgun.

I'm running up the stairs back into the mall at pace, heading for the fire exit out back.

They won't be able to fire through a crowded shopping mall. Got that wrong. There's one of the most terrifying sounds in the world behind me – an AK on full auto opening up. The mall erupts into screams, people diving everywhere as bullets smack into the plasterwork above my head, skid off the floor, smash the windows of shops. Whoever this geezer is, he's none too accurate, but I fear for anyone who's in the firing line.

It's a big mall with a central escalator which I use for cover as I head towards the rear fire exit. I slam into the doors and nearly knock myself out as they open about eight inches. Someone has parked a bloody car right up against them. It's probably just some rubbish driver, but I can't risk that being a deliberate ploy to cut off potential exits. I run hard left into a big department store. People are panicking now, running everywhere, some flat to the floor, some hiding behind racks, some screaming and running. Jesus, I wish I'd picked another way out. I've fought in Ireland, in Serbia, in Iraq and Afghanistan and I've never seen such recklessness – not only in terms of what's going to happen when those trucks full of Federales pull up with their assault rifles, but in the collateral damage he's doing to bystanders while chasing someone who is completely unarmed.

He'd be better chasing me straight than firing at the same time. I've showed no signs of returning fire, so he can catch me at his leisure, shoot me and save himself precious rounds.

I run up the escalators of the store, taking about four steps at time. As I get to the top, I hear the clatter of the AK again and a whole heap of plaster from the ceiling falls like snow. I can't go up the next escalator now; he'll be halfway up the first one while I'm going up that and have a clear view of me.

I dive out into what looks like a menswear section. I hear a voice.

'Yanqui! Yanqui!'

There's an absolute stillness in the store. Everyone has taken cover or fled.

But now I can hear a child whimpering.

'Yanqui! Yanqui!' He says something I can't understand, but one word stands out: *niña*. Little girl.

I'm crouching behind a counter, and through a gap in its construction, I can see he's holding on to a girl of about nine or ten. He's got the AK jammed into the side of her neck and she's weeping with fear and also with pain, because the thing's red hot and has to be burning her. His eyes are wild and it's obvious he's off his head on God knows what.

'Yanqui! Yanqui!'

I've got to stop this. There's no way of sneaking up on him, no way of getting hold of him – he's got his back to the escalator. Still, I can't let this kid die. Maybe if I give myself up he'll try to take me prisoner and then I can get near enough to take the gun off him.

I stand up from behind the desk. Immediately he

throws the girl away and levels the gun. There's a shot, and he stands there with a bewildered look on his face. Then he falls to the floor as the little girl screams and runs for cover.

A guy with a small-calibre pistol is coming up the escalator. He nods to me.

'My contact?' I say.

He shrugs and shoots at me twice – aiming into the centre of my chest. One of the shots misses, but the other smacks into the vest. It hurts like hell but it doesn't knock me down and I'm on him, slapping the gun away with my left hand and chinning him hard open-palmed with the right. He's unconscious before he hits the escalator, his head smacking into the edge of a step. I've punched him about halfway down, but the escalator brings the body back up to me – along with the gun. I'll have that, along with a clip of ammunition from his pocket. It's a Bersa Thunder 380 with a fifteen-round double-stock magazine – a cheap South American version of a Walther PPK.

I have to find a way out of here now, and I don't think the way I came in is going to cut it. More of these guys could be about. I am surprised that only two of them followed me. I'm even more puzzled that matey boy with the pistol shot the guy with the AK.

Ah well, we'll leave the debrief for later. I go up the next escalator on to a floor selling furniture. Here there is a fire exit and the door is open. Obviously someone's gone out this way before. I have to take the risk. It's on the back of the building, but if the gunmen have come round the front, I'll be a dead man once they get those AKs trained on me. No choice. Can't go back.

As I move towards it, I hear a noise. There's someone flat to the floor behind a kitchen display. It's a woman. She sees that I've seen her and puts her hands above her head, half pleading, half trying to fend away the bullet she imagines is coming. Some of my emergency Spanish comes into my mind. '*Venga!*' It means 'follow' or 'come', I think. I beckon her forward and she follows me as I make for the fire exit.

Suddenly there are a whole heap more people crawling out. I feel incredibly guilty that I exposed these people to this danger. I didn't have a lot of choice and it wasn't me opening up with the military hardware, but I have to shoulder some of the blame for what's happened here.

We go out on to the fire escape. We're three storeys up overlooking some tower blocks and residential streets. There's no sign of a police response yet, so I run quickly down the steps. I've got the gun in my jacket pocket but I don't touch it. Everyone is screaming as they come down the escape, the tension of their long minutes of silence on the floor spilling out of them.

I scream too. I have to try to blend in. At the bottom of the steps my phone goes.

I answer.

'I can see you. Don't move.'

A silver Toyota Camry pulls up behind the store. Now I've got a choice, haven't I? Third time lucky. I get in. Why? Because this is the first Toyota Camry that's come along without the blokes inside shooting at me.

This car has only two people in it, the driver and a

nine-year-old kid in the back. I keep my hand on the Bersa in my pocket as I get in.

The driver pulls straight out into the traffic and shoots a look towards where I'm holding the gun.

'You got some metal yourself, I see.' This guy looks like you imagine a Mexican to look like – white soccer shirt, baseball cap, cross on a leather thong around his neck. He has no real nose, just a sort of splodge in the centre of his face, and his eyes are scarred. Clearly a boxer, I'd say – straight out of the mould of those unhurtable Mexican lightweights who've been eating Europeans alive in bouts for the last fifty years.

'Yeah. Where are we going?'

'Away from here, fast.'

'Sounds good.'

I try to remember our route, but he drives quickly through a maze of back streets before pulling up behind a derelict general store built of blocky grey concrete.

Him and the kid hop out before another car pulls up – this time an old white Mitsubishi Pajero.

'Get in,' he says.

I'm thinking about just cutting loose here and walking back to the hotel, but I don't know if I've been compromised there too. I've got a gun if it all goes tits up. I get in the back. The Pajero is driven by an old bloke in a Dorados basketball vest.

We pull out on to a highway, leaving the Camry behind. I guess it must have been nicked.

We drive through the dusty bowl of the Rio Grande and then off the tarmac on to a smaller road. We've been going for about thirty minutes when we come across a weird sort of condominium. It's like a small town, low concrete buildings almost like Butlins chalets, but many of them derelict, quite a few burnt out.

'Factory houses,' says the young bloke. 'Factory closes, people go home. Crack addicts come in.'

Great. I wasn't expecting Beverly Hills, but I seem to have ended up in one of the few places on earth that looks as though it might be more dangerous than Juarez.

'Put this over your head,' says the young bloke. It's a black bag.

'Why?'

'Then people will think we've kidnapped someone. If we walk in chatting, they'll wonder why we're with a gringo and might get the idea we're talking to the DEA.'

Nice place, where you have to look like a kidnapper to blend in.

I put the hood on and the young bloke tells me to lie down.

I do. About five minutes later, we pull up. He drags me out of the Pajero and I feel a tidy smack in the guts. Normally it wouldn't hurt, but I've obviously bruised up or even broken a rib after taking the round in the jacket, and it's agony. The blow actually puts me on the floor.

'Sorry,' whispers a voice, and I'm dragged into a house.

When the hood is taken off, I see I'm in a bizarre scene. Or rather, a very normal one. There are three kids watching cartoons on TV, a woman in the kitchen rolling out tortillas on a board. I have to wonder about a society in which it would be considered plausible to keep a kidnap victim in this kind of place.

'Do you want a coffee?'

'Yeah, I do.'

I sit down and take off my jacket and my sweat-stained bulletproof vest. If they were going to kill me, they'd have done it already.

'I'm Juan,' the young man extends his hand, 'and this is Roberto. The rest you don't need to know.'

'What happened back there?'

'You tell me. Your phone was compromised, maybe. Maybe someone working for the DEA set you up for a little cash on the side, maybe maybe.'

'They knew what car to come in.'

'The phone then, very likely.'

'But one of them shot another one.'

'I don't understand.'

'The guy with the AK was about to shoot me and one of his buddies shot him.'

Juan smiles.

'Maybe not one of his buddies. A rival gang.'

'I don't get it.'

'This is a city of free enterprise. Maybe whoever wants you dead goes to one gang and says, "You need to turn up at one by the Paradiso in a silver Camry. They don't have a silver Camry, or can't get one within the hour. So your enemy goes to another gang who do have a silver Camry. In the meantime, the other gang carjack a white Camry that happens their way. That'll do, they decide, so they come too, thinking that if they can get you first, they can claim whatever price is on your head. And start fighting the other guys who have come to kill you.'

That would explain a lot. There were eight men got out of those vehicles, with a variety of weapons. And yet only two of them came after me. The others were caught up in a battle with each other. Jesus Christ, it's a tough town where a death squad gets mugged.

'So why didn't the Federales or the police turn up?'

'Who knows? Bought off? Didn't want to get involved in a gun battle? On their lunch break? Attending something bigger?'

'Bigger than someone taking an automatic rifle into a mall?'

'It happens, believe me.'

I start to wonder about whether I'm doing the right thing. I want to get Soto, need to get him for my own peace of mind. But is my peace of mind worth all this?

The news comes on the TV: a report of various killings, including the one at the mall.

'I caused that,' I said.

'No,' says Juan, 'this is Juarez. If not you, someone else. We are far beyond causes here, my friend. There is money and power and death. That is all. If not you in that mall, then someone else, somewhere else. Those guys are high on meth or crack and are going to use their weapons somewhere. If they don't chase you into a mall, maybe they chase someone else who runs into a school or a hospital or a party.'

He sips at his coffee.

'Besides,' he says, 'you have caused Soto a problem here. That mall belongs to a powerful man. He will want revenge for that.'

'Which powerful man?'

'Hugo Torres. He is the local head of the Rio Grande cartel.'

'So I've started a gang war.'

'The war started a long time before you got here. Now, do you want some guns?'

'Yeah, I guess I do.'

He takes me into a bedroom in the back.

There, under a baby's cot, is a holdall full of weapons.

He holds up a rifle. It's a Ruger Model 77 hunting rifle plus standard scope, with a detachable night scope at the back – the whole thing folds down to a concealable length. Not a military item, but a good civilian hunter's set-up – not far off the sort of scope some people use for fox culling in the UK.

I take out my wallet to pay him.

He counts out the money and passes me the Ruger.

'Welcome to Juarez,' he says.

Chapter 9

My first mission here is going to be locating Soto, clearly. That's not going to be all that easy. I need to build up a picture of his habitual movements, where he sleeps, who he associates with. I need to find him and then to follow him. Given that he's on turf he knows, he may even have blown my journalist cover story already and is likely to be surrounded by his *sicarios* – the local word for the assassins of the cartels – I'm going to have my work cut out.

I've realised very quickly that I'm dealing with a very serious organisation here. They compromised my mobile phone virtually as soon as I arrived. That means they've got a sophisticated surveillance operation of their own. They may have worked out I was trying to buy guns. This means that the best thing to do, bizarrely, is nothing for a while. I need him to stop thinking about me. If he thinks I'm a journalist and that I've gone home, that won't take long. If I've been compromised at the DEA or the sheriff's office, he might know I've come to bring him home and he won't relax as quickly.

It's time to lie low, make him believe I've gone away, that I've been scared or wounded or even died. There are two options. The first is to return to the USA. The problem with that is – as Juan says – every window washer, trinket seller, and newspaper boy on the bridges is working for the cartels. They'll know when I'm back in the US, they'll alert their secret contacts at EPIC and I'll have eyes on me.

The second is the harder course, but it's the one I'm going to choose. I stand out too much in the city at the moment. I need to disappear, to look rougher, to look poorer and more beaten up. Luckily, we're surrounded by miles of desert that specialises in beating you up. I'll take a month out there and come back to Juan when I'm ready to go. There is a range of small mountains which are quite well wooded. I'll head for those and should have everything I need.

Over the next couple of days, Juan sorts me out with the necessary kit. A bivouac, sleeping bag, a good knife, cheap mobile, a fleece and sweatshirts. I put together a decent survival kit and load it all into a rough old rucksack. I'll look like a hunter – there are a few out here chasing big-horn sheep and Rio Grande turkey. I have the pistol in my belt with one more clip of ammo and the rifle in a holdall. There's twelve rounds of ammo for the rifle too.

He also comes up with something I didn't expect – a little off-road Yamaha motorcycle.

The tank range isn't far, but it should get me into the mountains and out again. If I get desperate for water, I just have to ride to a fill-up area.

All precautions are taken and I'm smuggled out of the house into the Pajero in the middle of the night.

The motorbike's waiting behind an abandoned petrol station about ten miles south. There's a good big moon but I don't drive far the first night, because biking off-road by night is asking for it, and besides that, it's cold. It's November, and while the weather is pleasantly warm by day, it's freezing at night.

However, I can see enough to stay on the bike, as long as I go fairly slowly. According to the map, there's also a lake within about ten clicks of where I am. That'll be useful.

I stop after a while and bivvy down, then get going again as soon as it's dawn. It's beautiful country, the black ridge of mountains rising out of the scrubland. I head for those and find a hiker's trail when I get there. I hide the bike and mark its location on the map and in my mind. Then I set off up the trail. Obviously I won't be staying on this, but it's likely to go past some water sources. Excellent, it does. A day up and I hit a pleasant little stream. I replenish my water, drop in iodine and head off the track along the mountainside, through the forest. I bivvy down there and spend another day walking, giving the land a recce. I'm in pine woods, which is good news, but there's a big bluff of rock which enables me to see the land for a good way around. It also provides some shelter. Yup, this will do.

I spend the days looking out over the mountains, snaring some birds, boiling up dried noodles, making my way to the stream and securing my camouflage. It's great to live like this, watching the sun's movement in the sky, the lengthening and shortening of the shadows of the forest, listening to the stream, washing and drinking from it. Back to nature. It's corny but I do love it. Most of the time, though, my mind's on the job and I take the time to zero my telescopic sight.

I can't trust Juan. Not because he'll let me down, but because he could so easily have been compromised. They could have found the Camry, someone from the neighbourhood could have heard they were looking for a gringo, one of the kids could have talked to another kid in the street about this Yanqui Juan had in his house. No, any contacts I had when I came into the country, any contacts made through those contacts must be used extremely sparingly, if at all. I'm on my own here. It's far from ideal, but that's how it's going to have to be. At least my growing beard, sun-baked face and fucked-up clothes will change my appearance. But Soto's going to have to be found by me alone. I recall the file Maria gave me. He goes to church every Sunday at the central cathedral. Well, I know where to find him; it's just a matter of following him from there.

I've been three weeks in the desert when I see the trucks coming, hear the thumping music and, above it, the girls screaming.

Chapter 10

At first I think it's someone having a party. And I'm sort of right.

As they near the hills they cut the lights but not the music. More out of boredom than anything, I train the night sight on them. I've come to the bottom of the hill near dusk to check on the bike and decided to camp a little lower. Thank God I have.

They pull up about a mile away down the hill, fifty yards or so from the edge of the wood. Six men get out, along with two girls. The cars are big 4x4s – difficult to tell what type. Being a peeping Tom isn't really my style, and I'm about to turn off the night sight and get my head down when I notice the unmistakable outline of a Kalashnikov.

That interests me greatly. Really I should just ignore it and go to sleep. I don't know if it's guilt about what happened at the mall, or just some basic British instinct that you don't walk away from someone in trouble, but I start to make my way back through the trees.

They're building a fire, I can see, hacking stuff out

of the scrub at the bottom of the hill and lighting it the old-fashioned way with a can of petrol. This is all a bit bright for the night sight, so I switch back to the standard.

The music is still pounding out, so I don't really have to bother being quiet. I descend the hill quickly. Even with the long-range ammo, if I have to use the gun I really need to get close in – fifty yards through the trees probably, and I reckon they'll see the muzzle flash after two shots. There isn't a suppressor on this thing. Still, I'll worry about that when it happens.

I'm there quickly, despite the dark. The moon and the fire are bright enough to see by. In the end I crouch down exactly where I predicted – fifty yards from what's going on. As I sit still and watch, I can't believe what I'm seeing.

I don't know what went on before and I don't want to know, but one of the girls is down on her knees, the other being held by two of the men. Two more are huddled around what looks like a crack pipe, or maybe they're even using a lighter to chase the dragon – burn heroin on a piece of foil. It's impossible to tell at this distance. In front of the kneeling girl I can see the clear outline of a man with a pistol. Even above the music I hear the girl begging, her friend too. Their voices are high, hysterical, jabbering. I've heard that sound before. These people clearly think they're begging for their lives. The men are chanting, singing along with the song on the car stereo.

I lift the rifle to take out the gunman, but before I can, he's squeezed the trigger, there's a shot and a flash and the girl slumps backwards. Then – I can't believe my eyes. He takes a machete from his belt and hacks off her head in three swift movements, holds it up by its hair to the other woman, an inch from her face, jeering and tormenting her with it. Then he throws the head to the floor, takes a pace back and gestures for the two men holding the girl to stand aside. He levels the pistol and unhooks his belt, taking his dick in his hand, beckoning her forward to it.

I shoot him. He goes down flat and I know I've hit where I was aiming, straight in the side of his head. That spoils the party mood with the other five. One more shot, taking out the guy nearest the 4x4s, and I'm moving sideways. I can't allow them to get a fix on me.

They kill the music. That's going to make it much harder to disguise where I am. I have two shots left in the hunting rifle. The fire's still blazing, the moon's still bright and I see one making his way towards the car. I shoot him, dropping him. Then the guy with the Kalashnikov because I don't want that spraying the hillside any time soon. Four down. The other two start blasting with pistols into the darkness. You can do that all night, matey boys. You're going to be very lucky to hit me through the trees.

They obviously conclude the same, because one reloads and the other picks up the Kalashnikov and comes running into the woods. I can't reload because of the noise. Instead I crouch deep in the shadow of a rock and wait for him with my knife. I can still hear the girl sobbing down below. Why doesn't she run off? It's then that the search ends – not because they give up, but because they come too close. The man with the AK walks past within ten yards of me and stops to light a cigarette. This is the behaviour of someone who wants to die, so I oblige, covering the ground in a run and a leap to take him out with the knife, a hard strike to the side of the neck. I see the fear flash on to his face in the light of the Zippo as he sees me coming. He screams, and his friend, no more than twenty yards away, just starts blasting with the pistol. But I've got the AK, and at this range through the trees, he doesn't stand a chance. I give it him full auto. The trees erupt into splinters, and there's a shout from the man as he goes down. I check the guy I've taken with the knife. He's definitely dead. The guy I blasted with the AK is gone too, his face peppered with shards from the trees.

I shoulder the rifle, draw my pistol and walk back down the hill. It's a mess down there and I'm keen not to hang around. I can still hear the girl sobbing but I'll leave her a little while. Her hands were tied behind her back so she won't have picked up a weapon, and I don't want to approach her straight away after what she's been through. She needs a little bit of time to herself, I'd say.

The guy I shot first shows some signs of life. He has a substantial wound at the side of his head but he's breathing lightly. I check him for weapons. Nothing. Fair bit of cash, though. I'll have that towards the 'Get Soto' fighting fund. He's also got the key to one of the 4x4s. I collect all the weapons and put them in the back. Jesus, there's some kit in there. Six hand grenades in a box. These are improvised jobs – they actually have blue levers, which would indicate that they're training grenades –

but there are blobs of what looks like welding on the bottom. Someone's had them open, doubtless filling them up with something to make them lethal. There's a few boxes of ammo along with three full-on ballistic vests and what looks like a money-counting machine. There are two gas masks, along with eight tear gas grenades. There's also a MP5SD sub-machine gun – a sound-suppressed version of the MP5. Why you'd need a quiet gun in Juarez is anyone's guess, because from what I've seen, you could open up with an artillery piece and no one would come to investigate. There's also a load of cable-tie handcuffs, two black hoods and a whole heap of drug paraphernalia, including a couple of crack pipes.

In the other 4x4 there's something even more chilling – four Federales uniforms, right down to the black balaclavas. I know from my research that it's a favourite ruse of the drug gangs to dress up as the police. There's also a tarp and a packet of Marlboro. I light one up, put the uniforms in the other car, then lock the door. Why lock the door? Why not? I counted six of them, but I might have been wrong. Extreme caution. It's a good habit.

I look out around me to the horizon. No sign of lights, no noise of engines. In fact it's very still, the noise of the girl's crying aside. We're far enough into the desert for it not to matter too much about the noise of the gunfire. And from what I've seen, it wouldn't matter too much if we did it right outside the central police station.

I'm going to have to get this kid back to safety, which means my Grizzly Adams act will have to come to an end, for a while anyway.

The one with the wound in the side of his head, the guy who shot and beheaded the girl, is trying to say something. Sounds like '*Matai mai*.' I guess he's asking me to help him.

'Don't speak Spanish, mate,' I say.

'Kill me!' His voice is just a wet rasp.

I think of him dancing around waving that severed head in the girl's face.

'Sorry, I'm busy at the moment.'

The girl's sobbing still, hiding underneath the second car. I go over to her. Jesus, she has a black eye the like of which I last saw on Ricky Hatton. One side of her face is hugely swollen and her eye is reduced to just a slit.

My time with the Spanish recordings on the plane is not counting for much, to be honest, and I can't think of what I'm meant to say to calm her down.

'*Me llamo Nick*,' I say. My name is Nick. That's about the extent of what I can remember. Oh, one more word. '*Amigo*.'

Then she starts talking twenty to the dozen and I really cannot understand a word. I kneel beside the truck. What's 'hands' in Spanish? Actually I do remember, because on the recording the bloke makes a joke that the word for wife is the same as the word for handcuffs. '*Esposas*.' She nods and wriggles out from underneath the car.

Something I didn't notice from a distance is that she's naked from the waist down. I saw through the cable-tie cuffs with my Leatherman, then I open the car and bring her the smallest pair of the uniform bottoms I can find.

The bloke with the head wound coughs. That was probably a bad idea. If you've never been to Juarez, you'd probably think you couldn't be in any more trouble than lying with a paralysing head wound in the middle of the desert. You'd be wrong, though. The girl staggers over to him. His eyes are glazed but he still manages to say something.

'*Puta.*' I know that one – whore.

She's only a small woman, and she's been through a terrible, terrible ordeal, but from somewhere she seems to find an incredible strength. She grabs him by the shoulders of his jacket and drags him across the scrub. He's powerless to resist; the bullet's hit the 'off' switch on his ability to move. She gets him as far as the fire, lifts him under the arms and puts him in – not his whole body, just his head.

The fire's very low now. The petrol burnt quickly and it's just embers. He screams and wails for about two minutes. Then he's quiet. That's a bit rich for my blood, but he can't complain. He knew he was playing Mexican rules.

I don't want to watch him dying, so I make my way around the bodies collecting up wallets and mobile phones. I've noticed that this lot bear the tattoos of La Frontera cartel – a big tiger's head – and you never know what information they might yield.

I also use my pen torch to consult my Spanish–English phrasebook. Strange to be doing this at such a time, but these things are invaluable. I look up the word for 'where?'.

When I come back, she's sitting staring at the body of the man who killed her friend and, I should guess, raped and did God knows what else to hers.

'*Dónde?*' I say, showing her the car keys.

'Juarez,' she says. '*Llévame al Juarez.*'

She gestures to the body of her friend. She wants me to bring that with us.

I nod and point to the passenger door.

'You get in love, I'll do this.'

I take the tarp from the back of the other 4x4 and put her friend's body in it. She's naked too and I don't want her family to see her like that, so I take the clothes off the smallest of the corpses and dress her in those. I gather her body up and put it in the back of the 4x4, on top of the guns. Then I put the head in and cover that up.

The car is a big Land Cruiser V8 with blacked-out windows, for which I'm grateful. These cars aren't rare in Juarez – it's the transport of choice for the drug gangs.

The girl gestures that she wants to use a phone. Which one? We have seven. She may as well borrow mine, though; it's brand new and never been used. I turn it on for her and she dials, talks for a while. She's reassuring someone, I can tell.

There's a big gas station visible about a mile ahead and I guess this is where the main highway must be.

She puts down the phone and says something that I don't understand. I shrug.

'Stop-uh!' she says.

I stop and she makes a motion like 'calm down', which I guess means she's telling me to wait. We do.

After about an hour and a half of waiting in almost total silence, we see a car turn off the main highway.

It stops and flashes its lights. This doesn't always end well in Juarez, as I've found out to my cost.

She makes a gesture to me like I should do the same. There's one car, and that phone was bought for cash. It should be safe. I flash back and the car comes towards us across the desert. It's actually not a car but an old minibus. I have my pistol out and at my side.

The girl points at it and shakes her head.

'*Mi familia.*'

My family.

The bus pulls up and there's a kid of about sixteen at the wheel – her brother by his looks. The minibus has some Spanish writing on the side I can't understand – apart from the word '*Adicción*'. Addiction. This is some sort of rehab centre bus. I've heard of thankless tasks, but this one has to take the biscuit.

The brother gets out and they hug each other, weeping and cooing. Then his eyes turn to me and she seems to be explaining what's happening.

He speaks.

'You saved my sister.'

'Yes.'

'Thank you.'

He comes over and gives me a big hug.

'We must take Catalina.'

He obviously means the girl in the 4x4.

'You want to abandon the Land Cruiser?'

'It's too dangerous. It would stand out in our neighbourhood and someone would report it to the bad guys.'

I nod.

'I'll help you.'

We carry the girl's remains into the minibus. Thank God for the tarp.

'Your sister?' I say.

'No. Friend.'

He looks at me.

'Who are you?'

At this point I decide to tell him. Why? Because he thinks he's in my debt. These people obviously aren't gang members, and I need help to get to Soto. They run an addiction centre. Maybe they'll have contacts that could help me.

This will expose them to great danger, so I'm going to have to tread very lightly.

'My name's Nick.'

'I'm Miguel. Why are you here?'

'I've come to talk to Alberto Soto.'

'Why?'

'He killed my friend.'

'You're going to kill him?'

'Only if I have to. I'm going to take him to America. Hopefully he'll be sent to my country and face prison.'

'You are *loco señor*, he will kill you.'

The girl speaks to him, and he draws breath quickly, sucking in air through his teeth.

'One of those men you killed was Soto's nephew. He has many family, but this is bad.'

Strangely, my first thought is for their safety.

'Your sister should lie low for a while. I'm going to take some things from the back of the Land Cruiser. You might not want them in your vehicle.'

I open up the Land Cruiser and show him.

91

He takes out the AK.

'Well,' he says, 'if someone comes for my sister now, we will have an answer for them.' He lifts up the AK, pointing it in the air. 'We will have the devil's horns, *amigo*.'

Chapter 11

We load the minibus full of weapons and drive back into Juarez. I swipe a sat nav that I'm amazed to find jammed under the passenger seat of the Toyota as well – that could come in useful. Miguel explains that he's going to drop me at a respray shop his brother owns. That way I can be driven right into the building and get out and unload things without anyone seeing. His brother has a flat above it and I'll stay there until I've decided how to move against Soto. He warns me that it's at the edge of one of the big slums – the Colonias – but says I'll be OK because his brother's shop is '*intocable*'. Still, I need to get flat on the floor of the minibus.

This is adding one more person to the equation than I'd like, but it sounds like a necessary evil. I need a base in Juarez and this is as secure as I can manage. There's no guarantee that the brother won't betray me – there's actually no guarantee that the girl I've rescued, Liana, won't betray me – but at some point, when you're establishing a local network, you have to trust people.

Crucially, these people have a reason to hate Soto and a reason to be grateful to me, but I remember what Juan warned me: 'In Juarez there are three reasons for anything, three solutions too: money, power, death.' Not sure where my relationship with Liana's family fits into that.

There's no one at the shop – Miguel says his whole family is at his mother's house waiting for Liana. He leads me in past three cars, all of which have had their dashboards removed. No prizes for guessing what's going in there. The shop's '*intocable*' not because Miguel's brother is a nice guy who helps out at the addiction centre; no one's going to mess with it because it belongs to a cartel.

Miguel sees me looking. There's something else I see on the wall – the sign of La Frontera cartel, the tiger's head. These are the same people who abducted Liana.

'My brother is a good body repair man. The best. Soto and the cartel know that.' He gives a shrug.

'Didn't buy your sister any protection, did it?'

'There are many crazy people involved. Not all of them do what they are told. She should have been protected, but if the wrong people want her . . .' He shrugs again.

'I should go. I can't stay with someone who works for that cartel.'

'No. My brother will not harm you. You've helped us. Like I say, the cartel can't control everyone. He works for them because he has to.'

I nod.

'*Plata o plomo*?'

'*Si*. We will help you as much as we can.'

'You might pay a high price.'

'Someone rapes my sister and kills her friend. I'm not a man if I don't try to take revenge. My brother feels the same. If we can hurt La Frontera, we will.'

So I'm staying with an employee of La Frontera cartel – the very people I'm looking to attack. I'm beginning to realise that the line between good guy and bad guy in Juarez can be a very hazy one. It's easy to see why someone would want to take the drug money around here. Once upstairs in the flat, I peak out of the one dirty window. It's just about dawn, a pink light rising over the hills. The street is deserted apart from a couple of dogs, but I can see this place is dirt poor. The spray shop seems to be the only substantial building for as far as I can see. There are a few breeze-block-built huts, some with corrugated-iron roofs. Elsewhere houses have been lashed together out of what looks like plywood, or are just tarpaulin lean-tos. The desert wind is up, coating everything with sand. The skeletons of ancient cars and trucks litter the place. I see a running water standpipe. The place stinks too – a human fug of shit and piss. Can't imagine that the sewers are much cop here – if they exist at all.

It's unimaginable poverty. I, however, have a shower in the apartment, and a proper toilet. Guess working for the cartels in a useful trade – hiding drugs and money in vehicles – brings its benefits, namely a septic tank and a water supply.

I'm having to readjust my outlook.

'Who lives here?' I ask Miguel.

'The people who work in the *maquiladoras*,' he says.

'The what?'

'The big factories.'

'Drug factories?'

He laughs. 'No. Auto parts, air conditioners, TVs.'

As he talks, I notice people starting to assemble on the street. There's a mixed group of predominantly women and girls, aged from about twelve up to retirement. When I say a group, in the ten minutes I'm watching, hundreds of women appear. There are some blokes and boys too, but not nearly as many.

'These people are all going to work?'

'Yes.'

'The kids don't go to school?'

'No.'

'Who are they working for?'

'Big Western companies.'

'Which ones?'

'All of them.' He laughs again. 'This is where the people toil so you gringos don't have to.'

As I'm watching, buses pull up to take the people away. He sees the look on my face.

'They are the lucky ones, Nick. They have jobs. The wage is a dollar an hour here for forty-eight hours. In China they will work for a quarter of that. The factories might not always be here. Or they'll employ more of the illegal immigrants from the south.'

'Mexico gets illegal immigrants?'

'Plenty. It's richer than a lot of the other countries around here, and it's on the way to the US and Canada. People come through here from El Salvador, Nicaragua, Guatemala, Honduras, Ecuador, Colombia.'

'From Colombia?'

'Sure.'

'But that's two thousand miles and about six countries away.'

'A long way to come barefoot with no papers. Even longer if you're going for Canada.'

I think about that – a dollar an hour and you're considered well off. In my short time in the mall before all the shooting started, I was surprised to see that prices weren't far off what they are in the US. These people are the lucky ones and they're on starvation income. If I lived in that poverty and someone came to me with even a handful of money asking me to do something for the cartel, would I say no, particularly if I had sod-all education or other prospects? I hope I would, but I couldn't blame anyone who didn't.

Plata o plomo. It's not just the cartels who are making that offer, it's the whole system, from the starvation rates of the factories to the death run through the desert to the north and the US for the illegals. *Plata o plomo*, silver or lead. I'm surprised they aren't the colours of the Mexican flag.

Chapter 12

Miguel leaves and I take a shower. It feels good after my three weeks living rough. I see myself in the mirror for the first time. My face is baked brown, I have a decent beard and I've lost around a stone, I should think. Good. I don't want to look like a soldier; I'd rather look like a tramp.

I don't want to sleep, but I lie down on the sofa. About an hour later I hear a noise downstairs. I pick up my pistol.

In comes a man in paint-spattered overalls. He's unmistakably Liana's brother. Her family look very alike.

'*Buenos días*,' he says and shakes my hand. He looks around the flat and I'm glad I've hidden the guns under one of the beds.

'*Bueno*,' he says. '*Muchas gracias por mi hermana*.' I guess he's thanking me for saving Liana.

'*De nada*,' I say – which is the Spanish equivalent of saying 'don't mention it' but means more literally 'it was nothing'.

He laughs, probably at my poor accent more than

anything else. Then he signals for me to wait. He goes downstairs and comes back up with an aluminium box. He opens it and I can see inside a pretty extensive gun cleaning kit. Great, that'll keep me busy. Miguel must have told him about the weapons. He points to the fridge in the kitchen and to the cooker, and makes a gesture I take for 'help yourself'.

I do, banging together some eggs, which I eat on corn bread. It tastes good to have something fried after nearly a month of noodles and roast whatever bird.

After I've eaten, I examine the mobile phones. There are some pretty unpleasant pictures on these which, were the guy who took them not dead and were the police dependable, would have seen him locked away for a long time.

There are also a couple of texts. I don't understand them but I write them down anyway – along with all the numbers and names. Then I turn the phones off again. A mobile is a potential tracking device. Don't know how we're going to work this, but I'm guessing Soto's nephew will have his uncle's number in his contacts and the others won't.

But there's only one number there that has a name I can be sure of: 'Mama'. Guess even psychos like to talk to their mums. The rest of them are all nicknames and code words.

The sun comes up, the apartment fills up with paint fumes and becomes pretty hot. Still, I sleep. It's been a long night, and feeling properly clean means I'm out like a light.

It's getting dark again when I wake up. There's someone on the stairs and I reach for my pistol.

The door opens and it's Miguel and his brother.

Miguel says hello while his brother goes to make a coffee.

'How's Liana?'

'Better than she would have been if you hadn't been there.'

'So this nephew, what was he, an underboss?'

'You've watched too many *Godfather* films. He's his nephew. There is one boss of La Frontera – Perez. Soto runs the security and big intimidation. He's an important guy but he's trying to become number one. There's a small crew around the big guys who protect them. The rest is . . .' he searches for a word, 'like the *maquiladora*s when they want something made . . .'

'Outsourced.'

'Outsourced, that' s right. It keeps costs down, no one knows who to trust, the killers have to stay competitive.'

'I wonder if Maggie Thatcher knows what she started?'

'What?'

'Never mind.'

A sudden thought strikes me.

'Why do you speak such good English, Miguel?'

'I made a big effort to learn. One day I will go north and make a better life for me and all my family.'

'You know this could make things a whole lot *worse* for you and your family.'

'Things will be hard anyway. As soon as they find out that Liana survived, they will come asking questions. And their questions will be written on a bullet.'

'Well then, seems we better take it to them, give them something to think about.'

Miguel's brother Ernesto brings the coffee over and we start to talk. I know that Soto goes to church every Sunday and I can latch on to him from there. But we need to get closer to him than that eventually.

We decide to work backwards in our planning. OK, how do we get him across the border? The bridges are all watched and who knows which of the border police – on the Mexican or the US side – have been compromised? We have to assume that they all are. So we can't just stick him in a van and drive him over – that has the potential to go very wrong. There are crossing points into the US where the fence is either broken or non-existent. They're watched by the US authorities but people do get across that way – sheer weight of numbers overwhelming the border patrols. They might stop 95 per cent of them, but a one in twenty chance seems good to the Mexicans. I could get him to the border and have Maria pick him up. But that would involve making a call to EPIC, and I have to assume that any message might be intercepted by La Frontera and we'd end up with a very different reception committee to the one we were anticipating.

There's boat, but although I have a few quid, thanks to the money I took off the guys I killed, it's not enough to buy or even hire a boat for such a perilous voyage. And the sea's a long way away, though that is actually appealing because they wouldn't expect me to take him out that way.

Plane – forget it.

It's Ernesto who has the idea and Miguel who explains it.

Illegal immigrants to the US – if they can afford it – will often be smuggled inside cars like the ones Ernesto builds. If they can't afford it, they might be smuggled anyway, paying off the gangs by working for them as dealers, prostitutes, whatever.

They are sealed into compartments and take their chances – it's not uncommon to find them dead when they're taken out. However, there is a luxury way to travel like this.

A lot of the top drug guys have family in the US. Their wives, who as rich Mexicans find it easy to get visas and travel across the border, have their babies on US soil, giving them joint citizenship. The children go to school there to avoid the hell of their home town that their father is partly responsible for creating. When things hot up for Daddy, it becomes very difficult for him to see his kids. Family is everything in Mexico, so small details like being wanted by the FBI won't deter him from crossing to see the children – particularly if they're ill.

In the past, Ernesto has knocked up a tiny compartment in a car, complete with oxygen cylinder and breathing apparatus. The guy gets in, is sealed inside and breathes the oxygen all the way through customs and out the other side. Either that or his guys have been bought by his rivals and they take the car out into the desert and leave it there, but that's another story.

This is a way we can get Soto out. Bound, gagged, but with an oxygen mask on, he can be smuggled across the border.

So we've got that sorted, or rather an idea of what we might do. How do we transport him to the car?

Where do we take him? What time? No idea. That's the sort of stuff surveillance will need to tell me. But at least we have an objective in place – get him into that car.

'It's a shame you killed all those guys,' says Miguel. 'We could have got some information from them.'

'Not so much of a problem,' I say. 'We can take one of his men as a dry run, but first I need to get a good look at him, establish a pattern of movement. Where does he live?'

'Up at Campestre, but you won't be able to get in there.'

'Why not?'

'The cartel seals the roads up there – like with boulders and barriers. You can only drive so far before you'll meet a roadblock.'

'OK,' I say, 'we'll start with the cathedral and take it from there. Can you get me a car?'

Miguel translates and Ernesto lets out his big laugh before saying something back. Miguel nods.

'What colour do you want?' he says.

Chapter 13

Miguel gets me a decent old Plymouth Acclaim – a big blue boxy thing. This is a standard and unremarkable car that won't draw too much attention. I am going to go in carrying weapons for this one. The risk of discovery is too great and I don't want to be caught out like I was at the mall. I'll take the Bersa, which tucks nicely under my thigh, and keep the MP5 on the floor in a bag. I'm guessing that Soto's boys won't like anyone sitting parked up for too long, so I have to go carefully.

First up is a visit to the cathedral he uses.

Miguel drives me in the minibus for this – I'm flat to the floor as we leave the garage, and only sit up once we get into traffic. I'm looking enough like a local now not to warrant a second glance on the bus, and I make sure I borrow some stained jeans and an old T-shirt from Ernesto.

Miguel is quite complimentary when he sees me.

'Jesus, man, you look like one of my mum's addicts.'

That sounds good to me.

I check the cathedral downtown and look for times of the Sunday services. Great, there are eight of them, starting at seven in the morning.

'The benediction is at seven in the evening,' says Miguel. 'He'll come for that.'

'Why?'

'Why do you think a man who sends so many people to their graves, who tortures, robs and steals, wants a blessing? He's afraid for his soul.'

That Sunday we start surveillance. We're parked up watching from about a hundred yards away when a couple of guys in Ralph Lauren polo shirts start walking towards us.

Miguel stiffens and goes to start the car.

'Leave it,' I tell him. 'Move now and we're compromised. It'll be obvious.'

One of the guys comes over to the driver's side and knocks on the window.

He says something, and Miguel nods and starts the engine.

'What?'

'Says we can't sit there with Soto in the cathedral.'

We pull away and I get a good look at what's happening as we go past. The cathedral is a big mock-classical thing in the middle of a large concrete plaza. It's set too far back for a drive-by to be effective, par - ticularly when there's a cordon of Federales around the building. Yup, the balaclava-clad army are there in force so dear old Soto can speak to God without someone arranging him a face-to-face with the almighty via an AK-47 round.

There are a line of them facing the road, all with automatic rifles, and a group of four more outside the church frisking people who are going in. As we move off – we really can't hang around for fear of getting clocked – I catch a glimpse of Soto. He's wearing a polo shirt like the guys who moved us on, chinos and smartish shoes. His car has been allowed to pull right up to the front of the church. It's a Porsche Cayenne 4x4 with the obligatory tinted windows. The door is opened for him by another short, tough-looking guy who's openly got an AK in his hands. Soto gets out and is gone into the church in an instant.

'Which way do you think he came from?' I ask Miguel.

'I'd say from the east, over there.' I say, pointing past the church.

'OK, drive round there, go past it and park up two hundred yards down the road.'

'What if he goes the other way?'

'Then we'll know for next time.'

He does go the other way, as it turns out, up towards his house at Campestre, which is the country club area – or was before the narcos took over – so I guess he's gone there.

We watch for three Sundays.

By the fourth, I've established, by a process of elimination, that he always goes home after church. But there's an interesting thing. The guy who habitually opens the door for him doesn't follow him home. This guy peels off just before Campestre and, accompanied only by the guys in the car with him, goes to a club. He comes out with a girl around midnight and drives back to a plush place just outside the city centre. This is obviously his little love shack, because the other guys don't come back with him –

it's just him and the girl. She leaves the next day in a taxi – he's not enough of a gentleman to give her a lift, but he at least has the good manners not to kill her.

My test-run target does this three weeks running.

There are three problems. Number one is the girl.

I can kidnap him, but what happens to her? Kidnap her too? Let her go when we're done? That's a logistical nightmare. I only want to have one person to worry about. Also, she could be implicated by the drug gangs, and could end up dead if they know who she is.

Problem two is the dogs. Big dogs. He keeps them in the compound outside his house.

Now I'm not sure how vicious these dogs are – though they are a couple of pit bulls and look fierce enough. They do a good job of barking and snarling at anyone who comes past, diving at the fence, but as soon as he gets home they're coming up to him wagging their tails. Before the girl gets out of the car he chains them up, then takes her into the house before going outside and releasing them again.

The dogs aren't a massive problem, but they rule out plan one, which is breaking in and waiting for him to get home. He's going to expect to see those dogs there or he's not coming in.

I decide the best thing is just to shoot them on the way out using the silenced MP5. No problem. It'll tell people he's gone missing, but that's OK. A lot of these guys go missing, and it puts more pressure on him. I've no intention of physically torturing him, and he'll emerge on the street a week later looking fresh as a daisy and with a lot of explaining to do about where he's been. Some of these guys can be a bit paranoid, so we'll start to offer him ways out. Maybe he'll begin to realise that he might have an easier ride if his boss goes missing; his gang will suddenly have a whole heap of other stuff to worry about beyond where he's been and who he's been talking to.

Problem three is the alarm system. There's clearly one in the house, as he always spends time punching in a code when he gets inside.

So how are we going to do this? Take him outside the house? Then you've got a potential gun battle, and the girl to worry about. I don't want to kill any more people than is entirely necessary. I'm someone looking for justice; I'm not a hit man. We need a more elegant solution.

A knock on the door of the flat provides one. It's Liana, hotly pursued by Miguel.

They're having a right old row, though I can't understand a word of it.

'*Diga lai. Diga lai*,' she keeps saying, or something like it.

Then she sits on the bed and folds her arms and says slowly, 'I help.' I didn't realise she could speak English. Perhaps her near-death experience knocked it out of her.

'What sort of help?'

'Club Luz.' That's the gangster club.

I look at her. Her black eye has gone down and it's undeniable that she is a looker. A classic Latin beauty. If she can get into the club and manage to come out with the right man, that would get rid of the dog problem. Except, of course, she'd have to subdue him. Well, that's not impossible. You can buy what you like in the pharmacies in this town, and a fair dose of Rohypnol is quite easily available.

Her brother isn't having any of it. She is quite insistent, though.

'*Mi amiga. Los odio*' are the only words I catch from her sentence. My Spanish is getting better from being around Ernesto and Miguel, as well as playing the crash-course recordings on the drive to and from the observation point. I understand that. 'My friend. I hate them.' She's saying she wants to avenge her friend.

Ernesto comes in at this point and there's a very long discussion. Ernesto is quiet and serious. From little bits of translation, I gather that she's confident no one in the wider cartel would know who she is by sight. Only if she went back to the factory where she works would she be in trouble, because someone might report that two friends had been missing for a night, one had turned up dead and the other had come in clearly beaten up. Women don't survive those abductions, so it would cause people to talk. Then word might get back to someone who might start to think it funny that Soto's nephew and his boys – main hobbies rape, murder and torture – had gone missing on the same evening that she had clearly escaped from an abduction.

I say nothing. In the end, Miguel puts his head into his hands.

'She insist,' he says.

'What are her reasons?'

'The death of her friend. She can't go back to the factory in case people report that she has returned.

Someone will know that Soto's nephew was planning to abduct her and will start to ask what she's got to do with him going missing. She wants to see them suffer for what they have done. And for what they do.'

Money, power, death. The three reasons for everything in Juarez. Looks to me like she just got the full three limes on that particular fruit machine.

Still, I want to be sure.

'You could die,' I say.

'I am dead,' she says, very slowly. That, I think, makes her a very dangerous lady.

'OK,' I say. 'Miguel, make sure you translate what I say very carefully. There's going to be a plan A, a plan B and a plan C, because I don't want your sister stuck in there. If we have to, we'll kill this guy, but if all goes smoothly, we should be able to take him. Do you have anywhere we could interrogate him safely?'

'To the north, in Anapra, there are many deserted buildings. Some of them were built on a swamp. Not even the crack addicts use them.'

'We'll scout one of them tomorrow,' I say. 'In the meantime, let's run through these plans with maximum attention, because one mistake and we will pay with our lives.'

Chapter 14

Anapra is the American nightmare, within sight of the American dream. It's unbelievable, but here in Juarez's poorest district, where there are no roads, no pavements, where improvised electricity lines, stolen from the main grid, buzz – and occasionally smoke – overhead, where everywhere people look out with the intense stares of meth or crack addicts, where children run filthy and naked in the streets, you are only half a mile from the campus of the University of El Paso, Texas. A campus where beautiful rich young people stroll arm in arm on green lawns talking on mobile phones, mobile phones that people in this city have died and sweated to make, wearing clothes paid for by the suffering in front of me, passed by automobiles made by people who could never dream of affording them. Being an interrogator, I've done a lot of reading on psychology, and this reminds me of a human mind: the bright, untroubled reality of El Paso like the day-to-day consciousness, the stinking streets of Anapra like all those fears, hates and horrors the unconscious locks away.

I'm not political, not at all, never even thought about all that stuff. But right here, smacked in the face by the contrast between the two worlds, you can't help thinking that something is seriously wrong.

Ernesto drives, taking one of the drug cars that are in for repair, a huge Toyota SUV with blacked-out windows. He wears his Ralph Lauren. He wants to look like a bad boy, someone you don't want to mess with. I go fully tooled up and wearing one of the Federales uniforms, complete with black balaclava. This is a wise precaution for these guys, especially because they often work for the cartels themselves.

We drive further out, where the houses seem to be sinking into the floor. This place was built on a swamp, and the swamp has decided to take a bit of revenge.

There's not a lot around here, but we manage to find a burned-out house – probably a former crack den – that has two rooms relatively intact at the back. We'll have to do an in-and-out pretty quickly, because we don't want the car attracting attention, but I think we have our interrogation centre – one room for our subject, one for us to take turns sleeping in. It might take two or three days, but sleep deprivation is the way I'm going to go. It's not something I'd normally choose to do – softer interrogation techniques tend to yield a better standard of information – but we don't have long. Obviously I'll try to soft-pedal on him first. Just pointing out the level of shit he's going to be in with his bosses if we put it about that he's been talking to the Federales may be enough. But sleep deprivation is a useful tool. You can be a very hard man indeed, but without sleep, you effectively become someone else. Your reasoning deteriorates, your will falters and eventually you give in. It's almost impossible to hold out against, and I should know, because, in training, I've had it done to me.

Recce done, we pull out of Anapra, then I change out of the Federales uniform and Ernesto drops me in town – along with the sat nav so I can find my way back – where I steal a car: an old Honda Accord. I don't feel too bad about this as it's already clearly been stolen – the door lock's been banged out and the ignition has had a screwdriver thumped through it at some point. I use mine to get it going and drive it back to Ernesto's, where it's time for some improvisation.

We can turn this into a surveillance vehicle – if not a very comfortable one. These guys are suspicious of anyone waiting in cars, and have lookouts all over the place. Now the club's on a busy road, so that should provide some cover, but I just can't expect to sit in my car unnoticed in the same way I might conducting surveillance in the UK. This is going to be a hard routine. We drill two holes in the boot of the car and make a crawl space under the seats with a bit of judicious cutting. We also disable the boot lock and simply tie the lid in place. I want to be able to get out in a hurry if I need to. There's enough space for two people in there. It'll be hot, it'll be cramped and we'll have to piss in a bottle, which won't be nice, but we won't be discovered. We could even, given the fact that there's one hole for the muzzle and another for the sight, shoot from the car. I want Miguel in there with me for two reasons. The first is back-up.

The second is that I want to be able to control him. That's his sister in there, and this is an operation that needs to be governed by the head, not the heart.

We don't have the luxury of a lot of troops at our disposal and we're going to have to get inventive to watch our backs. I rig some firing circuits out of the car's rear brake switches and send Ernesto out for some pay-as-you-go SIM cards for the mobiles I took off the boys in the desert. I take the grenades to pieces – there is no way I'm going to use an improvised hand grenade without checking it; you never know how short the fuse has been cut. However, once I've dismantled them and performed a bit of jiggery-pokery, I've improvised two good-sized pipe bombs with plenty of nuts and bolts sealed around them. These are a weapon of last resort, but they're useful to have as a back-up.

My final little precaution is to put a big sheet of steel under the back parcel shelf, riveted to it. Ernesto rigs it so that with a good push from the inside, it comes up to armour the back window.

Sunday comes around and we're ready to go. The set-up is one of the most dangerous bits. Liana is to get to the club on her own ten minutes before our boy comes in. She's been given a good description of him – he wears distinctive green cowboy boots, so she should know him on sight. The problem is that a lot of Juarez nightlife is quite literally dead. In many areas the local people are just too scared to go out. So she's going to be in there with maybe eight or nine men, the bar staff – who will be in the employ of the cartels themselves – and whatever women are desperate enough to try to hook a rich gangster as a boyfriend, with all the risk that entails. We have one security measure for her. I use Ernesto's computer to set it up – starting by accessing the Hotmail account I share with John back at home. I compose a draft message and save it without ever sending it. He reads the message and alters the draft to reply, also without sending it. This way we never have to risk an insecure email communication. This is my first time on the computer since I've been in Mexico – I don't want even the slightest risk of compromise. It sounds paranoid, but the drug gangs employ very sophisticated counter-intelligence techniques, including scanning email communications from their henchmen. It's unlikely that Ernesto's computer is affected, but you never know.

It seems things have been hotting up in the UK since I left. Murders in Glasgow, in Manchester, in London, all with the same 'narco manta' message attached to them. The narco mantas are a Mexican tradition, I've found out – cloths, sometimes quite artistically done, that tell your enemies who killed their friends, and that they can expect more. The worrying thing is, if the gangs feel safe enough to be so brazen, have they already got people inside the police who are protecting them? Have they already compromised a customs point?

Still, can't be thinking about that. If I get Soto, all these questions will be answered.

What I'm really after isn't news, but a bit of software. John drops it on Google Cloud and I pick it up. It's not strictly legal for me to have this, but John has risked his neck for me. It's no more than an app, really, that I can install on both my phone and

Liana's. It lets me use hers as a listening device, even when the phone is switched off.

I just spark up the app and effectively I've got a bug I can tap into any time I want. We also use this on Soto's nephew's mother, sending her a text from his phone with a question mark on it. This is cruel and unpleasant, but it gets the app on to her phone and it's entirely consistent with the taunting behaviour of the drug cartels. The pity is that we hear nothing from it – just sounds of domestic life.

I also pass John the mobile phone numbers and the names, to see if he can get me closer to Soto.

I check that no one's looking – and it's safe to say they aren't; the streets are deserted – then get into position in the Accord and wait until I see the target go in. I leave it a couple of hours – our boy normally doesn't come out until at least midnight. No point exposing Liana to any more of his charming company than strictly necessary.

At ten I give her the call and her brother pulls up in the minibus and drops her off with a big hug. She looks absolutely amazing, if a little classy for a gangster's girl. She goes inside, and Miguel pulls off to find a place to park the bus out of sight.

About an hour later, he walks up to the car and gets in. Again, it's safe for him to take up position, so he climbs in next to me under the seat. It's going to be a long wait, in pretty grim conditions. It's not helped by the fact that I'm already wearing one of the military flak jackets, and that Miguel put one on as he got in – it doesn't leave a lot of room in there. Our boy normally leaves at midnight, but he has been known to stay in there until three or four. Midnight comes and goes, and the car boot is getting close to freezing. I can't help thinking that security here is a bit lax, but then again, these are not the top dogs.

Ernesto is here too – up on a fire escape overlooking the back of the club.

At one in the morning, two cars pull up – both big SUVs with blacked-out windows – one Cadillac, one ultra-blingy Range Rover Sport. Call it intuition, but I know immediately that something has gone wrong. This hasn't happened before, plus this is a kind of middle-market joint. These cars are a league above that – top-of-the-range stuff.

Two guys in the car, two on the pavement with AKs, and hello, it's only old Soto going in there. I feel my pulse start to race but I calm myself. There's a white guy with him – I can only see the top of his head because he gets out of the wrong side of the car.

Miguel looks anxious. 'What do we do?' he says.

Something might have gone wrong here – there was always a risk – but what I hadn't foreseen was Soto turning up. I pull out the phone and tap the app. All I can hear is Latin disco music, nothing more.

'I'm going in there to get her out!' says Miguel. His eyes are wild, I can see that even in the dimness of the boot, which is lit only by the small holes for the sight and the guns. He's making too much noise.

'Calm down!'

'You come up with something or I swear I'm going in now!'

'Leave it. You don't know why he's there. There's a gringo with him; it could just be a business meeting.'

It occurs to me to choke Miguel out, just put him

under for a bit to calm him down. I really doubt that they've recognised Liana. I curse myself for having brought him along. He's too emotionally connected to all this. Whatever's happened, too much has changed in this situation from our original plan. We can always try again another day – patience is the key to this sort of operation. I'll abort it.

I pull out the mobile phone I took off Soto's nephew and turn it on. I scroll down to 'Mama' and pass the phone to Miguel.

'Tell her there's a bomb in La Luz nightclub and that Soto's in there. She should call him and get him out.'

He nods and makes the call.

'Someone answer?'

'Yeah.'

'Good.'

Suddenly the *sicarios* on the pavement jump into action, leaping into the cars and starting the engines. I've a split-second decision to make, and I make it, putting a Ruger round into the front tyre of the rear car just before it pulls away. The noise and the smoke in the boot are terrible, but the guys in the car are too intent on screeching around the corner to notice.

'They're going for the fire exit,' I say. 'Reverse out and get ready to follow them.'

I've got a choice here. I'm trained for high-speed pursuit, but I have a feeling there's going to be a bit of shooting. If they've got Liana with them, then I'm going to have to be very careful in confronting them. I can't leave it up to Miguel to blast away as best he can.

Ernesto at the back phones in.

'He says they've got her!' says Miguel.

'Well tell him to head for the RV as planned and be ready to receive us. We're going to be transferring to his car according to plan B. He must not come to help us. Stress that. We need his car to get away in.'

The cars come screeching back round to the front, the one whose tyre I hit already slewing across the road, losing it as he goes around the corner and ending up facing the opposite way. The SUV behind goes crashing into it, and there's a pop of airbags on both cars.

I aim for the ones I can see, sticking a round into the driver of the car that spun and the passenger of the rear car. That's the most I can risk with Liana in one of the vehicles. I don't know where she's sitting.

'Reverse fast!' I shout at Miguel. 'Don't ram them!'

He hammers the car backwards across the road as I kick the armoured shield up into place to protect him and pull down my balaclava. The wheels scream in an arc of burning rubber. Shit, he's lost control and gone sideways instead of backwards, which is what I'd intended. So much for the armour. I open the boot and poke the AK out. Soto's got Liana, but she's struggling with him so he can't aim his gun. Has he kidnapped her, or is he just using her as a human shield? Three men in the other car haven't got out yet; they're arguing about what to do. I click the AK on to full auto and empty the magazine into the car without Liana in it, coming up to a kneel as I do so to get an angle on my shots through the window of the higher car.

I go to jump out, but as I do, Miguel pulls the car around hard to get the shield in place and I fall smack on to the tarmac. It probably saves me life. A hail of bullets zips through the air where I was. I see movement out of the corner of my left eye. Someone is coming out of the club. There were at least four *sicarios* – including the one we originally targeted. They got dropped off there, so they have no car.

But only one of them has emerged, and he appears to be bleeding. They haven't seen me, and one of them is shouting out in Spanish:

'*No era yo! No era yo!*' I can only just hear him; the gunshots have made me deaf, and everything's taking on that strange underwater slow-motion quality you get in battle.

There's a blast of fire from behind the cars, and he falls dead. I guess they thought someone had set them up. Too bad. From where I am on the floor, I can see four pairs of feet behind the car. Two belong to Soto and Liana, the other two to *sicarios*. I give the two guys a couple of shots each, and they're on the floor, screaming. Then I've got to move, because Soto has put his pistol on the ground and is returning fire. Liana makes a run for it. I hear her footsteps on the concrete. I hear Soto scream, '*Puta!*' Shit, Miguel's out of the car, his pistol in his hand. He comes screaming around the crashed cars, blasting wildly at Soto. He's dropped with a single shot. That means Soto's got to reload – he's been spraying bullets wildly and wouldn't fire just one at Miguel if he had more in the magazine.

I vault over the car. Soto is the only man standing, and clearly as deaf as I am from all the gunfire. He swings a briefcase at my head. I hadn't expected that. What's he doing with a briefcase? I block it and step in, seizing his wrist with both hands and turning my back to him. Putting his elbow against my shoulder, I yank down in a classic arm break. It gives way with a loud snap, but I don't let go. I turn on him, driving my arm up into his armpit and throwing him with a shoulder throw. Then I choke him out on the ground. From the moment I get hold of him to the moment he loses consciousness seems to take forever, but it's probably less than ten seconds.

Liana's come running back to Miguel. I join her. He's breathing, though he has a big wound in his leg. Soto's obviously used to dealing with people in ballistic vests and has shot low. I strip a T-shirt off a dead *sicario* and pick up Miguel to take him to the back of the car.

'Keep pressure on the wound!' I say to Liana, miming what to do. 'We'll get him to hospital.'

A burst of gunfire comes from the bottom of the street. Great, it's the Federales.

They're advancing fairly tentatively in a big pick-up, but it's bristling with guns.

I pick up a tear gas grenade and run back to get Soto.

He's conscious now, very groggy, but screaming out at the Federales, who seem reluctant to come on while I'm there. I grab him and try to get him to his feet, but he's having none of it. It's then that I realise. One of the guys lying next to him isn't a *sicario* at all. He's a rather pudgy gringo in tennis shoes and business shirt.

I'm not going to be able to move Soto, and I'm running out of time. I reach into my trouser pocket and he thinks I'm going to shoot him.

Instead I take out my phone and quickly photograph the gringo.

The engine of the Federales' Jeep picks up revs; they've obviously decided to come and get their boy. I have to get out of here; I'm completely exposed.

I could kill him now, but I'm not going to do that. I've got this close to him once, I can do it again.

It's amazing how your Spanish improves if you've got something you really need to say.

I stare into his eyes and say, '*Le conseguiré*.' I will get you. I didn't even know I knew that until that minute.

I grab his briefcase, toss a tear gas grenade into his lap, jump over the car and into the Accord. Then we're off.

'*No hopital. No hopital!*' Liana is shouting from the back seat.

'Why not?'

'Doctor dies *si le toca*!' The doctor will die if he touches him. These animals aren't beyond shooting up a hospital, that's for sure.

'OK.'

We hit the RV alley, but there's no time to change vehicles now. Liana calls Ernesto to tell him we're coming to the bridge. I call Maria.

A sleepy voice answers.

'Got a problem.'

'Who is this?'

'Your English friend.'

'Jesus, I thought you were dead.'

'No. I have a casualty, though, and can't go to hospital. Can you help?'

'Who is it?'

'A Mexican man. He's been helping me.'

'I can have an ambulance pick him up and get him treated in El Paso.'

'He can go across the border?'

'If he's in danger of his life. Happens all the time. Let me send it now.'

'I got to Soto but I had to leave him. Any info on his location, let me know.'

'Yeah. Where do I meet you?'

'At the Bridge of the Americas. How long will it take?'

'Five minutes; the ambulances have priority clearance.'

'OK. We have to assume that your office is unsafe. Maybe even your number. Soto knew I was coming to the US.'

'Right. So they might know you're coming to the bridge.'

'Yeah.'

'Drive right up to the border.'

'I have two other Mexican nationals with me. Can they come over?'

'Not without visas.'

'We could be caught in a fire fight on the bridge.'

'You'll have to deal with that. If they get shot, they can come over.'

Terrific.

'Can I trust the Mexican guards?'

'I don't know.'

Great.

We're screaming down a big road by the Rio Grande now, Liana directing by pointing. The Bridge of the Americas is in front of us. The early-morning traffic is already twenty or thirty cars deep in the queue for the turnstiles, and around the corner now. It's then that I hear the familiar rattle of an automatic rifle behind me and rounds smacking into the metal screen on the back window and the body of the car. I can't see anything there, and there's no point in looking.

'What? What?' shouts Liana.

She is asking me what she can do.

'Just keep the pressure on the wound and your head down!'

Another five hundred yards and the car starts to cough. They've hit something vital, probably the fuel tank by the way the dial's fallen to empty, and although we've been lucky not to go up in flames, the car's going no further.

I slam it hard left into the traffic lanes approaching the bridge. I can't see the ambulance, but we have to go for it.

I can't let the car grind to a halt and this isn't the time or the place to be seen to be shooting back. Mexico, unbelievably considering what goes on here, has very strict gun laws.

There's a Mexican military outpost here, and some of the boys from that are starting to wander forward in curiosity at all the noise.

Liana jumps out of the back of the car and I pass her the briefcase – we want whatever's in that because Soto seemed keen enough to hold on to it. Then I ditch the ballistic vest – going to have to run for it and can't do with the weight. Luckily these new American jobs are quick release – designed for paramedics to be able to get them off you quickly if you're wounded.

I grab Miguel, put him over my shoulder and run for the line of cars. At least we'll have some cover there, and if the Mexican army do their job and shoot back, it should put the *sicarios* off from shooting at us.

I've reached the very first car when the bullets start to zip past my ears. I hear Liana cry out and I turn but I can't see her. The ambulance is coming, blue lights flashing, but it's on the other side of the road. I have to get Miguel over there.

Thank God the Mexican soldiers are coming towards me, four guys with automatic rifles. They don't look particularly certain what to do. People are screaming, jumping out of their cars, and the air's thick with the smell of gun smoke and gasoline.

I carry Miguel between the cars and realise there's a mesh fence between the two lanes of traffic. It's only one of those builders' temporary jobs but I won't be able to go across. Smack. One of the soldiers goes down. I look around. Two SUVs, two pick-ups, both blasting away, but now the army lads have been piqued by the shooting of their friend and start to return fire. That at least makes the *sicarios* keep their heads down. People are running from their cars, some towards the US, some back off the bridge, anywhere to get away from the *sicarios* and the army boys.

I put Miguel down and crawl to the fence and pull the mesh panels apart. It's only resting on bricks, so it's not too difficult. The US paramedic is showing unbelievable nuts to keep his vehicle there. The doors are open; Maria is there.

'Get in!' she screams as the paramedics pull Miguel under the fence.

'No, I've got to do one more thing.'

'You'll die!'

'So will you if you don't move. Now go!'

I duck away from the ambulance, running back down the line of cars.

The *sicarios* aren't going anywhere and have advanced on foot on to the bridge as far as the Accord. There are five of them, chewing away with automatic rifles. All the civilians are long gone, but most of their cars remain. I take out my mobile phone, select 'Bertie' from the address book and hit dial. Bertie is Bertie Bomb. The two pipe bombs in the Accord go off to devastating effect, the first triggering the second. The Accord is lifted about three feet off the floor, exploding in a ball of flame and shrapnel.

It's an awful sight. All the *sicarios* next to the car are killed, along with two in the back of the pick-up nearest to the explosion. An SUV starts into life and squeals off over the bridge. That was enough for the remaining *sicarios*. They've decamped.

I turn around. The ambulance is gone. I phone Liana.

'*Si.*' I can hardly hear her through the ringing in my ears.

'*Es mi. Dónde?*' It's me. Where?

'*Aquí.*'

I turn round. She's right next to my elbow. The case is still in her hand.

'*Poco a poco,*' I say to her. Little by little. That's the Spanish expression for 'gently', I've come to understand. I take the case from her and lead her off the bridge. The carnage and confusion are terrible, and ambulances are now pouring in from both sides of the border. Some of the *sicarios* are calling out for help, and there seems to be a new battle between the army, who have arrived in force, and the paramedics about whether they get a kicking or treatment.

We walk down into Juarez. This city is incredible. A small act of war has just taken place on one of its major thoroughfares, but already the traffic is impatient and honking in the gridlock that blocks the avenue beside the Rio Grande, windscreen wipers and snack salesmen running between the cars. Nothing shocks this town. Nothing.

Chapter 15

We take to a back street and cut up away from the main drag.

'At disco. *No necessito*,' says Liana. She seems to be saying that I shouldn't have made the call at the club.

'No danger? *No peligroso*?'

'No. Soto has big business. Happy.'

So Soto had come there to celebrate. To celebrate what? I wish we could communicate a bit better.

'Your brother. Miguel. *Hermano*.'

She nods and gives a sad shrug. '*Si*.' She understands, I think, that her brother was coming in there to get her no matter what, and I had to stop him.

I still have the case, so as we get to the centre of town, I duck into a mall. In the gents' toilets I open the case. Well, there's something. It's a gun I don't recognise, along with a set of night goggles. There aren't any marks on this thing at all – no serial number, no manufacturer's stamp. It's an assault rifle and grenade launcher combined – clearly fires 5.56

128

rounds. It's an impressive bit of kit – it reminds me of the Daewoo K11. Daewoo make assault rifles that could never be issued to the British Army; the number of times squaddies would say 'That'll be the Daewoo' when shooting one would render whole divisions clinically insane within weeks. But it is really similar; maybe I'd go as far as to say it's a rip-off. It has a laser rangefinder that tells you the distance to a target absolutely accurately and automatically adjusts the shell so it bursts on top of the target. It's linked – wirelessly it looks like – to the goggles, which give a thermal display, ranges, night vision, you name it. A quick check shows that this one's loaded with a thirty-round magazine and six 20mm airburst shells. It's also got a built-in bipod for stable shooting. It's said that in Mexico you'd be in trouble for a single spent shell casing on the floor of your car. If that's the case, I could be looking at about twelve life sentences for this thing. It's a frightening bit of kit.

Out in the street, we call Ernesto. He's pleased to hear from his sister and we reassure him about Miguel. We head back to the garage, and I'm glad to get out of my sweat-soaked clothes and have a shower. The amount of dirt you pick up in combat still never fails to amaze me. My whole body aches too, as the adrenalin subsides. I realise I've thumped my knee big-style at some point, and I have livid bruises all the way from my hip to my ribs on the right side. Have to count that as a win, though, considering the amount of lead that's been flying my way today.

Liana hangs around and cleans up herself. She's a beautiful girl for sure, all the more beautiful for how tough she is. The average Westerner, having been through what she's been through, would need months or years of counselling. She doesn't want counselling. She wants revenge.

Now the conversation can go a bit more smoothly because we have the laptop to help us translate, and we get a much better idea of what we're saying to each other. It's not perfect, but it's a damn sight easier than trying to get by with pointing.

Seems Soto was in a good mood because the gringo had given him the money.

They were celebrating with the club girls, booze and coke. Soto was saying that the Araña cartel were in for a big surprise.

Looking at the gun, I'd say he was right. Now I've had a chance to experiment with it, I can see how the goggles work. They've actually got a heads-up display linked to a camera below the barrel. You can aim the rifle without the goggles through the sights – which also have day/night options. But if you pair it with the goggles, the laser finder works to give you a crosshair over your target when you're aiming correctly – it's like *Call of Duty*. An experienced soldier would find it difficult to miss with this, and even the *sicarios* would have their accuracy improved massively. Add the airburst shells into the equation and you've got the capability to take out people hiding behind barricades or shooting around corners.

Another amazing thing about this gun is that you don't have to expose your whole head from behind a barricade to fire it. You could hold it above your head and aim using the goggles streaming live video from the muzzle. You also have the ability to link the guns: a command can show what you're up to, and you can immediately patch in to one of your buddies to see what he's seeing. Impressive.

If Soto's got a shipment of these rifles coming, I'd say he was right to be happy. They're top-grade military hardware. In urban warfare or house clearances, one of these would give the shooter a tremendous advantage. To be honest, I wouldn't trust it compared to a tried and tested gun if I was going to war, but its weapons system could come in very useful.

I wonder where he's getting this stuff from. The British Army hasn't got it, nor the Yanks. And as much as this gun is similar to the Korean one, this represents a stage beyond it in evolution. Clearly La Frontera have some serious backers. I wonder who they are and what they want. These boys buy a lot of guns, but not in military quantities. And the risks are too great for any firm supplying them, compared to the rewards. Mind you, a corrupt executive might not turn his nose up at ten million dollars in drug money.

I upload some anonymising and encrypting software from the Internet. I then send the picture I have of the gringo who was with Soto to a private Posterous account. I use the Hotmail box to contact John in England to tell him how to get to the account, along with instructions to ask Maria how Miguel is. I want that gringo identified asap.

I sleep on the sofa at Ernesto's while Liana takes his bed. She's decided she's going to stay here until she finds out what's happened to Miguel.

It's good to sleep, but I can't allow myself a long one.

When I wake up, I check the email. The dead gringo's been identified. He's Per Van Rooyen, a South African former National Intelligence Service guy. He left that service in 1981 – well before the end of apartheid – and had been working as a freelancer for arms companies in trouble spots around the world ever since. He was regarded as a safe pair of hands to carry out negotiations in war zones around the world, and was very well paid. How do the DEA know him? He was also a former CIA operative. When the US wanted to get money through to the far-right Contra rebel death squads in Nicaragua in the early eighties, Van Rooyen was their man on the ground. He set up links between the Mexican drug cartels and the Contras, funding the war against the Socialists in Nicaragua with the proceeds of cocaine that ended up fuelling the crack epidemic in the US. He was a US state-employed drug dealer according to the DEA, who, as John points out in his email, have a dim view of the CIA.

Whether all that murky stuff happened or not, the DEA IDed him immediately. They hadn't known he was there. Maria tells me to proceed with extreme caution. Van Rooyen played every side in the drug wars, and it's impossible to say what friends he might have. I might not just be stepping on the toes of La Frontera cartel. The presence of Van Rooyen hints at links to a wider world.

Maria has come up with one further piece of information – Soto's been taken to the central hospital and is, according to sources, still there. In theory he's a sitting duck, though this particular duck is going to be surrounded by some serious protection.

It's not practical to get to him in the hospital. However, this arms connection has intrigued me.

Kidnapping one of Soto's men doesn't look like it's going to work. I take out the dossier Maria gave me on him – along with details of three known safe houses. One is his main house in the west. I don't think he'll be going back there. There's a place up in the mountains in the national park the Americans call the Big Bend, but the most interesting looks to be El Porvenir. This is – or was – a prosperous little cotton- and alfalfa-growing town near to the border, east of Juarez. It's just opposite the Texan town of Fort Hancock. Unbelievably, the narcos have virtually emptied the place. They gave the entire population two months to get out or be killed. So it's an entire town taken over and run by La Frontera. There has, typically, been serious trouble there too, as the Araña cartel made a push against it as soon as La Frontera got there. It appears the army has either joined in on the side of the drug barons, or just stood by and let the narcos get on with it.

It makes sense that he'd go here while he recovers. It's out of town, easily defendable and roadblocks can stop anything heavy coming in. Anyone else is either going to have to drive across the desert – in which case they'll be seen or heard – or walk, in which case a quick getaway becomes difficult. It's also where I would guess he'd want to keep any incriminating evidence of his dealings. If you can see your enemy coming, you've got time to destroy anything you don't want him to see. That's where I'm going to look for him, anyway. If he's not there, I can still gain useful information on the kind of forces he has at his disposal.

I've been thinking a lot about La Frontera and concluded that it's losing its grip. If it's been forced into such extreme measures as attacking the UK drugs market, opening new routes by basically staging an act of civil war, then it's obviously behaving desperately. It's also taken steps to secure some major arms supply. That should boost its manpower, because it will be able to offer the gangs access to the best weaponry.

It's getting dark when there's activity out front. Something is thumping along the road. I don't want to look out, but there is the sound of motors and it stops outside our door.

I take up the MP5. There's a lot of noise downstairs, even more than normal from the repair shop. Someone's laughing and joking. I relax slightly and return the MP5 to the rest of the weapons, which I've placed under the bed in the back room. There are footsteps on the stairs, the sound of a man's voice. It's not Ernesto. Liana and I look at each other. Quickly she leads me to the bedroom, closes the door and gestures for me to lie on the bed. 'Sicarios,' she says.

I do what I'm told, pushing my pistol under the pillow. She quickly strips down to her underwear and lies down beside me. We're both face down. I can't at first work out what she's doing.

Then I get it. I've spent the whole time fighting La Frontera in a balaclava – apart from at the mall. On the off chance someone recognises me, she's giving me the perfect excuse to cover my face – by lying face down on the bed.

I hear the guy pissing heavily. Then he starts to take a look around the flat.

He opens the door. I have my hand on the gun beneath the pillow.

He says something in Spanish, which I think translates as 'nice ass'. He walks into the room and squeeze's Liana's backside.

Laughing deeply, he says something to me. I hear the word '*hermano*' – brother. Then he walks out and I hear him going down the stairs, and she says a word that needs no translation.

That's what power does to you – you think you can do what you like.

There's the sound of an engine driving away, and Ernesto comes up the stairs.

'*Carro*,' he says, '*carro, tenemos su carro.*' Which, in Mexican slang, means 'we have his car'.

I walk down the stairs into the main bay. There, its front end smashed in, bullet holes across its doors, is the Range Rover Sport that Soto rolled up to the club in. Next to it is a brand new Cadillac, in need of similarly urgent attention.

'When does he want them back?' I say – because I'm planning on including a few optional extras he might not like.

135

Chapter 16

Ernesto is a genius. The one good thing about operating in a criminal economy is that the kit you need for a bit of skulduggery is never far away. First thing up, he clones the key to the Range Rover. Then, using a black-market BlackBerry with GPS, we build ourselves a bug, disabling the phone's speakers and ringers but wiring it directly into the car's electrics so that it's taking a permanent charge from the battery. It's installed in the actual body of the car, under the repair that Ernesto does to the front. He's a miracle worker in straightening the thing out, and conceals the smartphone in its own little weatherproof case inside the wheel arch. I've been around cars my whole life, and if I came across that while I was working on it, I'd just assume it was part of the manufacturer's design. Now I can get its exact location at all times. We also fit it with a remote kill switch, so that I can turn this engine off whenever I want to just by using an app on my phone.

Finally Ernesto modifies the car's existing secret

compartment – in which there is, conveniently, an oxygen bottle and mask. At the moment, the under-seat area can accommodate one person, just about. The idea is that the stowaway is actually screwed in with no way of getting out. Ernesto drills out the screw holes so that the screws simply rest in them. Then he installs a magnetic sealing system. It looks exactly the same from the inside, but now the person in the secret compartment can get out by themselves. This all falls in with my kidnap plan. He also pops a little explosive device up inside the inner front wing of the Cadillac for good measure.

Ernesto irons out the cars in a couple of days and they are ready to be picked up by Soto's *sicarios*, good as new. A message from John comes in. DEA sources say Soto will be going to El Porvenir as soon as he's out of hospital, which won't be long.

I need to be waiting for him when he gets there. Plan of exit is pretty much straight over the bridge to Fort Worth. The guards on the Mexican side may well have taken either the silver or the lead, but if I can conceal him until I get him to the US, I'll be fine. This is a stealth operation. I'm going to hole up in El Porvenir, where I can watch him up close for a while. Then I have a plan that, if it works, will allow me to just drive him into Texas unhindered.

While I'm waiting for the car to be fixed, Ernesto drops me in town and I nick an old Honda Civic. Then I research the town on the Internet. It takes me a while to find the international bridge to the USA – it's actually about six kilometres north of the town, and is nowhere near as big as the bridges in Juarez.

The satellite maps on Google are very useful,

though Google Earth doesn't reveal much more. I expect it's quite hard work to find someone willing to drive around narco country with a video camera stuck on the outside of his car.

According to my briefing, Soto's set up in the mayor's house on the north-east corner of the town. This is a pain in one way, because I'm planning on coming out of the desert hills to the south-west, so I'll have to skirt the town. On the positive side, the mayor's house seems to have a view of some trees. They'll provide me with cover as I scout the area looking for a decent observation point for my close target recce.

I have to travel light for the trip. I take the mysterious rifle and the goggles, replacement batteries for both and three more home-made pipe bombs, linked to the phone names Bertie, Chloe, who's my daughter, and Catherine as in Catherine Zeta-Jones, as I wouldn't mind having her number. I also take the Leatherman, the Federale uniform and balaclava, a big water bottle, my smartphone, pistol, knife, and pen and paper to record my observations.

Then it's out down the big Federal Highway 2 for about twenty kilometres. That's about as far as I dare go in the car. Any further and I'll risk narco roadblocks. I turn off the highway and take some dirt tracks into the desert, then park up and wait for night to fall.

I drive east as soon as the sun goes down, not using my lights. Clouds have rolled in, blotting out the moon and the stars. I can't see much but I go forward slowly – no more than ten miles an hour in the poor light.

After about an hour I have to stop. There are people in front of me, lots of people.

They're only shapes at first, flitting through the darkness, but as I press on, I can see men, women, some kids, trudging across the desert in the dark. Jesus – migrants trying to get into the USA. How desperate do you need to be before you'd try a hike through such uncompromising land? At least they seem to have some sort of armed guide with them. I wonder how far they've come this way.

I drive on for another couple of miles. Then the windscreen shatters. At first I think a rock's been thrown up, but in a heartbeat I realise that there's nothing in front of me to throw up a rock. Another crack, and a flash in the dark. I'm under fire. I duck down right into the footwell, putting the engine block between me and the shooter. Then I accelerate. There's a whole lot more rattling around the car, and then the sound of shooting stops. I look up to see not very much – the windscreen's blown and the desert dust means I can't really open my eyes. The car's thumping and grounding on the uneven floor, so I slow down. Another half an hour of going forward half blind at twenty miles an hour and I think it might be OK to stop.

I get out of the car, assault rifle ready. I turn on the scope and scan the horizon. A few distant heat sources, nothing more.

I guess that I must have been attacked by one of the city gangs that come out here by night. My research showed up that they wait in the desert to prey on the immigrants who are trying to get over the border. They rob them, rape the women and kill them. Nice bunch of guys. If I wasn't focused on Soto, I'd go back and pay the bastards a visit.

It's about time I ditched the car now anyway. I can see El Porvenir up in front, a dim glow on the horizon. I turn off the scope, shoulder the rifle and make my way across the desert. I've no reason to believe that the town's on lockdown, but I know I'll stand out like a cat in a dogs' home if I just walk in. So it's got to be a very careful approach.

There's maybe another fifteen kilometres to go, but I don't want to get too close tonight. I need the maximum hours of darkness for my purposes. Instead I turn towards the hills overlooking the town. I can wait the day out there and sleep. I drink the last of the water I brought from the car. Now I just have five litre bottles in my backpack. That's a luxury amount based on the fact that it's only about six kilometres to the hills and I can ditch some there. I won't be carting it all with me into El Porvenir. I put the assault rifle into a big cheap holdall to disguise its outline and make for the hills.

A good day's sleep later, I'm ready to go, setting out a couple of hours before dusk so I'll arrive within clear view of the town as night falls.

It's dark when I get there – darker than it would normally be if this was a fully inhabited town. It really does seem that a lot of the people have left, because there are very few lights on here – maybe twenty in the whole town. The narcos want this as a base to store their drugs, somewhere with excellent communications and roads, a stone's throw from the desert. They're not exactly into community building.

Five hundred metres from the town, I stop and

check things out with the night sight. There are some people moving around, but not many – just a couple of solitary figures walking between the houses.

I can see from the scope that the south-west corner of the town where I am – the north-east approach being blocked by a large obstacle known as 'the United States' – is practically deserted. I wonder if I can get an OP here. I put on the rifle goggles. They're a decent set of IR goggles, combined with the heads-up display. Any movement is now completely obvious to me. I make the outskirts of the town and immediately encounter a large storage barn – no walls, just a roof supported on pillars, really. It's not a pretty sight in here. There are seven corpses lying around the place, and signs that they've been executed in the centre of the barn – the signs being a lot of blood and worse. There are some large bags of seed here too, and as I come forward, I notice that there are a lot of cigarette butts around them. You don't have to be Sherlock Holmes to work out that this is the seating area for people witnessing execution and torture. I use my knife to open one of the bags and push in a phone-operated pipe bomb. These bags are natural cover, and a ditch just behind me tells me that if I'm running, I can use the bags to hide behind, make the ditch and pin my pursuers down behind the bags. I can then explode the bomb. Just as I plan my way in, I plan my way out, and it's good to know I might be able to spring a few surprises.

Up in front I can see the exhaust of a car glowing bright green in the IR goggles. Someone has just arrived. Don't think it's Soto, because he hasn't got much of an entourage with him. Directly in front of me is a burned-out house. I quickly duck into that. Now I can see that most of the houses with lights on are grouped quite close together. This has its advantages, but it wouldn't work if the town came under sustained attack from a rival cartel. They've already surrendered the outskirts, giving their enemy plenty of cover. Better to take them on when they're stuck out in the desert and you're behind the nice thick wall of a house.

Just across the street I can see what I'm looking for. It's a tall building – looks like some sort of municipal facility, maybe a gym or a swimming pool. It has two floors and an apex tile roof. At the apex on this side is a small porthole window. I'm willing to bet it's got one on the back too. The entrance is in deep shadow so I can get into it unobserved.

I check the terrain again. Nothing. I crawl forward to the doors. They're glass, and I can see an empty reception desk. I click the goggles to image-intensification night vision, away from infrared. It's clear the place has been ransacked. I check the door for signs of a booby trap. Can't see any. The door is open and I go quietly in and up the stairs. I come to a balcony overlooking a basketball court with a climbing wall to one side. There are nine bodies in there, all young people, two children, clearly executed. The smell isn't pleasant and there are a good number of flies. Perhaps someone didn't leave town fast enough for the narcos' liking.

I make my way around the floor and come to a series of doors arranged around a large square area with a set of stairs in the middle. I listen at each and there doesn't appear to be anyone inside. I go in, opening each door with my foot, gun levelled.

Offices. I check them all out. All have been tipped upside down and none contains anyone. I come out of the last one and go up the flight of stairs. Here is a smaller floor containing one office. There are big skylights in it, which I couldn't see from the street, and the two porthole windows at either end. This will do well as an OP. The desk is in front of the porthole that faces the town, the chair roughly level with the window. I have to take precautions against being seen from the street. The window isn't huge – about three feet across – so it should be difficult to see into it, particularly in the bright sunshine of the Mexican autumn. Not moving while observing should be enough for me to remain undetected, but you can't guarantee it. I need to break the outline of my body. I very quietly remove the chair and push the desk nearer the window. Then I arrange some box files, some on their sides, some standing upright in a sort of mini-Manhattan effect on the desk. If I reduce the swivel chair to its lowest level, I'll even have the luxury of sitting down while I watch. Add to that a little kitchen area, which gives me a sink to piss in, and this is a pretty cushy OP.

The window at the back doesn't face much, but it'll make a good point to check if anyone's coming up behind me. I also check out a place to hide if things do get serious. There's access to a water tank here, through a small door in the side of the office. That's not going to work, as the space around it is small. However, there is a possible use for it, for which I do a little collecting in the basketball hall, trying to ignore the horrible sight of the bodies in front of me. I also put a box file on the floor in the entrance to the building and place a pipe bomb in it. It occurs to me to put this on the reception desk, but I'd prefer it to explode at leg level. Their upper bodies may be protected – I've seen they've got some serious body armour at their disposal. At the foot of the stairs to the OP I put a towel – pipe bomb in there too. Let's hope I don't have to use them.

Then it's a matter of settling down to watch. Ideally, of course, this is a two-person job, but since there's no one I can trust for this sort of thing, I have to do it myself. That means accepting that I can't do as thorough a job as I might.

I watch throughout the day and into the night, but as I start to tire, I know I'll need sleep. I set my phone to wake me every forty minutes. I can't enter deep sleep or I'll be vulnerable to someone sneaking up on me.

I sleep next to the water tank with the door shut.

What I do observe during the day is that there appears to be something like an electricity substation building about fifty yards away. The magnification on the rifle scope is good enough for me to pick out the 'Danger of Death' electrocuted man symbol. The doors are closed but I wonder how substantial they are. Substations are delicate things – you can take one out by just heaving a couple of metal rods or even throwing sheets of foil in there if you've got the nuts. Personally I'd prefer to blow it up from a distance. Electrical power of that magnitude frightens me – you never know what exactly it's going to do.

Better to be safe than sorry is my opinion. It's good

to know that the substation is there, though, because that enables me to tip things substantially to my advantage, should I need to.

The surveillance goes well. I can see a fair bit from here, and I note that the bulk of the *sicarios* are living in three big houses – doubtless the nicest ones where they found the most mod cons. There are about forty of them, armed with a variety of weaponry. I count fifteen AKs, and two other assault rifles. This is only the stuff they're wearing on the street; there may be a lot more weaponry hidden away in the houses. There's one Jeep mounted with what looks like a Browning M1919 medium machine gun. This has been around a long time – it's very similar to the gun used on the Spitfire in World War II. It takes a 250-round belt and fires at 600 rounds a minute, and can hit things up to just under a mile away.

That would be bad enough, but on day two something else pulls up – it looks like a Range Rover on steroids, except it's a light sandy colour and has a remote-operated turret on the top. This is a Plasan Sand Cat. I knew they were building them in Mexico, but I've never seen one in the flesh before. It's a modern armoured vehicle designed as a replacement for the Jeep. Its turret has a minigun – a multi-barrelled machine gun that can fire up to 4,000 rounds a minute – the relatively heavy 7.62 calibre. Its range is a bit shorter than the Browning, but given the fact that the car's well armoured, you can afford to get a bit closer – especially when engaging infantry. It's also got a grenade launcher on the roof-mounted turret. Clearly there's some collusion with the military going on here – you can't go into a shop and just buy one of those. Anyone coming at Soto over the desert here is in for a shock.

The guy driving it goes into one of the houses to my right, where he appears to stay. They don't post a guard on the car, but the door does seem to have an external lock.

Night-time is interesting. Nothing really happens until about midnight, at which point loud music starts and cars begin to pull up, disgorging *sicarios* and girls. This is a party, narco-style. I can see one guy sitting outside clearly smoking crack, and at some point during the evening I hear gunshots.

I've been there a day, living off muesli bars, when I notice a build-up. There are several army units coming in – the black-clad Federales. I'm in my Federale gear myself, so I'll be able to blend in if I'm making a run for it. Only problem is, these guys are clearly not worried about being identified by the narcos, because they haven't got their balaclavas on. That's possibly because they *are* the narcos. There are eight cars in total – a mixture of pick-ups and Jeeps. I know I'm in trouble when I see from the rear window that they're throwing a cordon around the town. There are three cars behind me, and I can see lights towards the edge of town. Big clouds are rolling in off the hills and lightning is flashing around.

I have to get out of here, but that's not going to be easy. They've effectively sealed the whole place off. It's pitch black in the office and there are lights outside so I have no chance of being seen. I squint through the rear window and immediately hit the floor. A man with a shock of blond hair is taking a rifle from one of the Jeeps. It looks exactly like the one I have. He puts on the goggles, and now I know things are serious. He can see me as easily as I can see him. I put on my goggles. The HUD reads 'Pairing. Accept or reject?' These guns are clearly part of a set. If I press 'accept', I'll know exactly where he is and be able to split my screen to see what he's seeing. As I know bloody well where he is and know he's looking up into the town, that's no good to me – particularly as he'll also know exactly where I am. I don't press anything. To reject it would be to show that I'm here.

Big raindrops start to hit the street, and thunder rumbles in from the hills. The cordon of lights remains at the edge of town, but now I can see torches coming forward, building to building. There have been no battles here; these aren't soldiers attacking the narcos, they're criminals hunting – what? Me? Could my presence here have been compromised? I didn't even tell Ernesto or Liana where I was going. But I did tell John, and he may have told Maria. If her computer has been hacked, then they'll know that I'm here.

The rain rattles across the roof and I can hear the men in the street shouting out: 'Gringo! Yanqui!' I stop myself marvelling at their lack of discipline and remind myself that there may be nearly eighty of them, some of them high as kites, heavily armed and looking for me.

Someone obviously has them under control, though, because they're not going into any of the houses, just combing the streets.

Then I hear the voice through the megaphone. He's

speaking English, heavily accented. Israeli? Arab? Can't tell what it is.

'Mr Kane! We know you're here. Your American friends have given you up. Surrender now and I can promise a quick death.'

I imagine he's scanning with the goggles, looking for any heat source. He knows full well that anyone who takes a shot at him is signing their own death warrant.

'Tomorrow we start setting fire to the buildings,' he says. 'We'll search any scrub, flush out any drain. When it's light, we will find you. Manhunting is my game, Mr Kane; we will find you.'

The thunder booms closer and the wind howls through the town. I've got to get out smartish. I walk down the stairs and halfway down again. Through the external doors I can see a major heat source. There are three of them right outside the front door. I don't know if they're planning on coming in or are just sheltering from the rain, but I can't go out that way. The emergency exits are possible, but I can't see beyond them. Someone could be on the other side.

This calls for extreme measures. I go down on to the basketball court and pick up the body of the only adult in the group. It's not nice work – he's a guy of about forty-five, quite heavy, and though he's not that long dead, he is starting to smell. I get him up to the top floor and put him into a climbing harness that I liberate from the gym area, clipping him to the rope before securing it around the water tank. 'Sorry, mate,' I say to the corpse, 'but this might help get a few of the bastards back.'

I had planned to escape this way myself, but that's

not going to work. To do what I need to do, I have to get the *sicarios* inside the building.

There's a really easy way of achieving that. I go back to the foyer entrance. The IR lights up the men outside like Blackpool at Christmas; the HUD crosshairs stop dancing and sit still over their huddled forms. One of them lights a cigarette and I give two squeezes on the trigger of the rifle. Two bursts of three smash through the glass door. Two of them are down, the other diving for cover. I retreat into the darkness upstairs and take out my mobile phone.

There's an awful lot of shouting and, as I would expect, a couple of grenades come flying through the doorway. I hear them explode, triggering the first pipe bomb. Ah well, no plan survives first contact with the enemy, as they say. I've got other concerns for the minute. The emergency exit at the back's being rammed through. I put three rounds into it to dissuade anyone from coming any further and jump into one of the offices. It's dark, but the *sicarios* have torches and the reception area is on fire.

I hear shouting and a confused argument at the bottom of the stairs. I dial Chloe, and the stairwell erupts as the second pipe bomb goes off.

I don't waste a second, running out of the office and up the stairs. To go out on to the street at the moment isn't practical. Others will be coming in through the door and will want to know why I'm going in the wrong direction.

It's time to make a little escape route. I go into the top office and lock the door, shoving the desk up against it. Won't do a lot of good, but better than nothing. I look out of the porthole window at the back, then open it quietly. The cars still have their lights on, so make a good target. The rangefinder seems unaffected by the rain. If it is, I'm about to find out. I fire an airburst shell into the first car. Then a second at the next one, and a third. Three huge explosions, screams, and the lights of the cars are out. Someone's shooting into the door now. I go to the front porthole. The street's crawling with *sicarios* and the turret on the armoured car is moving, as is the machine gun on the Jeep. I can't think about the consequences. I select my targets for maximum effect, one on top of the Jeep, another above the thickest group of enemy, a third a car whose lights I can see.

The door of the office is being cut to ribbons by machine-gun fire now, and I've got to expect a grenade before long. I crawl for the little door with the water tank in it and wriggle inside next to the dead body, then start kicking out the roof tiles. Bang! The grenade goes off, shredding the cheap wooden door to the water tank space. Luckily I'm behind the tank, which starts spewing water all over the place. I don't have an angle of fire, so I shove myself, belly to the floor, around the tank and push open the door. As the first Federale comes into the room, I give him three from a single squeeze of the trigger, then I'm crawling out of the hatch, laying down fire. There are four of them here but they're surprised to find me alive, and I advance on them firing accurately with the IR in the smoke and the darkness. They're down.

I take an AK from one of the fallen men and go back into the tank room. I strap the gun around the body, then kick it out through the hole in the tiles. I've tied the rope so that the body will dangle about halfway to the ground. Sure enough, withering fire goes into the side of the building and a big cheer goes up. I hope they'll think I'm dead, at least for long enough to allow me to slip away.

I'm down the stairs and on to the balcony. Federales are finally pouring through the fire exit. I empty the magazine of the advanced rifle at them, then throw the rifle down. As soon as the vision clears a bit, I ditch the goggles too. Back to old-school stuff now.

The building's on fire and I stagger out of it, picking up an AK and a couple of grenades from a fallen Federale as I go. I'm covered in the grime of the smoke. Maybe it saves my life. Like I said, I can just about pass as a Mexican if I keep my mouth shut. Like any modern nation, they're a diverse group. But here it wouldn't be so easy. Many of these guys might know each other, and anyone paler-skinned would probably stand out. As it is, I can see by my hands that I'm the colour of a chimney sweep and no one could really tell if I was bright green underneath.

I shoulder the AK and start to get out of there. I'm going to head for the desert. I should make the hills before dawn, and then it becomes much harder to find me. I'll have to run for it as soon as I get clear of the town.

I skirt back around the burning building and crawl across into the shadow of the barn. I roll behind the seed bags, but suddenly there's a rifle butt in my face, a flash of white light and I'm on my backside. I try to level the AK, but I'm stunned and the rifle butt comes down again, and that's the last I remember until I'm jerked to my knees and my vision clears to see a pistol pointing at my head.

'Nice try, Nick, but you've got too used to fighting crackheads. I figured you'd come out of the village the same way you went in.'

It's a tall blond guy in a Federales uniform, the advanced rifle slung around his body, the goggles down around his neck. Two men have hold of my arms and a cable-tie cuff is around one wrist, though the other is free. Guess I must have put up a struggle even though I can't remember anything about it.

A kick goes into my guts, but not from him. He shouts angrily at the Federale who did it – doubtless telling him that if they kill me, they aren't going to get any information out of me. Either that or he thinks hitting me is a job he wants to keep to himself.

'Who are you?' I ask.

'I think you'll agree questions are my prerogative at the moment. Tell me, why are you here and who are you working for?'

I say nothing.

'I get it, the grey man. Well, in five seconds you're going to be the very grey man, dead along with the rest of the men you did for tonight. My brief was to find you and kill you. Information is a bonus.'

I say nothing again. I think I could throw one of these guys on my arm; the problem is that I'd be shot before he hit the ground.

'There are methods, aren't there? I'm sure you've seen the YouTube videos of how the cartels like to kill people. I can shoot you, or, if you're uncooperative, I can let one of the army boys here

152

peel your face off and you'll be a viral Internet hit all over Mexico by tomorrow.'

One of the Federales comes up and frisks me. Pistol, knife, smartphone are tossed out on to the floor. Blondie takes the phone and looks through it. Thank God there's next to no information on it.

'Who's Bertie?'

No reply.

'Chloe?'

No reply again.

'Catherine?'

Same answer.

'OK, this is a nice phone. Video calling. Let's see which of your friends wants to watch you skinned alive. That's what I'm going to do if you don't talk. The friendly offer of a bullet to the head has been taken off the table. You choose. Skinned alive with your friend, lover, daughter watching, or at least listening; or maybe just skinned alive. Not much of a choice, but more generous than most people get.'

I say nothing.

He taps the screen of the phone.

Nothing happens.

I glance at the sacks of seed. I'm too near to that bloody pipe bomb if it goes off.

'Chloe.' He taps the phone . 'Hello, Chloe, I've got your husband on the line.' He smiles. 'Are any of your friends ever in?'

I am going to be blown up by that bomb. There are three Federales sitting on top of the bags, smoking, but they're not going to take the full blast. I'm all of fifteen feet away. Those things have about a five-metre killing blast. I might survive. But I probably won't.

'Catherine.'

He presses the screen.

Nothing.

Wisps of smoke start to issue from the bag. It didn't go off. The Federale sitting directly on top of it hasn't noticed in the smell of the burning building.

'We can video it and send it later,' says Blondie. He says something in Spanish to one of the Federales, who comes forward with a big sharp knife. He grabs me by my hair and sinks the blade into my forehead, just above the hairline. Blood spurts down into my right eye, and I can't see anything out of it. For the first time in my life I start to shake with fear. Blondie was wrong: I haven't seen the YouTube clips, though I did come across them in my research. I know he's going to use the hair under the knife to get a grip on the skin so he can pull it down like unpeeling a sock.

'*Lento, lento!*' says the Federale.

I know what that means all right – 'slowly, slowly'.

I'm not going to sit here and be butchered, though I'm certainly going to be killed. I can't break the grip of the guys on my arms, but I can use them as something to swing off. I pull down hard on both arms, lifting my body into the air to deliver a good kick to the kneecap of the guy with the knife.

My Federale boots are heavy and tough, and he goes down hard, dropping the knife and screaming. It's open day at fuck-you farm then from the Federales, as kicks and blows come raining in on me.

'Stop!' It's Blondie.

'You didn't like that way to go. These guys have plenty of others. How about breaking every bone in

154

your body? You've read about the guys who are found at the side of the road like that?'

I'm wrestled on to the floor, two guys on each arm, more on my legs. I feel the pistol come down hard on my right hand.

'*Numero uno!*' shouts Blondie.

'Hey!'

There's a shout from behind us, laughter.

'*Fuego!*'

'*La bolsa se arde!*'

I understand '*bolsa*'. It means 'bag'. I think he's saying that the bag's on fire.

The Federales seem to find this very funny, although one still takes the opportunity to stand on my broken fingers. I don't give him the satisfaction of screaming.

There's some more joking in Spanish. And then, finally, the pipe bomb goes off and the joking stops.

Chapter 17

I'm running as soon as the blast sweeps over me. I'm shielded by about six bodies, the guys standing right next to the bags, the men sitting on my legs and arms, even Blondie crouching to smash my hand again with the pistol.

It's chaos for a second and no one knows what's happened. I'm going hard for the cover of the buildings. In the desert I'm a dead man – they've got cars, lights, IR. In the buildings, among all the fire and the smoke, I have a chance.

There are too many Federales lying injured, too much smoke, to risk blasting away, but this doesn't seem to stop some of the boys who weren't affected by the explosion firing wildly. Ambulances are pouring into the town now. I run around the grid system of the houses, avoiding the ambulances. There are some areas that are lit, but most aren't, and my pursuers have very little chance of identifying me in the dark. I hear a car sweep around the corner, and dive for the shadows at the side of a house. It hammers past me.

To the north-east, up where the border is, I can see helicopters hovering. The Mexican response has been non-existent. These are the badlands. The only army that comes here is bought and paid for by the cartels.

There's an ambulance in front of me now, I could be off and away in that in no time. The paramedic has just closed the doors, but there are too many men around it, helping to load the wounded or waiting for evacuation themselves.

I need to get out. I have the advantage of the uniform and the dark, even if people are chasing me. They don't know quite what to do, having lost their leadership. Some are searching the houses, some running madly through the streets or cruising around in cars. I cut across some waste ground and come across the body of a Federale lying in the street. It's the second time today that the idea of using a body for a diversion occurs to me.

He has an AK, but I can't carry that and him, especially with a mashed hand. I drag him into the shadows and take his pistol belt. It's then that I realise he's still breathing. He has a big ugly wound in his side, which indicates to me that I got him from the top floor of the gym or that one of his mates shot him in the confusion. That makes up my mind. I'm going to save him and save myself in the process. He's a scumbag, but who knows what brought him to be doing what he's doing. And I'm not here to randomly kill people. I'm after Soto and I also want to stay alive. Anyone who gets in the way of those aims better watch himself. But I'm looking for justice, not revenge.

I get him up across my shoulder in a fireman's lift.

It's agony on my hand, but I've got him and I carry him up towards the ambulances. The fact that I'm taking one of their mates to get help means the Federales don't even look at me twice in the confusion.

There's a massive squabble going on near one of the ambulances as various people try to get in, but I push my way to the front and the medic takes one look at the guy who's with me and screams at the others, presumably to get back. I carry him up into the ambulance and drop him on to the bed. There's a guy lying on the other bed unconscious. A paramedic climbs in and says something to me, which I presume is an instruction to get out. I just point to the pistol on my belt and he gets the message. He shouts to the driver, goes to close the doors and there's a rush. Two Federales get in, one with a badly burned face, another with a bloody leg that's actually bad enough to soak the floor. The one with the bloody leg closes the door and just sits on the floor. The other one slumps down at the paramedic's feet.

The ambulance begins to drive, its siren blaring. We hit the highway, which is deserted apart from another ambulance in front of us. Great, Mr Leg has taken a glass pipe out of his top pocket and is inserting some crystals into the bottom of it.

'No *fumar*,' says the paramedic who is tending to our unconscious friend, waving at him to tell him he can't light up in here.

'*Chinga tu madre*,' says the bloke. He runs his Zippo under the pipe and takes a big hit. He's just told the medic to fuck himself.

'No *fumar!*' says the medic.

At which point the Federale takes out his pistol and shoots him. The noise is terrible, the smoke overwhelming. The ambulance swerves, the paramedic falls on top of me. He has a big wound in his ribs, just under his arm. The Federale drops the pistol wearily to his side.

It's at this point I do something I shouldn't do. I lose my temper. I shove the paramedic off and plant a big kick right in the middle of crack boy's face.

His head goes back into the wall of the ambulance and he's spark out cold.

I open the door and shove him out.

The other Federale looks at me, his eyes widening.

'Yanqui!' he says, going for the pistol in his belt. I can't mess about here. There's no way I can draw my own pistol; the belt's set up for a right-hander, and I'll never get it free in time having to fiddle with it with my one good hand.

I give him the best left hook I've got, right on the tip of the chin, diving down into it with all my weight behind it. I feel my knuckle break as I hit him, but he collapses like someone's hit the off switch.

He's going to have to go too. I relieve him of his mobile and kick him out the back of the ambulance, taking his AK as I do.

The driver shouts something at me in Spanish. I'm going to get him to drop me in the desert and then he can take his mate on to the hospital. Jesus, my hands hurt.

The driver shouts something in Spanish again.

'Drive, drive!' I say.

'You're American.'

'Yeah.' No point complicating stuff.

'How is my friend?'

'Not good.'

I look at the medic closely. The big veins on his neck are sticking out and he's a sickly blue colour, breathing shallow and rapid. He's collapsed a lung, for sure. I've seen this enough times.

'I'm going to aspirate his lung. I need a syringe.'

'You know what you're doing?'

'Yeah, just drive, get to the hospital. Where's the syringe?'

'In the bag hanging up above the bed.'

I take out a syringe, cursing with the pain in my hands. I can barely manage the bag, but thank God this operation doesn't require much beyond stabbing him with the syringe. I stick it into him just below the collarbone. There's a big hiss as all the trapped air comes out, and the guy's breathing starts to stabilise.

'Drop me in the desert,' I say.

'You're in pain.'

'Yes.'

'You should go to hospital.'

'I'll be killed if they find me there.'

'They won't find you. I can make sure.'

Juarez is approaching, and we're waved through the Federale roadblocks.

I sit back in the ambulance and find that I've started to shake. It's a natural reaction to the adrenalin wearing off. The city zooms past us, the streets quite empty at this hour.

We pull into the casualty entrance of the hospital, and now it is perfectly OK for me to pull down my Federale balaclava. Juarez is full of rival gangs, and even the army who are in league with La Frontera won't want to be seen by anyone working for Araña.

Nurses rush out to grab the paramedic, and the driver speaks to a doctor. He nods, and it's like I'm on a conveyor belt. I'm taken out and up into a lift by the doctor.

'You saved one of our ambulance guys,' he says in English as he examines my hands.

'Yes.'

'What are you? DEA? CIA? Border? FBI?'

'Do you think I'm going to tell you?'

We reach the top floor.

'You're going to need an X-ray,' he says. He presses another button on the lift and we go back down to the ground floor where we came in.

'Keep your mask on. I'll make it quick,' he says.

I see that he's used the lift as a sort of instant private consulting room. I'm whizzed through into X-ray, and then he leads me out through some swing doors and I find myself in a big car park. He sits me inside his car – a beaten-up Daihatsu Fourtrak. No one drives a snazzy car unless they're prepared to defend it around here.

He gets in next to me and cleans up my head wound, cutting back the hair. He injects the area around the cut, which hurts like hell, and then stitches it up.

'I'll be back in a minute. Help yourself to a drink,' he says. It's his idea of a joke. There's half a can of Coke wedged down the side of the seat.

I would like to drink it, but I don't think my hands are up to it.

He returns with the X-rays, some bandages and a bowl of water.

'You've fractured three fingers on your right hand and the little finger on your left. You'll need a cast on the right and strapping for the other one.'

'Which fingers are broken?'

'These.' He counts them off on his own hand. It's not the trigger finger.

'Can you make it as light as possible around the palm?' I say.

'You need to shoot a gun?'

'Yes.'

'We get that request a lot,' he says. 'I can leave the trigger finger free if you want.'

I have to laugh. Bespoke casts for gangsters.

'You're lucky,' he says. 'This is the best teaching hospital in Mexico for fracture management.'

'And gunshots,' I say.

'We're all good at gunshots,' he says. 'Get ready for a little pain.'

That's clearly doctor's code for 'brace yourself for nearly unbearable agony'. As he straightens my hand out, I say nothing.

'Tough guy,' he says.

'In my experience, screaming gets you shot,' I say.

He nods. Then a thought strikes me.

'Was Alberto Soto treated here recently?'

'No. He went to the Borunda private hospital. Worse treatment, better view,' he says.

This sets me thinking.

'Do you know anyone who does shifts there?'

The doctor puts his hands in the air.

'I'm not getting involved in this,' he says.

'I just want to know when he's going to have his cast removed.'

'They'll go to him,' says the doctor. 'A guy like that won't risk being out in public too much.'

'Do you think you could find out when that will be?'

He puts his head into his hands.

'No,' he says. 'I'm not endangering my friends.'

'These guys kill doctors, don't they?'

I know this from my research. A couple of years before, all four plastic surgeons who operated on one cartel boss were found dead. If they bring their buddies in for treatment and that buddy dies, some of the cartels tend to think it's the doctor's fault, rather than the guy who put six bullets in him in the first place.

'What do you want?'

'I want someone to send him an email from the hospital telling him he needs to have his cast removed. Then I want to know when and where I have to go to get to him.'

He finishes wrapping my hand in the wet blue cloth.

'Not interested. That'll take about ten minutes to dry,' he says.

'Do you know the name of the doctor who treated him?'

'No, but you can find that out.'

'How?'

'Just ring up and say you're not happy with how your hand has been set and ask for an appointment with the top guy.'

'Will I definitely get the right doctor?'

'When a gangster like Soto phones up, he doesn't have the medical directory open in front of him. He asks for the top guy. You know what the narcos are like. He'd have a gold-plated doctor if he could. He judges things by how expensive they are.'

'OK. Well, thanks for your help and your bravery.'

I take out my phone and use the one good finger on my right hand to call Ernesto.

'Would you mind translating for me?' I ask the doctor.

Chapter 18

As soon as we get through to Ernesto, I can tell from the doc's face that something's wrong. There's awful news – Miguel has gone missing from the US hospital where he was being treated.

Ernesto had a silent call from his brother this morning. He tried to call him back but didn't get a reply. Then he called the hospital and it was discovered that Miguel had disappeared.

Ernesto's been in hiding in the north of the city ever since, his mother and the rest of the family too. If they find out Miguel's identity, they'll kill his whole family to teach him a lesson.

'We should go after Miguel,' I say.

'No use,' says the doctor.

'Why not?'

'He's already dead. Or gone. Look for him in heaven.'

There's a chance Maria's phone is compromised, but I have to call her. She's says she'll get on to it.

When she rings me back, she tells me that she's contacted the sheriff's department and they've told her that they are looking at the CCTV at the hospital. There's no record of anyone coming or going. But if Ernesto and his family can make it to the border, she'll get them at least temporary asylum granted. I call Ernesto to tell him, with the doctor's help.

The doctor speaks to him and gives me my phone back. 'Someone's coming to get you,' he says.

I don't think this is a good idea and try to call Ernesto back, but there's no reply.

'I think you're going to have to get me some serious painkillers,' I say. 'I need to be able to shoot and I need to be able to do it very soon.'

He nods, goes away and comes back with six packs of needles. 'You're going to have to do this regularly,' he says. He slides an injection into my hand. It's briefly agony, but I can soon move my trigger finger without any pain. I pick up the pistol. No chance with the cast on, but I might be able to shoot the AK I picked up from the ambulance.

The doctor says I can wait in his car and leaves. Twenty minutes later I see the addiction centre minibus come into the car park. Liana is driving.

We have to get rid of that bus – it's a liability now they're looking for Ernesto. Liana's taken as much as she could from the garage: the Ruger, tear gas, mask, the laptop, several phones and all the ammo, a toolbox, the cash and the dead men's IDs and credit cards. She's also brought a change of clothes – thank God.

I load up the Fourtrak and hotwire it with a screwdriver through the ignition, not so easy with my broken hands. It starts up straight away and we're out into the traffic, Liana driving. The laptop has its dodgy 3G dongle in, so I dial up and get on to the smartphone tracing site. Soto's car is moving.

'I think Soto could be going to get Miguel,' I say. 'We could try to get him back. Get Miguel. Soto has him?'

She understands what I'm saying.

She shakes her head and then says very clearly, 'Miguel dead. Too late.'

I ring Maria again.

'Soto's moving,' I say.

'How do you know?'

'I've got a guy on him.'

'We've had word from the sheriff's office. They've got a Black Angel informant who says Miguel is alive and they're taking him across the border via Big Bend National Park tonight. That's very near one of Soto's main houses – you've got the info on it in the dossier. There's an unguarded crossing there. CCTV only.'

'What's a Black Angel?'

'They're the Frontera gang over here – their prison arm. Plenty of people on the outside too. They did the kidnapping.'

'Is he alive?'

They won't kill him this side of the border if they can help it,' she says. 'They can't buy the cops or the prison guards as easily in the US. But I think he's crossed the border already – the CCTV shows an El Paso registered SUV going over earlier tonight.'

'So you think this might be a set-up?'

'That would involve the corruption of officers on this side of the border.'

'Right. What about that CCTV from the hospital?'

'Sheriff's office took it, they got there first.'

'Can't you see it?'

'They're saying it's their jurisdiction.'

'Is it?'

'Yeah.'

'So they're helpful with the contact but not with the CCTV.'

'Bureaucracy, what can you do?' There's something in her voice that makes me think she thinks it's something more than bureaucracy.

'Will you go?' she says.

'I don't know.'

We motor around Juarez and I try to think. It is impossible. We can't let emotion intrude on the plan.

Liana puts her hand on my arm. She has tears streaming down her face.

'*Está bien*,' she says. It's OK.

There is nothing we can do – I can't run a suicide mission, this isn't *Saving Private Ryan* – but as I imagine what's happening to Miguel, I become more determined than ever to take out Soto, and soon.

Chapter 19

Five hours later, we're at a service station in the desert, drinking sickly Jarritos mango fizz and munching on tortillas. This is dinner. We've been plotted up in the desert for most of the day – somewhere to hide while we think what to do. While we waited, I searched the Internet news. My set-to in El Porvenir the previous night has made the US local news and been reported as a gun battle between the Araña cartel and the La Frontera boys.

It reports that around twenty *sicarios* are believed dead, with many more injured. There's footage which looks like it was filmed from the US side of the border. You can't see much, just a series of explosions as the airburst shells go off. This news chills me. I had no alternative, but it's not a particularly clever feeling to be responsible for so many deaths. Beyond that, it makes me wonder what will happen when La Frontera get their hands on the airburst shell technology.

I was disguised, in the dark, well armed with IR and a fairly fearsome gun, but I was still just one man. Imagine what a platoon could do armed with those weapons and that technology. And then there was the armoured car. Things are getting very serious. If these guys can take over whole towns, what next?

I've been thinking carefully about my tip that Miguel is being taken to Big Bend. I wonder who that came from. Soto's car arrived at Big Bend hours before and is still waiting there. For what? For Miguel to be delivered? No. Maria said he'd already crossed the border.

For me, I think. It's clear there must be a leak in Maria's office – if it's not Maria herself. I'm discounting her because she has tried to help me too much. But every time I call her I'm compromised in some way, and now I'm pretty sure someone has used her to get a message to me.

If Miguel has told them about how I saved his sister, they may think it worth a shot that I'd come to save him. And they'd be right if I was running this thing purely on emotion. Miguel's a good kid and he's helped me. But I know – and amazingly, his sister knows – that it's just not operationally possible.

Waiting in the desert, I get in contact with John and mention the presence of the blond guy. How he was injured in the bomb blast, so it's my thinking that he might have ended up in the hospital. Which means he might be on CCTV. John gets a request over to Maria, but this time he asks her to go to a call box and text him the number, and then he calls from a different line at SOCA. She says she can ask Mexican law enforcement to get hold of the recordings.

She has good contacts with – apparently at least – good people in the police. The day's digital recording is downloaded to her and to John. We get the blond guy IDed. Again, this is interesting. He is Evan De Waal, also former CIA but he was thrown out of the agency for unspecified reasons. He's worked as a mercenary everywhere from Angola to Peru. Interestingly, he has some contacts with arms manufacturers, again on the sales side. He's not the guy doing the selling, however; he's a security consultant assessing and protecting the safety of the salesmen.

He gave a false ID at the hospital and claimed to have been injured in a road accident, according to the medical records. He was concussed and a little burned but otherwise unharmed by the blast.

Something he said makes me wonder. He had instructions to kill me. Have they brought in a specialist just for me? I suppose I should feel flattered. Can't say that I do.

I'm beginning to wonder what I've stumbled into. Someone is supplying La Frontera with top-grade military hardware – someone whose operations I am clearly messing up. It isn't a surprise that they're prepared to kill me, but it is slightly odd that they've brought in a specialist to do so. They clearly know who I am, as De Waal addressed me by name. And they knew I was in El Porvenir. I told no one I was going there, but I did call Maria from my new mobile. Could they have got a track on that?

'What next?'

With a combination of my computer and sign language, I manage to get Liana to phone the private hospital and ask for the top fracture doctor. I hear the words *'más caro'* – most expensive – and we're told our man is a Dr Ramires. So he's very likely the guy to target if we need to get hold of Soto. Liana is put through to a secretary and explains that I've had a fracture fixed, I'm in pain and I need the doctor to look at it because I think it's been set wrong. I'd like to pay in cash.

The secretary tells me the doctor will see me first thing tomorrow morning.

I shake my head and type 'last appointment' and show Liana the computer screen. I'm pleased my index finger is usable without too much pain.

Twelve midday is his last one tomorrow. I nod. Liana engages the secretary in chat, as I've asked her to. She asks what appointment system they use, because she's always telling her dad, who is a plastic surgeon in Mexico City, he needs one. The secretary says it's Medi-Right. We'll download the free version of that later to practise on.

I've tried to think of a way to get into the offices at the hospital but I just couldn't see one. Hospitals are busy places and it's difficult to go breaking through locked doors in them.

The trouble is, in a city like this one, security is quite a high priority. I might be able to blag my way in pretending to be a patient or a guest but I'm not going to be able to disable an office lock, use the computer system and leave unnoticed.

So I've decided, after a bit of lateral thinking, on straightforward deception. We go into town and spend some of the *sicarios'* cash on good clothes, nothing too flashy but Liana recommends I buy a

Ralph Lauren polo shirt. She says I should try to look like a narco because it will be good if Ramires is nervous when he's seeing me. We also buy a memory stick.

Liana ducks into the hospital on the way back. She tells the receptionist she just wants a chat with Carla, the consultant's secretary, about my visit the next day. The receptionist says she can go on up. There she gives Carla some concerned-partner bullshit, saying she's from out of town, her husband is an important guy and she wants to make sure the hospital is up to his standards. Carla shows her around.

I've told her to notice everything she can about the waiting room, the secretary's area and the consulting rooms. Everything, particularly in the waiting area. She does a very good job of briefing me with the help of the translation site. The waiting area contains twenty-four chairs, a yucca plant, a TV and one of those fancy coffee machines. It has a bin, magazines and a central coffee table. The secretary leaves the door of her office unlocked when she goes out. It's a straightforward Yale-type doorknob lock – what we call a Kwikset lock. This is a massive relief. You can pick one of them with a couple of paperclips, a box of which we obtain from a store after she's finished the recce. We're hoping not to have to pick the locks and just rely on distraction, but you can't guarantee this sort of thing.

We drive into the desert for the evening. I've slept in more uncomfortable places than the Fourtrak. I look at Liana in the deep purple glow of the starry night. She's beautiful, but she's been through so much. I hope things are going to turn out OK for her. I should marry her and bring her home. But then, I think, laughing to myself for the first time in a long time, the poor woman has suffered enough.

The next day we wash and change at the petrol station and are ready to go.

We park the car in the hospital's car park and make our way into reception. We're asked for an impression of a credit card. I give them my real one. I'm clearly a gringo as soon as I open my mouth. If someone comes asking questions, then the scheme's blown anyway. I can't see why they would, though. Liana has the laptop in its bag, freshly charged from the car, and I have the Federale service revolver in my daysack. We are going to be winging it big style here.

We're told to go up to the top floor. There is the waiting area, just as Liana described – the coffee machine, the secretary's office with its Kwikset lock and, through that, Ramires's consulting room. The computer, which is what we're interested in, is on the desk. The secretary welcomes us and goes back to her work. I see my chance with the coffee machine and go over to it as if I'm making coffee, my back to the secretary. She's engrossed in her work and not looking anyway. The fuse is in a little plastic clip at the back of the machine. I lever that out with the screwdriver on my Leatherman and pocket it. Liana takes out the laptop and starts tapping away on it.

We're alone in the waiting room, which is why I chose the final appointment of the day, and after about ten minutes the last patient leaves. Now it's down to Liana. I'm called in. What should happen is that Liana will complain that the coffee machine is broken and ask for a cup of coffee like a self-important narco girl. The secretary will have to leave the office to make it. If this doesn't work, it's plan B.

If it does work, then Liana sticks in a USB drive, loads up a remote-control programme, activates it to allow control from our computer and gets out of there. Then the computer's ours via the web. Simple. In theory.

Ramires is studiously uninterested in anything about my life. He speaks good English but asks me nothing about what I do, who I am, why I'm here. He does ask me how I broke my hands and I just smile at him. He nods.

I can see he thinks I'm a complete idiot and a crybaby and he explains that it's normal for my hands to be hurting on just the first day in the cast. He says he can send me down for an X-ray if it pleases me. It doesn't. I complain and whine for a bit longer and eventually – after about half an hour, during which he's too polite to tell me to shut up and get out – I eventually leave of my own accord.

Liana is still playing on the laptop. A good sign.

I smile at her and we go to the lift. 'Down the stairs,' I say. I hope the Internet connection holds, because Carla will need to give permission to establish a link again if things go down, and she's not likely to do that. In a metal box like a lift there's more chance the connection will break.

In the reception, we pay for our appointment – at £80, cheaper than I thought. Liana waits with the laptop in the hospital while I go out and move the car around to the front of the building, opposite a very

175

pleasant big green park. This is the park that gives the hospital its name. Liana gets in and we wait.

At 1 p.m. the secretary emerges from the building with another woman and a man and goes over into the park. I'm amazed by such a sight in Juarez. But normal life does carry on. The sun is shining, there are birds around. It'd be a nice day if it wasn't for the drug war going on.

I look at the laptop. The link is still fine. We access the remote-control programme. Yup, there it is.

We find Soto's code name really easily. On exactly the date I broke his arm, all appointments in the afternoon are cancelled and a 'Señor Lopez' is put in instead.

The follow-up appointment is Wednesday and, glory be, he has an X-ray booked in for 11.30. He's the last patient of the morning too – clearly the doc doesn't want to feel he has to hurry him out. So Soto will have to come to the hospital because they can't take the X-ray to him. There's one thing I'm worried about. I check the web. Yup, there are such things as portable X-ray scanners, but they're quite new technology. It's a worry, though.

I get Liana to call the hospital. She says she's calling on behalf of a patient who can't visit the hospital for 'reasons of security'. She says he's broken his arm and his doctor says he needs an X-ray. Do they have a portable unit that could be sent? She's put through to X-ray and told that they did have one but it was sent out to a 'special patient' and stolen, the doctor accompanying it never heard from again. For that reason, says the radiographer, the hospital hasn't got one and the demand for them is understandably low in hospitals in Juarez. She says to talk to a doctor about other possibilities. She knows that vets have been used before.

With a bit of toing and froing, the gist of the story emerges from Liana. OK, what we do know is that Soto has to leave his compound that day. We don't know that he'll go to the hospital; he'll probably meet the doc at the nearest X-ray facility to him. I google it and there's nothing even close to where Soto's staying in the national park. There's a small town called Praxedis, which has been the centre of a lot of marijuana smuggling – dope accounting for a surprisingly high level of the cartels' income.

I would have thought there would be a vet's practice there, but there isn't. The nearest is Juarez. One way or another, Soto's coming home on that day.

While we have the connection, I scan the rest of the computer. Well, well, there's Soto's mobile number. It won't be too useful in terms of evidence gathering because he'll have a clean mobile on which he never talks business just for stuff like this, family matters. Others he'll change more often than most of us change our socks. However, it gives us a whole network of people we can potentially tap, once we see who he's calling. He might be guarded about his business dealings, but not every member of his family might be. His nephew who I killed in the desert, for instance, was clearly off his head half the time. Heavy crack or crystal meth use tends to reduce your ability to remember to be careful about what you say.

Surprise, surprise, there's no address on file but there is an email. Again, not too exciting, I doubt anything major goes down on that. However, it might give us the chance to do some computer forensics and find any other accounts that were created at the same time. The UK police couldn't do anything like that, but the Patriot Act in the US allows all sorts of skulduggery.

We sit in the car for the rest of the day, waiting for an email reply. Nothing. At five the connection goes dead; the secretary has clearly shut her computer down.

I have to plan my attack on Soto. This is going to mean close surveillance on his property. He could go about his Juarez visit in two ways. The first is to tip off all his boys and come in with his full entourage of people. That's my favourite. The Araña cartel have been squeezing him in the city and he needs to put in an appearance to show people he's still in command. These guys are all about front, killing and money.

My second bet is that he'll come in incognito in an unremarkable car, have his X-ray, get his cast removed and get out.

Either way, I need to know the full extent of what I'm up against at his ranch near Big Bend. This means a surveillance operation. After that, I have a decision to make.

Chapter 20

The X-ray appointment is in a week's time. This raises the problem of what to do with Liana until then. Luckily Big Bend – or the Mexican side of it – provides us with the answer. This is a sparsely attended national park – fewer than 300,000 visitors a year on the American side and probably not nearly as many on the Mexican. The whole thing's about 120 miles wide. 'Mountain, river and desert environments, unmatched for solitude,' says the website. Suits me.

Soto's house – which was referred to in Maria's dossier – is at the appropriately named Rancho Los Alamos. It's actually inside the park, halfway up some minor mountain range. The tracer confirms that he's there – or at least his car is. The house is convenient for all sorts of stuff, no doubt, and with a terrific view. For me as well as him. It's scrubby desert in the park, easy to get up close, which is what I intend to do. I can see no evidence of tracks on Google Maps – until I switch to satellite view. There's the house – more of a compound, really – with a single road in and no roads out, unless you consider dying an exit. I love this satellite view because it shows me so much. Shame you can't order up the images in slightly better resolution and in real time, but you can't have it all. I can see four buildings – a big one with a terrace, I should imagine, two smaller ones by the road – guard houses? – and some sort of outhouse. I'd guess this is either the generator or the oil tank. This place won't be on the grid and will need deliveries of heating oil. The big building looks to have solar panels on the roof too. Very green.

It's halfway up a small mountain, which is a strength from the point of view of resisting assault – no one's going to be coming down from behind.

Soto's journey to the doctor's is still in my mind. I figure that he'll pick up some boys from El Porvenir on his way in, and that even more will join him as he gets into Juarez. Can't really see any weak point in this operation that doesn't involve huge casualties, with me very likely being one of them.

We drive out into the national park, past Soto's house by thirty miles. We've bought enough supplies for two weeks, and the river here – which flows through a spectacular canyon at points – will provide us with water. I've brought enough in the car to last Liana two weeks – twenty-eight litres. I'll take two with me, but after that I'll risk the naturally available stuff, particularly as we bought some iodine from an outdoor supplies shop. God knows what else is in this river, but to be honest, if I live long enough for it to poison me, I'll be a happy man. I also picked up a bit of climbing equipment, fairly basic stuff – a harness, a rope, karabiners and a few other bits and bobs –

but up in the mountains, you don't know when it might come in useful. I got some big strong cable ties too. Liana also went into an army surplus store in Juarez and bought a couple of sleeping bags. She didn't buy a tent because I want her sleeping in the car with the doors locked at night. She'll have a pistol, but you want to be doubly safe.

She also got something that's worth its weight in gold, something I asked her to look for – a couple of big US military casualty blankets, which I was delighted to find they stocked. These are like the space blankets you see given out to people at the end of marathons but they're backed by a drab olive canvas. While I'm observing Soto it'll confuse, distort and mask my IR signature. If he has IR scanning, he'll need a real pro to understand he's looking at a man under a blanket and not just an animal or part of the landscape. They're good enough to fool the military out in Afghanistan. Finally I bought a pair of binoculars and a survival kit – fishing line, hooks, small compass and surgical sutures.

I'm going to be spending a week on surveillance, so it's time to leave Liana in the park. There are some old mines and caves out here, and we manage to get the Fourtrak into the mouth of one of those. It'll be a lot less visible to passers-by now – should there be any – particularly so at night. I also get her to set up a tripwire with the fishing line and attach it to a couple of Coke cans. At night, it will at least give her an advance warning that someone's coming. We check our mobiles before I go. Good, there is a signal, albeit a weak one.

I recce the caves a little. Some are no more than

crawl spaces under the hill – though one drops away into a dark shaft after a short way. Nothing immediately usable there.

I have the Ruger and the AK-47 with me, along with one of the Glocks I got in the desert back when all this began. The rest of the kit, including the MP5, I leave with Liana. I give her some brief instructions on its use, but recommend she uses the pistol in self-defence – a sub-machine gun's not an easy weapon to use if you're not very experienced in handling them.

Then I set out for Soto's compound, heading high up over the mountain behind it. I have to scout the trail as I go and make sure I'm unseen, travelling well below the horizon and keeping off the very tempting footpath that goes the first part of the way. I've blacked my face and dulled all the shiny surfaces with gaffer tape – my belt buckle is a particular risk – but I don' t bother with camouflage quite yet.

The going's hard for the first part, particularly with my bad hands. The left isn't too bad, but all the fingers on the right are screaming under the cast. Never mind, best thing is just to get used to it. I still have the anaesthetic, but I'm not going to use it until I really need it. I'm navigating using a map I drew off the satellite image. It's doing me well so far.

The country here is spectacular. I'm on a wonderful, if sparse, black mountain, and I can see the river winding through the scrub away to my right. The cactus is coming into bloom and the landscape is dotted with reds and yellows. Glad I took the higher route here, where there aren't as many of the spiky bastards. Pretty as they are, I don't want an arse full of spines if I can help it.

A day's walk brings me near to the compound. I have to be careful here, travelling in the shadow of the mountain at dawn until it moves away at about ten, and then spending a long, boring, though not cold, day holed up waiting to get into position. I'm not travelling far at night because I don't want to risk breaking a leg. So I have about three hours to move in.

On the Saturday I find an OP about a mile away and lie down to begin the reconnaissance. It's a hard routine now, no movement, short naps, woken by the vibration of my phone. I live beneath the blanket, eating rarely – just muesli bars and chorizo. There are a few things I didn't see on the satellite – there's a whole mobile phone mast there, for a start, a proper commercial job. That explains why we had no problem getting a signal out here, despite the mountains and the remoteness.

The evening of the day I arrive sees a major party going down; with cars coming up the track, girls getting out, music blaring. The next day, though, the revellers go home and something really interesting happens. Soto drives off with just a driver in the Range Rover and two guys in the Cadillac following him. This is safe country for him, if he's going a short way and doesn't need all his heavies with him. He controls here, he controls the local town of Praxedis; what could go wrong? I can see for quite a way with the binoculars and it seems to me he's turning towards the town – is he going to church? He drops out of sight as he goes down towards the canyon. Well that's a weak point, and I need to think about it. An ambush consisting of just me and an AK is going to be tough. I don't have the kit to take out one of the cars with an IED, but I do have the remote kill for both vehicles. This raises possibilities.

I watch for another few days. Trucks come and go, unloading stuff, and I notice that the cases look big enough to contain rifles. Cars come to pick them up, and the people in them bear the gang tattoos and flashy clothes of the Juarez street gangs. It looks to me as if Soto is gearing up for a major war. There are a lot of guys here now – maybe a hundred or so, all milling around the house, coming and going. Some are dressed in army uniform and one, as he takes delivery of a case, splits it open to reveal a ground-to-air rocket launcher. My blood freezes. Soto's main rival is known as 'King of the Skies' because he commands a fleet of aeroplanes that ply the route between Colombia, Mexico and who knows where else. Is Soto planning to shoot one down? The cartels don't have access to military aircraft, they don't really even seem to use heli-copters, so what else would it be for? He's gearing up for something huge.

I have a long time to think. I can't take him here, I can't take him on the road, I can't take him in Juarez. I should have shot him when I had the chance; at least then he wouldn't be free and I wouldn't be here.

The only weak spot I can see is the dip between the house and the road leading out to Praxedis. It's about two miles out from the main house. You can't see the car from up here on the hill once it's in the dip, so you won't see it from the house either.

But I'll have no chance from the roadside and I'll risk killing him. I'll need the AK to take out the guys in the car, and you really can't predict where those bullets are going to go.

There is the option of the compartment Ernesto built into Soto's car. But I'd have to get in there somehow. I then realise I've been thinking in lumps, as one of my old instructors put it. There is a way to Soto, and I think I've just found it.

Chapter 21

Tuesday night and I'm in position up on the mountain, ready to go. I've ghosted back to check on Liana and to exchange some weapons. She now has the AK. I have the MP5 and four magazines, two grenades, two tear gas grenades, the gas mask, a knife, the scope and the suppressed pistol we found on Soto's nephew.

The cast has been on my hand for ten days now, but I can't afford its luxury, so I've cut the palm away and replaced it with gaffer tape. It makes it much easier shooting the rifle, but I still can't grip the pistol correctly. Looks like it's going to be southpaw stylie on that one. I've only got one magazine of ten anyway, so I won't encounter the problem of trying to reload with the wrong hand.

I've timed the cars into the dip and it's roughly ten minutes from the house to when they disappear. That means that once the firing starts and the boys get into their cars, I'm going to have at most five minutes to get Soto moving, factoring in the increased speed of pursuing vehicles and a bit of time for them to react.

I'm going to head straight into the park, RV with Liana and get Soto into the Fourtrak, then drive out of there and hit the crossing at Boquillas del Carmen. That crossing is an old one that's being taken out of mothballs; they say they're installing a bridge though it's not actually ready yet, but I've checked out the river on the web and it's easily fordable in the Fourtrak. If it's not, I'll drag the bastard across swimming. It's really not wide, and, even if he has to spend a little time underwater, he won't drown.

I found Liana in remarkably good physical nick at the car. She looked down, though, and I can't wonder why. She's been a week out here, worrying about her family, worrying about her brother.

Waiting for darkness on the mountainside, I reflect that there were some positives that came out of my surveillance. No dogs, excellent, the party on the Saturday night was a big and noisy one, and – this is ironically a very low crime area depending on the crimes you're looking for – none of the car drivers lock their doors when they park up here. Also, all the surveillance the narcos were doing – and there were a few guys with binoculars looking out over the landscape – was out to the front. If they're expecting an attack it's from the Araña boys, and they'll come mob-handed, probably with their own armoured vehicles. They're not coming over the back of the mountain, solo.

My aim is to get very close to the house when Soto's in Juarez for his X-ray and has taken most of his boys with him. There's extensive, quite old solar panelling on the roof and an access ladder to get up to it. I'll wait up underneath that until he gets back.

I'm hoping that this Saturday there'll be another party, so I can use it as cover to sneak into the boot of the Range Rover. It'll be four days up on the roof. Thank God I don't snore.

I haven't seen anyone open the boot whenever he's gone out in the car, and there's no reason why they should do that. If they do, well, they'll get a surprise. I could get into the secret compartment, but it's very small and I don't want to risk making a clumsy exit. That'll be for Soto, should I get the chance. I have a cloned key for the car and I might be able to get myself out of there using the MP5 and some lively driving. Might not, either. It'll mean the mission ends in failure – quite possibly with the death of Soto rather than his capture – but, at the end of the day, if it's him or me, it's going to be him.

Obviously this isn't my first plan, but it's all I've got. Soto hasn't stayed out of bother for so long without knowing a few tricks, and it's going to take something really audacious to get him.

The next morning Soto pulls out in a column of twenty cars. I find myself wishing him luck, hoping he gets back. I scan the building with the IR sights. Can't see anything at all. In fact I think the house is completely deserted. Down the valley I see there's only the boys at the gatehouse and they don't seem too bothered, sparking up a fat spliff as soon as the column pulls out and then going back inside.

I watch for a while. No movement at all.

The mountain's still in shadow when I descend, but I have to be very careful. I move slowly, fifty yards at a time, until I'm at the foot of the service ladder. There are three doors on the ground floor and a long window, rather pointlessly built very close to the rocks – I suppose it might let a bit of light in. I can see a big, expensive modern kitchen in there. I shouldn't go in, I could compromise the mission. But it's too good an opportunity to miss.

I try the first door. It opens straight away. A smell of dope, sweat and cooking hits me. I have my silenced pistol drawn. God knows what I'll do with the body if I have to kill anyone, but we'll cross that bridge when we come to it.

There's no one here, and no telltale alarm pads on the doors either. The kitchen is a bit of a mess and there are one or two crack pipes strewn about, along with a lot of other drug paraphernalia. A short hall leads off the kitchen. There's a living room through one door, and another is steel and carries a heavy lock – probably a storeroom, I should guess. I'd like to explore it but there's no way that's practical now. I make my way upstairs – modern glass ones supported by wires hung from the ceiling. The first floor is much tidier, and I find an office with an iMac on the desk.

I waggle the mouse and the computer flickers into life. There's a spreadsheet on the screen, full of Spanish terms. I don't understand any of them. I call John.

'I'm in Soto's house. I have his computer in front of me. What do I do?'

'How much time have you got?'

'Four hours, maybe.'

'Just email all the Excel and Word files over. Use the Safari search engine, the one that looks like a compass; choose private browsing and send them over as a whole folder using the following YouSendIt file. Got a pen?'

There is a chewed biro next to a load of Post-it notes. For some reason the normality of that seems jarring, doing what I'm doing. I copy down what he says.

'How good's the Internet connection?' he asks.

'Pretty good, I should think,' I say. 'They don't tend to go big on economy packages.'

I do as he tells me, John directing me as I go. I have had to learn about computers – anyone in my previous line of work can't afford to be ignorant of this sort of stuff. But I'd admit, I'm no natural at it, and it's good to have a bloke like John giving me instructions.

I hit send, and I'm waiting for the files to go when I hear a noise at the front door. Someone's coming.

I have no idea what to do, so I just dive behind a sofa, taking out my pistol. I can hear the guys downstairs. There are two of them, doubtless the guards, come up to check the house. I hear them on the stairs. If I kill these two here, then it's game over.

One calls to the other and I hear him sit down at the computer. Shit, he's going to notice the files still uploading. He calls to his mate. There's a conversation in Spanish. I hear the click of a lighter and the room fills with the smell of a spliff.

Don't suppose it's the sort of thing Soto will remark on when he gets back.

More talk in Spanish, and the bloke at the bottom of the stairs shouts something followed by the clear words 'Poker Millions'. I feel my mouth go dry. He's going to start playing online poker on that computer.

I know from experience that that can eat six hours like it's a couple of breaths. Nothing to do but sit it out. There's a large rug on the floor here, and any claret on it is bound to draw comment – especially when allied to the lack of guards on the gatepost.

One of the guards comes and sits on the sofa for a while. Then he draws up a chair alongside his mate and they sit arguing about cards, smoking dope and drinking beer for five solid, painful hours. I need to close that browser before Soto gets back or he's going to notice. On the bright side, he might blame one of these goons. I can't rely on that, though.

A few hours later and the only thing stopping me from nodding off is the hunger pangs in my stomach. It's getting dark and they're still at it. Suddenly one of them calls out. 'Shit!' I nearly jump out my hiding place. He's spoken in English. They both get to their feet in a clatter and I hear them go downstairs. I look out of the window. Down in the valley there are lights, lots of them.

I stand up, quickly stretching out my legs and back and go to the computer, wake it and close Safari. I hope that's enough. Then I go to the big sliding glass doors at the back of the room. My swollen hands are unwieldy on the door handles and it's one of those double-glazing-style locks you can never work out how to turn. I try up, down, down, up. Finally it opens, I slide the door just far enough and slip through. I click it closed and go out on to the veranda, which is more of a storage area for chairs and tables – owing to its view of a very large rock only twenty metres away.

The ladder is not too far off the side of the

building. I stand on the rail of the veranda and move one foot on to it. Then I transfer my full weight and climb up on to the roof, keeping low behind the solar panels. I don't look up to satisfy my curiosity about the returning cars. That would risk being seen.

Chapter 22

Three days later, the familiar Saturday night rave is starting, girls spilling out of cars, music thumping. I'm relieved the noise is so loud, and I wonder if Soto's done me the favour of parking where he always does – out of the sight line of the main house.

The clouds are rolling in again and I look up into a hazy purple Mexican dusk. I'd love to be able to enjoy it. One of these days I'll travel abroad and just lie on a sunlounger, have a few beers. Not today, though. It starts to spit with rain, then to rain more heavily. This is good for two reasons. It'll keep people in the house, and it means I can have a piss in relative safety. It sounds funny, but that's a big concern in this sort of close reconnaissance.

The rain, of course, is bad in that it makes me soaking wet. The party isn't going to stop any time before dawn, if last week's is anything to go by. Unlimited supplies of coke and crack tend to ensure that. I'm starving and I'm cold and dehydrated. I've been on minimum water rations, and I can't even drink from the puddle I'm lying in.

I have to make a move exposed by the full lights of the house. This isn't as much of a problem as it sounds. They've got a good sight line out of the house but it doesn't cover Soto's car, which is in the parking area to the side. It makes it much easier for them to see into the area the house lights illuminate but almost impossible to see into the shadows, where I'm going to be. The music's banging away, the girls are laughing and shrieking; it's been two or three hours since they went inside. It's time I made my move.

I go very slowly down the ladder until I get to the office. My heart's in my mouth as I see that Soto is in there on his computer. Whatever he's looking at, thank God, he's too engrossed to see me.

Then he stands up, goes to the window. But he doesn't look out, only draws the blinds. Don't know why he did that. Reflection on the screen maybe? Whatever, I can now go down to the ground unseen.

There's no point messing about once I'm at the car. The music's loud enough, everyone's having a good time, I just have to go for it. I go to step forward and something flares in the shadows in the lee of the building. A girl is there, her face lit up by the lighter she's put to her cigarette. I level my pistol but I can see she's no more than fifteen years old, bare-shouldered in her party dress. She inhales on the cigarette, and in its glow I see she has a big black eye and she's crying.

She looks at me, looks at the gun, lets the cigarette fall to her side. We're just two shadows facing each other now.

I should kill her with the silenced gun but I know I can't.

She opens her mouth and says softly,

'*Buena suerte.*' Good luck.

Then she walks slowly back to the house in her high heels.

I hear the noise of the party increase as the door opens and closes. Five minutes later, no one has come out. I take out the kill switch remote for the Cadillac and press it. No noise, no indication it's been tripped. Just as Ernesto built it, but it's agonising not knowing whether it's worked. I crawl to Soto's car and try the boot with my good left hand. It's open. I lift it; the light comes on in the car. I crawl inside the boot and pull the tailgate down. I'm curled up in the darkness, hoping no one's seen the internal light, hoping that no one heard the boot closing, hoping no one opens it tomorrow. I think of that young girl, the one who has just spared my life. I'm not a religious sort myself, but that, if anything is going to, would make me believe in God.

I'm in there a long time. It's a huge boot, but it still falls short of what you might call spacious. I have a couple of bouts of cramp, but I just have to put up with them. On the positive side, it's the warmest night I've had in a while.

The back parcel shelf isn't an absolutely perfect fit, so I can tell when it gets light.

It's a long time after dawn before Soto comes to the car. As he approaches, he seems to be arguing with someone. I hear '*Las ventanas!*' Oh Jesus, the windows! They must be steamed up. I didn't think of that. I'm soaking wet and I've been breathing in here all night. I can feel my heart pounding now.

I hear the other guy say something in Spanish

which I roughly understand is about Range Rovers and the merits of BMWs.

Then something else chilling.

'*Ese tipo que había en el trunk, debe haber pissed en el.*'

Lots of laughter.

It's that weird Mexican English. 'That guy you had in the trunk must have pissed in it.'

The doors open and I hear two people get in, hear the car behind trying to start. Some conversation. I make out the words '*las luces*'. They're asking if he left the lights on.

Soto says something that contains the English word 'later'. I think he's telling them to follow him once they've got it started. He doesn't want to miss church.

The engine starts, the air conditioning clicks on, but they don't get going immediately. I tell myself they're waiting for the windows to clear. Yes, they are. Then the car lurches forwards and we're going. The stereo starts to blast out. I don't know how he does that on a hangover. I count out the seconds in my head. After ten minutes I start to feel the car going downhill, rattling and rumbling on the road.

I press the kill switch and hear a '*Qué?*' from the driver as the car comes to a halt. I stand up, knocking the parcel shelf into the air and putting four shots from the suppressed pistol through the driver's seat into his body. He slumps forward, no movement. Soto's eyes are wide as he sees me. He gives a sort of resigned shrug.

I level the MP5 with my dodgy right hand. I don't need to say anything. He knows enough about guns to realise that he's dead if he tries to run from a sub-machine gun. I climb over the back seat, gun on him all the time. He doesn't try to move.

I make him cable-tie himself to his seat belt, take his mobile phone. His arm is free of the cast, I notice. Then I carry his mate to the back of the car, slump him in, put the parcel shelf back as best I can and get into the driver's seat, the MP5 on my knee. I press the kill remote, start the engine and get driving. It's taken about two minutes from the time I hit the kill switch.

Soto says nothing until we reach the bottom of the hill.

'You are the Yanqui?'

'English, mate.'

'You sent to kill me?'

'You'd be dead already. You're coming home with me.'

And at that, he actually laughs.

Chapter 23

We drive down the rest of the track at a nice sedate pace. I know the trouble is going to start the moment I turn right, if his boys are watching. They'll expect to see their boss make a left turn towards Praxedis, not right down towards the river and the canyon basin. The good thing is that the land is uneven going into the canyon and it's difficult to keep a good sight line from the house.

Once I drop down to the mine, I'll RV with Liana and transfer to the Fourtrak. If no one's found us, then it's less than an hour's drive to the border.

I glance up towards the house as we make the right. Nothing moves.

'Seems your boys are still in bed,' I say.

'You have twenty minutes,' says Soto. 'When I don't turn up at the church they will begin to look for you, and when they find you, you will die. If you are clever, you'll kill me before you're taken hostage. That way you will die quickly – maybe a day. I have more patience than my men. If I live, you will go to my special place.'

'Don't worry,' I say. 'If your boys start to close in, I will kill you.'

'A good idea. For you I would be careful. Down there in the dark, you would take many years to die.'

'You'd be better off shooting me.'

'You have made yourself an enemy, and I give my enemies no such favours if I can avoid it.'

We start to descend towards the canyon. Here, the road is cut into the side of the hill, making us invisible from Soto's house. It's a beautiful blue day and the park is deserted. We crest a ridge and Soto's phone vibrates. Six messages.

'Seems you've been missed,' I say.

We wind on down and then I pull off, up a track that's scarcely a track at all. After ten minutes we come to the mine. The Fourtrak's in the cave entrance. I pull the Range Rover in behind it. It's a squeeze, but it gets in.

'You got him!'

'Yeah. Come on.'

There's a noise in the distance.

Liana walks up to Soto.

She speaks quickly, but I can tell she's telling him she's getting her revenge on him.

He replies in English.

'Your brother isn't dead.'

'Where is he?'

'In my special place. I don't give my enemies an easy death, Yanqui. He's in the house, in the cellar. He will be there in the dark and cold a long time. We keep him alive, and others too.'

He speaks to her a bit more in Spanish, and Liana shakes her head violently – it's clear she doesn't believe him. But I do. I saw that metal door in his house.

'We'll sort this,' I say.

I need to think fast. The vehicles are now a liability; they'll mark us out. I take out my holdall from the Fourtrak, cut Soto free, get Liana to tie him again. All the time he has this look of amusement on his face. He's not so amused when he sees what I've got planned for him. I make him get into the climbing harness. I gaffer-tape his mouth. I attach the climbing rope using a karabiner. Then I gaffer him up properly, with Liana's help, winding him like a fly in a web to the rope. He has to be sitting upright, because if he's not there's a risk he could pass out, slump forward and asphyxiate. The technical term for this is suspension trauma, and it's a real risk when people knock themselves unconscious falling when climbing.

Then I fireman's-carry him up the hill to one of the smaller caves I recced earlier.

I put the gun to his head and take the gaffer tape from his mouth.

'OK,' I say. 'I'm going to leave you suspended in here, over a large drop. Now you have a stake in my survival. I live, I'll come back. I die, and you get a taste of your own medicine.

Now, I want you to make a phone call. Liana here will be listening. You tell your men to get the prisoners out and ready for collection.'

'It doesn't work like that.'

'Why not?'

'How long does a boss live in this business? Ten years if he's lucky. They accept I might die, some might welcome it. You tell them you want the prisoners and they will start shooting them one by one until you deliver me back. If you are easily threatened, believe me, you're in the wrong business.'

'So how do I get to them?'

'You don't. This is the business of death. You accept it. Leave your man. Take me over the border. He is dead already.'

'I'm not about to do that. Where are the keys to the cellar?'

'You have them. You took them off me.'

'Right.' I gag him good and proper and roll him into the cave. Then I drive a couple of wedges into the rock, tie him on and lower him into the darkness. He's dangling ten feet down.

You have to hand it to this bloke, he's a hard man. No struggling, not even an attempt to shout out. I guess he's right: he never expected to live and probably always thought he'd die a horrible death. It comes with the territory. Now he's potentially facing that death, he's not going to whine about it.

As we exit the cave, we see three SUVs hammering past on the lower track. They obviously think I'm headed for the border crossing. Good.

Plan B comes into operation. I'll take Liana to the nearest point on the river. This isn't a crossing, but just an access point into a deep canyon. She'll make her way back up the river, clinging to the south wall of the canyon. They shouldn't be able to see her there. As soon as the land levels, she'll swim across the river and run into the US. She'll be picked up, but she'll claim asylum.

Me, I'm going back for Miguel.

We drop down to the canyon floor and she gets out

of the Range Rover. I hug her tight, and she plants a big kiss on my lips. I squeeze her and tell her: 'If he's there, I'll get him.'

'Come back,' she says.

'Be there for me to come back to.'

Now I've got work to do.

I pull the body out of the boot – not easy with my fucked-up hands – and strap it into the passenger seat. The last pipe bomb goes under the driver's seat.

Then I hammer back up the trail towards Soto's house. I'm banking on most of the boys being out looking for him, and most of them having already gone past.

I banked wrong. Cresting a ridge, I can see a good ten cars around the entrance to the house. Plumes of dust are going up all over the plain of cactuses.

They're bound to have seen me.

I take out the binoculars. Outside a big tricked-up Humvee, a familiar blond head is directing people into cars.

They're coming for me. I have one thing on my side. They expect me to be running away from them, not towards them.

By moving the cars out, they're making my job easier.

I back down the ridge out of sight and get out of the car, leaving the keys in the ignition. I take all the sniper kit I can and run for the scrubland. There's a good few hours until dark, so I need to just go for it, keep low and bide my time. Luckily this isn't quite desert environment. The scrub is deep and green and shot with vivid purple flowers. Very easy to get lost in.

As I run, I call Maria.

'You mentioned some contact in the Mexican drug enforcement.'

'Yes.'

'Well I have Soto. He's separated from his men and I'm going to be bringing him in. I'm near his house at Big Bend.'

'They won't come that far into La Frontera territory.'

'Anyone at all you can get. His boys are all over the land and I need some way to take their minds off this. Have you seen the documents I sent through?'

'Yes. The shipment times don't correspond to commercial flights. Someone is helping him in and out with whatever he's smuggling. We're still decrypting the rest.'

'How long will that take?'

'I don't know. Let me see what I can do.'

'One last thing. Liana is going for the border on foot – I don't want her turned back in cuffs,' I say.

'Don't worry, I'll make sure that if she gets there, she will be looked after,' Maria replies.

I reach a small ravine, no more than a ditch really, and decide this is as good a place as any to plot up until nightfall. The emergency blanket goes over me, along with a whole load of rocks and scrub. I'm well camouflaged, but the outlook on the land isn't as good as it might be.

I can hear them hunting from down here, mostly by car. I'm a good mile from the road, but the mountain air is still. I hear them find the car and begin to fan out. They're searching mainly down by the river, though. They shouldn't find Liana, I tell

203

myself, the ravine is too deep to see the river from the top. Thinking about her won't help, so I put her from my mind.

Dusk falls and the hunt doesn't stop. More cars are joining in now, their lights sweeping the land. Obviously the US border people think something's going on, because I can see helicopter lights in the sky over that side, cars and trucks too. Maybe they think some enormous incursion is about to happen.

I start to crouch and crawl towards my objective. It takes three hours cross-country, by a much more direct route than the roads go. Eventually I find myself on the southern slope overlooking the compound. I'd love to get around to the mountain and cliff side again, but that's not going to happen. From here the climb rapidly becomes too difficult for someone with hands like mine, and the risk of exposure is too great.

I can see three guys in the office room on the first floor of the house. Blondie is one of them. The armoured car is out front, along with three flashy SUVs, Soto's Range Rover, which has been brought back, and the still kill-switched Cadillac.

There are about ten guys milling around, all carrying AKs. If I take care of them, then I'll alert the others, who will come back up the mountain. Not a lot I can do about that.

I call Maria.

'Any luck?'

'Only bad. Look, when you bring Soto in, you must get him into our jurisdiction. You must get yourself into DEA jurisdiction too. If you're taken by the local sheriff or the CIA or FBI, there's a chance he might walk, or at least get a very soft deal. Soto's a CIA informer.'

'He's a murdering bastard.'

'That too. The bottom line is that if we get him then he stays in jail. If they do, I can't guarantee it.'

'OK. I'm overlooking the house now. I'm trying to work out a way to get in.'

It's then that I realise – Blondie has a set of earphones on and is looking at the computer. Oh my God, he's listening in to communications that are going through Soto's personal transmitter. He may have heard what I said, and if he can get any sort of trace on that, he'll know I'm here. He rips off the earphones, picks up his assault rifle and dives to the floor.

We are now officially off plan. I take out my mobile phone and dial Bertie. The Cadillac explodes, and all hell breaks loose.

Chapter 24

I have to work with what I've got now, which isn't much. They're going to find where I am as soon as they get on to the front foot. The answer is not to let them get on to the front foot. I take the pin from a grenade and throw it, pretty badly, with my bad hand. It goes up as much as forward, but it creates confusion and I'm running down the hill into the *sicarios*, the MP5 clattering in my hand. I see men diving, running, taking cover, and I know that in very short order a serious amount of fire is going to be coming back my way. At the moment people are too busy getting into cover to return fire. Another grenade into the confusion and a stitch of machine-gun bullets rakes into the ground around me. Shit, someone's trying to get into the Sand Cat. It's facing uphill. My gun's empty as I hit the side of the vehicle. AK rounds slam into the open door, which thank God provides a shield between me and the house.

I smash the guy who's trying to get into the armoured car over the head with the MP5. A couple of blows and he's down. I tear him aside as someone tries to get in the other side. I take out my pistol and shoot him over the seats, jumping up into the driver's seat and locking the door behind me.

Someone else tries to get into the Cat, but I squeeze the trigger on the pistol, there's a suppressed, pneumatic sound and he slumps away. I slam that door and lock it too.

Suddenly they're all around me, hammering rounds into the Sand Cat. But this thing has ceramic armour and is pretty much immune to small-arms fire – at least on its body. The windows, though, are starring as I dive over the back seat into the gunnery compartment. I turn on the system, which seems to take for ever, while the truck rattles like a can in a shooting alley.

The video screen blinks into life and the image whirls as I shift the joystick. I engage the grenades to minimum range and fire – no idea what they are. Clearly anti-personnel, looking at the mess outside. I move the joystick, put the house in my sights and open up with the machine gun, rapid fire into the windows. It's as if the house has been hit by an explosion, the front caving in, lights going out, blinds on the windows crashing down. I can't tell if I'm hitting anyone but use the grenade launcher targeting system to stick two grenades straight through the big front windows. A couple of SUVs come hammering into the compound beside me. I turn the machine gun on them and they seem to crumple inwards, to implode.

The bottom floor of the house is where the kitchen is. It too has those big, light-grabbing windows. I jump into the driver's seat, put the vehicle into gear and ram them. The noise is incredible as glass and wood splinter around me. For an instant I can see nothing, just dust, but I can't hang around for it to settle.

I get out of the Sand Cat.

This is my chosen route out of here. I'll get Miguel, get him in the Plasan and then blast my way out. Unless they've got some real armour-piercing capability, I'll be all right. No time to hang around. The lights have gone, the air is filled with dust. I can see nothing, but I blunder forward to where I remember the steel door to be. I'm down to my pistol now – I left the Ruger on the hill when I charged.

Someone's looming at me out of the dark, but he doesn't shoot because he can't be sure I'm not one of his men. I don't have the same problem and double-tap him. He collapses to the floor. I take up his AK.

I click on my pen torch. Not much good – the beam just reflects off the dust particles. I hit a wall and then feel my way along it. The door. There are about twelve keys on Soto's key ring. Five of them could be padlock keys. I feel for the lock. There's shouting from upstairs. First key. No. More shouting. Second key. No. If I could see better I could read what sort of lock it was and match it to the key. There's a smell of burning from upstairs. The grenades have obviously ignited something. Footsteps. Someone's groaning above us, just saying, '*Por favor*' over again. Third key. No luck.

Cars are pulling up outside. I go out and give them a rattle on the AK to make them think twice about approaching the house too quickly. Then it's back inside.

I've lost count of the keys I've used and have to start again. The first one turns the lock – my first piece of luck all day. It's worked. I open the door and immediately – above the smell of burning, through the clogging dust – the stench hits me.

I take the padlock with me – not having someone sealing me in. The pen torch is more use here – the dust hasn't penetrated this far in. There's a set of stone steps going down into darkness.

I look for tripwires, booby traps, anything suspicious. Can't see anything. When I get towards the bottom of the stairs, it's like a vision of hell. There are three dead bodies rotting, all manacled to hoops on the wall. Miguel is there, half starved, beaten but alive, his eyes blinking fearfully up at the torch. There is one other guy, no more than skin and bone, shackled alongside him. They look entirely numb, almost mad as they stare at me.

No point messing about.

'Be quiet,' I say. 'I've come to get you out.'

It's obvious which are the handcuff keys on Soto's key ring, and I quickly free both of them.

'Can you walk?' I ask Miguel.

He just shakes his head and points to his knee. Shit, even through his jeans I can see that it's swollen up and covered with blood. I know these narcos go in for bone scraping – where they take an ice pick and run it down your leg. I hope that hasn't happened to him. The other bloke's in no better state.

OK. I leave the AK at the bottom of the stairs and fireman's-carry Miguel up over my right shoulder, pistol forward in my left.

I open the door and immediately have to hit the

floor again. There's more noise in the house now. People are coming in.

'Can you shoot?'

He nods. I give him the pistol and go downstairs for the AK.

The house is definitely on fire upstairs. The situation is becoming serious.

I swap guns with Miguel and go back for the other guy. He's no problem to bring up – he clearly wasn't a big bloke to begin with, but now he must be about six stone wringing wet.

There's a burst from the AK at the top of the stairs.

We need to get to that armoured car, but there's suddenly a revving of an engine, a splintering and thumping, and the Sand Cat is driven free of the building. Not good. This means that as soon as they get their guys out, there is going to be a siege here, with them equipped with anti-personnel grenades and a machine gun, me equipped with however many bullets Miguel has left in the AK, some tear gas and a pistol.

Miguel is shaking where he sits, pushing out the AK in front of him as if he's going to bayonet an imaginary opponent. I take it off him.

'Any ideas?' I say. 'Our ride home has just left.'

Miguel speaks in Spanish to the other guy.

He seems hardly there, but says, '*Túnel, túnel.*'

'What?'

'Tunnel,' says Miguel. 'There's a drugs tunnel here.'

'Where does it go?'

'Over the border? I don't know.'

210

'Where is it?'

He shrugs.

Someone comes thumping down the stairs, clearly wounded. I shoot him and he slumps forward. He's got another AK and I crawl forward to take the magazine.

I can't see anything upstairs, but there is the steel door next to us – padlocked like the other. I don't know what I'm going to do if this is full of prisoners. I can't take any more people with me.

Fifth key unlocks it. I open the door. The smell of dope hits me hard. I make a phone call. They're not monitoring me now.

'Maria. I'm going to be coming out somewhere on the US side of the border. It'll be at some sort of building. I think I've found a tunnel.'

'Think?'

'Yeah, think. I need DEA agents where it comes out. It'll be a series of farm buildings or a warehouse, and it won't be far from Soto's gaff.'

'Gaff?'

'House.'

'Right.'

The armoured car machine gun starts up on the front of the house, seeming to shake it to its foundations. We're too far back to be hit, but if a grenade comes, in we're done for.

I grab Miguel and bundle him behind the steel door, the other guy too. Then I pull it shut. There's no way of securing it from the inside, so no point thinking about it.

We go down into another big basement area – this one full of compressed bricks, the dope that's been causing all the smell. There's a tiled floor with a huge hole in the middle and a ladder leading down.

The hole is very tight indeed, and I have no idea how I'm going to get both of them down. Miguel comes good, though, crawling to the hole and half hopping, half jumping down the ladder before collapsing with a scream at the bottom. Good on him, though, he quickly rolls away. I can't mess about with the other guy, and I lower him as best I can into the tunnel, dropping him the final four or five feet because I can't hold him any more. He hits the floor with hardly any noise. He's in a bad way, too messed up to even complain.

I go down after him and check he's still breathing. He is.

'We have to move. One grenade down here and we're dead!'

I shine the pen torch down the tunnel. It's amazing. It's only about four feet high, but it has a railway track running down it, along with a little open truck. I've seen these on the Internet, but encountering it in the flesh really does make you marvel at the sheer amount of resources at these people's disposal. Still, before I get carried away thinking about their engineering prowess, I better consider the battalion of maniacs who are no longer swarming around the countryside looking for me but all zooming in on this tunnel like dogs after a fox.

'Can you hold him if you get on the truck?' I ask Miguel.

'I'll try.'

Miguel climbs on to the truck and I shove the other guy up on top of him, my hands agony.

Then I put my back to it and start to shove. It's slow work, but I'm covering the rear with the AK. I turn off the pen torch and push forwards in the dark. The place is fully electrified, but I can't find where the lights turn on. Even if I could, I wouldn't. We need the darkness.

But the darkness doesn't hold. A flash light in the distance, voices. I stop pushing and tell Miguel to lie still.

We're about two hundred feet into the tunnel now. There's conversation. Then a rattle. An ear-splitting bang. They've thrown a grenade down the length of the corridor, but we're too far away for it to harm us. The tunnel concentrates the blast, though, sending a shockwave over us, shaking down dirt and causing the guy with Miguel to cry out. There are other voices too, screaming and shouting.

A grenade's not a good weapon in a space like this. You can't be sure of throwing it far enough, particularly once you take into account how the tunnel focuses the blast. Basically, they've just blown themselves up.

I put my back into the cart again and keep pushing. I estimate I've got about a kilometre to go to get under the Rio Grande. The tunnel starts to dip and the effort of shoving the truck forward is replaced by that of trying to hold it back as it falls. We go down and down. I am knackered already and can't bring myself to think about how difficult it's going to be to push the cart back up.

From the Mexican side of the tunnel I can hear more people coming down. I move on as quickly as I can. How far have we gone? Difficult to tell in the darkness; just have to keep shoving until this thing ends.

Torches are flashing now, beams up above me from where the tunnel began to dip. It makes me realise how far down we must be. Well at least there'll be no need to bury me if they kill me in here.

The roof explodes around us, the noise almost unbearable. Someone's opened up with an AK from on top. I kick back hard and lose control of the cart. It goes trundling away into the darkness. There's a gleam from back down the tunnel, a barked instruction, and all the lights go out. Did I see what I thought I saw? The blond hair, the goggles. If Blondie's in here with his IR vision, then I can start making my peace now.

I hear him crawling forward in the dark above me. I have only my pistol, and I fire a couple of rounds, the flash briefly showing that the curve of the tunnel means he's not in my eyeline any more. But in about a minute or less I'm going to be a dead man.

I fumble with the zip on my daysack. My fingers have no real feeling and it's difficult to open. Then, as I do pull it down, it gets stuck. Close again and tug again. This time it comes free. I can hear Blondie breathing now. I put on my gas mask and take out the tear gas canister, throwing it only a few feet in front of me.

I hear coughing, spluttering, retching. He's got goggles on, which will offer him some protection, but he's still got to breathe. Special forces train to be able to cope with tear gas, but in concentrations like this the gas is completely disabling – no matter how used you are to it. I flick on my pen torch, but I can see nothing through the gas. I should advance and shoot, but I'm blind in the gas and the dark and can't be certain of hitting anyone. Just press on and hope the pool of gas delays them enough for me to get out. I hear Miguel and the other casualty retching their guts up behind me. How far to go now? Who knows?

I'm going to have to get rid of the gun. It's one thing popping people off in the lawless zone outside Juarez. There's a five per cent conviction rate for murder in the city and the police are said to control that. The conviction rate doubtless falls to sod-all out here. But once I'm in the USA, things change. As a foreigner I can't have a gun, and if Maria's right about the inter-agency rivalry north of the border, I don't want to give the sheriff's office or the CIA an easy excuse to nick me.

I crawl down the tunnel towards Miguel, breathing hard through the gas mask, feeling incredibly claustrophobic in the blind, tight space.

I bump into the truck. No point asking them it they're OK; they're quite clearly not. I can hear them heaving for breath. I start to shove again. The track is slightly uphill here. It seems like an age that I'm pushing. Down the corridor gunshots go off like Chinese crackers. Someone has made it through the tear gas and is firing blind.

Shove, shove and shove again. Suddenly the truck comes to a halt.

I climb over the truck, over Miguel and the other guy, to feel steel rungs hammered into the rock going up. The tunnel hasn't sloped up steeply at any point, so I guess this could be a serious climb. I can't make it with Miguel; I'm not even sure I can make it myself. The *sicarios* are closing in now and I'm down to two shots in the pistol, my knife and one tear gas grenade. I don't know how many are behind me or what state they're in. I've got no idea what's above, and I can't hear a thing owing to the noise of the gunshots. Looks like this could be it.

Chapter 25

An AK flashes in the dark, horribly close. He's obviously blind, because he's sent the shots into the floor. They go ricocheting around the tunnel, pinging off the metal of the truck. I feel a thump in my leg. Not good.

I bang a couple of shots into the shooter over the top of Miguel and the other hostage. Then I crawl back around, picking up his rifle. It's the modern version of the AK-47 – the AK-103. I push down the fire select lever to 'semi auto' and fire a single shot into the darkness. The flash briefly illuminates two people crawling forwards, clearly unable to see. I squeeze the trigger four times, using the flashes to adjust my aim. I've no idea if I've hit anyone.

I have one remaining tear gas cartridge now. Sorry, Miguel. I pull the pin and send it scuttling down the tunnel. Tear gas in such a confined space could easily kill you. But there again, so could a bunch of armed narco thugs. There's noise and confusion from down the tunnel. The hostages are spluttering and heaving. I clamber around them, then feel for the rungs and start to climb. My leg is numb, my right hand can hardly grip. I only have my index finger and thumb healthy on that hand. Still, fear and adrenalin drive me on.

Up, up, up. The gas mask is stifling and I really want to take it off, but I can't yet.

Another ten metres and I'm convinced I'll be OK, above the gas. It's heavier than air so it'll pool below rather than climb the shaft with me.

I really, really, really want to take a breather, but I can't. On, on, on. Is someone behind me? Can't hear, can't see. I just hope the tear gas will hold them off for long enough. I throw the mask away and it's like I've surfaced from being underwater. I breathe in, my eyes already starting to water. Some of the gas is trapped in my clothes. Can't let that worry me.

Bang! I've hit my head on something. A ceiling. I shove with my bad hand. The hatch weighs a ton, but it slowly shifts. I blink as my eyes adjust to the light. I'm in an office, of all things. It has a tiled floor, desk, photocopier and a Pirelli calendar on the wall. A light has been left on.

I pick up the landline and phone Maria.

'Yes.'

'Trace this call, this number. I'm on US soil, get to me quick. I have casualties with me, still in the drugs tunnel. Pursuers down there.'

'Where are you?'

My head clears and I look at a sheaf of A4 on the photocopier.

'Jackson Farm Supplies, 1032 Farm to Market Road.'

'The sheriff's right there.'

218

The phone goes dead and I stagger out into a big warehouse full of agricultural machinery. Sirens outside. Shit, it's night, they can't get in.

I run to the front doors. Loads of cops, their guns all trained on me through the glass.

'Open the doors! Open the doors.' I can only just hear them after all that noise in the tunnel.

'Well I haven't got the bloody key, have I?' I say.

I have to say this for US cops, what they lack in subtlety, they make up for in lack of subtlety. They tell me to stand back and just reverse a car through the doors. Then they're pouring in, some running past me, some forcing me to the ground.

'You need gas masks down in the tunnel!' I shout, but no one's paying me much attention.

I'm frisked and they try to cuff me, but the cast on my hand makes that impossible, which they seem to find hugely annoying. Not sure why. I'm one bloke, unarmed; there are about a hundred of them, and the lightest thing they're carrying is an automatic pistol.

I'm taken outside by about six cops.

Lights in the sky. My eyes are watering so I can hardly see what they are. A big wind and the sound of a helicopter's blades beating the air into submission.

Someone's talking to me in Spanish.

'I'm English, mate,' I say.

He looks surprised.

'What happened to your leg?'

'Someone shot me, I think.'

It's weird. Ten minutes ago all my senses were turned up to eleven, my focus absolutely complete. It's as if the body can't sustain that. Now I'm struggling to make sense of what I'm seeing.

People are talking to me, but the ringing in my ears is turning into a roaring and I'm starting to feel sleepy.

Blood loss? Oh yeah. The world swirls, the lights merge and everything goes black.

Chapter 26

I wake up to bright light, the smell of disinfectant and the feel of clean sheets.

I'm woozy, but my head quickly clears. There's a cop outside my room and a bizarre thought comes into my head: 'Who's paying for this?'

Then all thoughts are replaced by one word: 'Soto.' And another. 'Liana.'

I have a drip in, so I take that out. My clothes aren't anywhere to be seen and I'm in a hospital gown.

I go out to the cop, who, amazingly, draws his pepper spray on me.

'Easy, tiger,' I say. 'I just want the bog.'

'The what?'

'Washroom.'

'In your room. Get back in your room, now!'

I look left and right. No, there definitely isn't a dog in here, so I must assume he's talking to me.

'Are you familiar with the word "please"?'

'I will pepper-spray you.'

'Yeah, you could do that, or you could just say please.'

'Don't be funny with me, mister.'

I can't be bothered with this. I go back into the room, use the loo, come back out and lie on the bed. I can see there's no point in asking this idiot about Liana, so I content myself with:

'Fetch us a cup of tea, will you?'

'You watch your mouth.'

It seems I'm a prisoner here. I wonder exactly how much trouble I'm in.

The cop is on his radio, calling someone.

I check my leg. There's a large bandage on it, though it doesn't feel too bad. A superficial wound, with any luck.

A nurse comes in and is much more friendly than the cop, which isn't hard. She takes my temperature, pulse and blood pressure and says that a doctor will be along to see me shortly.

'You've been in the wars,' she says.

'Yeah,' I say. 'Where am I?'

'El Paso Central Hospital.'

'In El Paso?'

'That's right. They weren't playing coy when they named it.'

I'm a long way from Soto, and every hour counts. I reckon he could survive three days down there, tops. It's cold and it's dark and he'll have nothing to drink. I need to get to him.

'Could you call the DEA in El Paso, at the EPIC offices, and tell them I'm awake and need to speak to them.'

'Ask the cop.'

'I'm not sure that'll be possible.'

'I'm sorry, it's up to the police.'

At that minute there's a commotion outside and a familiar large figure appears. It's Sheriff Macmillan, red in the face, sweating like a roasting hog and pretty angry, if the bulging veins on the side of his face are anything to go by.

'Is he well enough to go to prison?' he asks the nurse. She tells him that that's down to the doctors.

'What am I meant to be going to prison for?' As far as I know, I haven't committed a crime on US soil.

'Re-entering the US without going through border control, for a start,' he says.

'I've done nothing wrong.'

He comes up close to my face. I normally only allow dentists and attractive women this near.

He speaks very quietly. 'You done something very wrong. You pissed off the wrong people. That's why you're going to jail. Word's got around what's been going down over the border and there are some boys in there who just can't wait to meet you.'

'So you're going to have me killed,' I say, loudly enough for the nurse to hear. 'Nurse, please phone the DEA in El Paso.'

'Get him out of here. We'll argue with the doctor later,' says the sheriff. From outside, four cops come in.

Not looking good. Again they attempt to cuff me. It seems they do that on reflex in the States. The cast comes to my rescue once more. The nurse goes running out of the room. I'm taken down in the lift in the gown I stand up in.

'Did you get the guys I rescued out of the tunnel?'

'Yup, and I hope they'll be joining you behind bars before long. You can form an invalids and

223

cripples gang, it'll help you survive for nine or ten seconds.'

He leads me out to the emergency room entrance, where there's a cop car waiting. I'm stuffed into the back and we begin to drive out of El Paso. It does occur to me that I'm going to be dumped dead in a ditch somewhere, but there's no need for that. After twenty minutes we approach a long mesh fence, sentry towers rising along its length. This is clearly the prison.

We drive up to some gates and are signed in. It's a long way up to the main building – a massive brick warehouse-like structure. I'm not meant to come out of here, it's pretty clear from the smirk on the sheriff's face.

'Can't say you wasn't warned,' he says cheerfully as he gets me out of the car. 'Don't worry, this ain't maximum security, this is mid level. You get to sleep in a dormitory here.'

Again, it's plain he thinks any sleeping I might do will be of the permanent variety.

We're met by a prison guard and taken through a steel door into a sort of reception area. It looks like a run-down bus station waiting room, except there's a sort of service window in one corner.

I'm taken in and searched, and the sheriff pats me on the back.

'Good luck in here,' he says.

I know from watching a documentary that these county jails are often more dangerous than the full-on prisons. Everyone goes through here, so you can have people who are in for multiple murder alongside those who've been done for driving violations.

The guards and the sheriff seem chummy but not overly so, and the guard who processes me is businesslike; a bit aggressive, but I'm used to being shouted at – you get that stuff in the army.

I'm taken into another holding area. This is an actual cage and it has about ten other people in there – all of them Hispanic. This should be interesting. The door's unlocked and I'm put in. No one does anything, but it's not exactly a 'welcome aboard' party either. I get slow stares from everyone. I'm white, I'm in a hospital gown, I've got a cast on my hand. They've stopped short of pinning 'kill me' to my back, but only just.

I go to sit down on a bench, but a kid of about nineteen, tattoos and bandanna, slides his foot along. This is the bit in the movie when I'm supposed to beat him to the floor and earn the undying respect of my fellow inmates. I need to save the fight for if I ever manage to get out of here – not that I can see how that's going to happen.

'*Voy a esperar allí*,' I say. That surprises me. I just said 'I'll wait over there.' Didn't even know I knew how to say that.

The kid's eyes follow me.

'*Vas a morir*,' he says – you are going to die. Either that or it's 'Happy Easter' and my translation's off.

I'm left standing there for about an hour. No one bothers me; whether that's because they're not as tough as they look and are in for minor crimes, or because the guards are everywhere around this cage, I don't know. I'm then called out and taken to a room where I'm given a prison uniform – like all-white hospital scrubs.

The guard looks at the clipboard he has in front of him and says, 'OK!' in a way that sounds like he's not sure whatever he's read is a very good idea.

I'm taken up two floors and along a row of dormitory cells, all fronted with bars. I try to calm myself. Grey-man tactics are the best here: just say nothing, keep a low profile, sit on your bunk and bother no one.

I'm put into a cell and I can quickly see it's not going to work like that. There are seven or eight blokes in there – all young and Hispanic – and they're all immediately on their feet.

This isn't going to go well for me, I can see. The guard locks the cell door, and I'm on my own. I can't believe this is allowed to happen, but I've seen the documentaries. Step outside the law in the USA and you're a bad man. No one cares what happens to bad men.

I sit on a spare low bunk, hoping to defuse the situation by not offering a threat.

A bloke sits down next to me. He's very young, no more than twenty, but he has gang tattoos all over him . I feel sorry for the kid in some ways. If you've finished up in a place like this before you're officially allowed to buy a beer, then what's happened to your life?

'You Nick Kane?'

'No.'

'What you in for?'

'No insurance on my car.'

He nods, very slowly.

'You're Nick Kane.'

'No.'

'We've been told you're coming here.'

There isn't really very much to say here. We both know the way this is going.

'Then you better do what you have to do.'

I look around me. There are three men close by. Four others look less interested. They don't have the same gang tattoos, and one of them even looks a little studious.

Could I take them? No, but I could probably make a mess of two of them. Not much compensation if they kick me to death.

'We got time,' he says.

I stay seated on the bunk. I'm aware that sooner or later I'll have to go to sleep. That's going to create a considerable problem. I keep thinking about Liana too. I wonder if she made it. And Soto? If he dies in that black hole, then all my effort's for nothing. I could have just popped him the first time I got a clear view of him.

What to do now? The classic army thing is to take the fight to them. I'm trying to think of a way around that when another prisoner is delivered into the cell. From the punched fists and the gang hands that greet him, I'd say the guys already here know him pretty well.

He's older and bigger than they are – a real gym rat by the look of him, aged around twenty-six.

The guard leaves. The new guy doesn't even look at me, just wanders off into the back of the cell, out of my view, but I note a change in the atmosphere. My cellmates are visibly more tense, all stealing little glances at me, which is odd, because they've had no problem with staring right in my face up till now.

I breathe deeply, because I know what's coming. In

fact, bollocks to it, I'm not going to sit here and wait for them to take the initiative. The big guy has his back to me and is putting his hand into a big square-mouthed litter bin against the wall. I run the length of the cell and just smash his head into the wall. He screams as I hit him, but he's taken the full force of my charge on the thick part of his skull – the forehead. It doesn't put him down, though, and as I drag him back to drive him into the wall again, I see he's pulled a toothbrush handle with a razor blade stuck in it from the bin. He takes a swipe at me, but I manage to get my arm around his, enveloping it and stepping back to break it at the elbow. He lets out a huge scream, but I still have hold of his arm. Normally I'd drive him into the floor, smashing up his shoulder joint as I went, but I can't afford to be on the floor in this situation.

The kicks and punches come raining in as I throw him at his mates, kissing him goodbye with a strong upward kick into the face. I'm taking a lot of blows, but I have my hands up and I'm catching most of them on my arms, the cast providing a good blocking weapon against fists. I take one guy down with a good knee stamp and he goes screaming to the floor, but my leg feels like it's going to give way itself. Someone's picked up the toothbrush and comes slashing in at me. I block with the plaster cast and take control of his hand, sticking the improvised knife where it's safe – in his guts. His arm's bent against the crook of my elbow, and though I can't grip his hand with my fingers, I can push it with the palm of my hand. A line of red is opened up across the white of his belly, and then the razor blade comes out of the toothbrush and falls to the floor.

I take a heavy punch to the back of my head, which sinks me to my knees, and then a kick comes in to my face which I block with both my arms.

Then there are sirens and screaming and the cell is full of guards. I fall to the floor to shield myself, but I'm dragged upright and bundled out of there.

Next thing I know, I'm being dragged down the landing and thrown into an isolation cell. It's incredibly small – hardly big enough to lie down in, with no furniture at all – but it's the safest place I've been in a very long time.

I sit on the floor and catch my breath, my hands screaming once again – God knows what permanent damage I'm causing them. I'm expecting a royal kicking from the guards any time soon, but I try not to think too much about that. I sit there for what seems like hours, the light unchanging, the noises of the prison outside. Is this my life from now on? Soto's going to die, Liana could be anywhere. I've screwed up on every level. My body aches, my head's thumping from the bang I've taken and the wound on my leg is starting to hurt as the painkillers wear off. I'm tired too – as much mentally as physically. Eventually I sleep.

I'm woken by the big metal door of the cell sliding back. It's the guard who brought me in, still with the clipboard in his hand.

'Nick Kane?'

'Yeah?'

'Come on,' he says. 'You're leaving.'

Chapter 27

I'm taken off down the landing and back into the lift in which I came. I go back past the holding cell and out into the first reception point. Maria's waiting for me there – in her full DEA uniform. I'm so pleased to see a familiar face, I barely notice the identically dressed Hispanic guy standing next to her.

'Hello, how are you?' says Maria.

'Top of the world,' I reply.

'This is Special Agent Martinez,' she says. I hold up the cast.

'I won't shake your hand.'

I'm brought a form to sign with a box that acknowledges I've been well treated while inside. I tick it. It's just like the Ritz, give or take a short sustained beating.

'Are they going to bring your clothes?'

'I haven't got any clothes.'

'What?!'

'We have a charity box for prisoners without clothing,' says a guard, 'but I'll get to get a form.'

'No time,' says Maria. 'You'll have to come like

230

that. We'll find something for you later.'

'Those clothes are prison property,' says the guard.

'We'll make sure they get back to you,' says Maria. 'I'll bundle them up tight as well so you can stick them up your ass. Come on.'

'If he goes outside in those, he'll be arrested,' says the guard. 'That's why we have prison uniforms, so escapees can be identified.'

'We've really got to move,' says Maria. 'What did you come in wearing?'

'A hospital gown.'

'Can you bring his clothes?'

'Take a while for them to be brought up,' says the guard.

'Can't do it,' says Maria. 'Gotta go now.'

'You gotta do it,' says the guard. 'I can't let you out like that.'

'I've got a pair of gym shorts in the back of the car,' says Martinez.

'OK, let's have those.'

Martinez brings the shorts, along with a T-shirt, and I go into the changing area.

The clothes are a bit too small, but if they'll get me out of here, I'd go in an Action Man uniform.

We're halfway out of the door when a sheriff's cruiser surfs to a stop on a wave of gravel.

In it is the permanently pissed-off figure of Macmillan.

'You ain't leaving,' he says.

'Beg to differ,' says Maria. She holds up a piece of paper.

'I don't give a shit about that. This guy is wanted, and I have it on good authority we'll be receiving a

Mexican extradition request very soon. You let him go, you're going to cause an international incident.'

'Yeah. Well you'd know all about those, wouldn't you, Sheriff?'

'I'm not sure I catch your meaning.'

'You've got a lot of houses for a guy on a sheriff's salary.'

'And I got all the documents that say where the money came from.'

'Yeah, make sure that you do.'

'My domestic arrangements are not the issue here. I'm more worried about where he's going.'

'Well I'm sure that if you contact the DEA liaison officer, you'll find out. Can I ask exactly how you discovered this prisoner was being signed over to the DEA?'

'Can I ask you to stick to your own business?'

'Corruption by drug cartels *is* my business.'

'Big words.'

'I got a couple of short ones if you'd like them,' says Maria.

I get into the car, can't see the point of this conversation. Maria's come to the same conclusion, because she gets in too, as does Martinez.

'I ain't finished with you!' shouts Macmillan at the car as we pull out.

'Where am I going?' I ask as we drive back into El Paso.

'We need a debrief. After that, we have to decide what we're going to do with you.'

Chapter 28

We make our way back into town. It's surprising that the Texas side doesn't look so massively different from the Juarez side. Gas stations, burrito joints, office blocks, highly visible policing. It's just that here the police are – mostly – doing their jobs and there's an air of complete calm.

I'm driven to an anonymous office building.

'Not at EPIC?'

'No, this place is a little more secure.'

'I've got Soto on ice back in Mexico. I need to get to him quickly.'

'Or?'

'If I don't get there in the next twelve hours, I think he's dead.'

'I'll see what I can do.'

'Yeah, and that girl, Liana. Should have come in around where you found me. And Miguel and the other guy.'

'We've got Miguel.'

'The other guy?'

'He's on life support.'

'Likely to recover?'

'I don't know.'

We go in to the offices and I'm walked down to an interview room which is pretty much like interview rooms all over the world – a desk, plastic chairs, false ceiling tiles. They fetch me a couple of sandwiches, which are very welcome, along with a coffee. This is a marked improvement on the reception at the jail.

'We're going to get a doctor come and look you over,' says Maria.

'I've only just got out of hospital.'

'Yeah, and if what I'm told's true, then you should still be there.'

A doctor does come in and gives me a couple of pills to take. He also gives me the news on my right hand.

'You know those fingers require some urgent attention.'

'The cast isn't all right?'

'No. You're meant to take it easy on the hand.'

'Yeah, that hasn't been exactly possible.'

'Well you need surgery on your fingers, and even then you might not get the full use of them ever again.'

'I'll bear that in mind.'

No time for that now, I have to get to Soto.

The doctor leaves, and I wait about twenty minutes before Maria comes back, with a little wiry guy in glasses. They both sit opposite me at the desk.

'Nicholas Kane?'

'That's me.'

'OK. We've become aware of your activities south of the border. You know that you've broken the law in a most serious way in Mexico.'

'I've only been defending myself.'

'I hope you can make that case in a Mexican court.'

'And you are?'

'DEA, rank unimportant. I understand you say you have Soto?'

'Yes.'

'Where?'

'In a hole in the ground.'

'He's secure there?'

'He could be found, but I think he's more likely to die than be discovered. I've left him in an unenviable position and he needs someone to help him out of it.'

'In Mexico?'

'Yes.'

'That complicates things for us considerably. It's sovereign territory.'

'I understand.'

He taps his fingers on the desk.

'Which is why you're useful to us. We want you to bring Soto back, understanding that this case has total deniability if you're caught.'

'I never thought it had anything else.'

'Good. Do you need some help?'

'I need to get to where I'm going. I need some weapons and a transport to as near to him as I can go. Beyond that, guaranteed extraction.'

'You need to go across the border yourself and get back out yourself. We can offer you an RV on this side, but beyond that, nothing.'

'And weapons?'

'Yeah, weapons. And men. I think I can give you six of them.'

'Weapons I need, men I don't.'

He looks nonplussed. 'Why not?'

'To be honest, I don't know who I can trust. There's already been a leak in the El Paso office. Every time I called Maria, the information went straight back to La Frontera. Six extra men is six more chances to be compromised. I'd rather do this on my own.'

There's another reason, of course. I've had to use forceful measures so far. If that continues, I don't want anyone there as a potential witness. The word of Mexican gangsters counts for nothing. Guys with direct links back to the DEA – no matter how much 'deniability' is involved – can complicate matters. I'm convinced I've done nothing morally wrong – I've been fighting a war against a vicious cartel that ruins people's lives. But I'm not sure a court would see it that way.

'You can't do it on your own, you're too beat up.'

'I'm going to have to do it on my own.'

'I could go,' says Maria.

Mystery Man shakes his head.

'You're a DEA agent.'

'There are stories to cover that. He could have kidnapped me. I could have gone rogue. No one's going to believe you stuck one agent in there on her own.'

He thinks about it for a moment.

'OK. No ID on you, no service-issue guns. In fact, I'm going to formally suspend you now, pending a corruption inquiry. If you get caught over there, you're labelled as a drugs dealer.'

'I'm not sure about this,' I say. I don't want to play

the 'I'm not going on an operation with a girl' card, but there's a big difference between being an effective policewoman and going on a special forces-style incursion into enemy territory.

'Why not?'

'I'm British Army trained. I've operated in four separate theatres of war, undercover or behind enemy lines. No offence, but I can't be carrying a passenger.'

Maria doesn't look too happy with this. At all.

'Do you know what a special agent's training involves?' she says.

'No.'

'Let's say I don't think I'll let you down. Anything you've been doing, I'm trained for too. And my hands work.'

'What's in it for you?'

'The files you downloaded from Soto's computer are yielding information,' says Mystery Man. 'We've got enough to link him to arms smuggling and we've got details of bank accounts that we think will lead us to something when we've followed the money trail. That could take a while, but I'm confident we've got enough to charge him. If the guy you rescued survives, we may have a little more. And if that doesn't stack up, which frankly it might not, we've got an extradition request from the UK.'

'Who's the guy I rescued?'

'That's Jorge Mendoza. He's one of Soto's closest associates.'

'Not that close.'

'He got caught skimming deals.'

'And put on the naughty step.'

'Soto's famous for giving people time to die. He thinks a slow death in the dark is worse than any other punishment.'

'Which, ironically, is what he's facing,' I say.

'So you guys better get going.'

'Yeah.'

'Well at least there's no paperwork to fill out,' says Mystery Man. 'Maria will take you to where you need to go.'

'And the gym clothes?'

'I'll have something sent over. But let me warn you. La Frontera will know that Soto hasn't crossed the border. They'll also know that you've been freed from jail. And they will wonder why. They'll be convinced that Soto is still alive and somewhere around Big Bend on the Mexican side. They'll be waiting for you.'

Chapter 29

We take a small helicopter as far as Big Bend. Mystery Man's been as good as his word with the weapons. We have two M4s fitted with what's known as SOPMOD kit – special operations peculiar modification – in short, day/night sights and grenade launchers. I take six high-explosive grenades, two of them armour-piercing. Maria takes the same. I have a SIG Sauer 225 9mm; she has a Smith and Wesson M&P .40, because that's what she's comfortable with. We're not arsing around this time and have full Kevlar body armour on, with front and back ceramic plates, as well as Kevlar helmets. If we weren't inserting so close to the target, I'd think twice about taking all this kit, but it's a luxury we can afford. It would be tempting to wear the full-on fireproof overalls as well, but you never know. If our main exit's blocked, we might need to blend in at some point. So we both wear basic hiking trousers and shirts underneath our armour.

We've also got a bit of climbing gear – getting Soto out of the hole might not be as easy as putting him in.

With my hands the way they are, I'll have no chance of just hauling him up, particularly in that confined space, so I'll need some options. Favourite would be to set up a bunch of pulleys, but there's not much to attach them to there. I may have to go down to him and ratchet him up. Not easy, but the best I can do.

All this stuff comes from who knows where. It's kept in an industrial unit on the edge of town. We don't sign it out, we don't see anyone there – though the strongbox security is formidable. There are no serial numbers on the weapons either. I get the impression that the DEA is well used to the problems of operating on Mexican soil without the permission of the government.

We have a good GPS and I've pretty much pinpointed the location of Soto's cave. On top of this, we've had the benefit of satellite recon. Nothing obvious going on in the area, although plenty of movement around Soto's house. The place seems to have been pretty well trashed, from the photos I see, but there are plenty of people moving around it still – lots of coming and going by truck. We have to assume there could be a reception committee.

We disembark at night on the US side within ten kilometres of Soto's house. From our insertion point we take a kayak across the Rio Grande and go south across the scrub to the mine. Soto is going to be in a mess, no question. We have a lightweight folding stretcher with us and a saline drip if he needs it. I'll tuck the salt bag into my rucksack and the fluid will drop from there.

The first part of the trip goes smoothly – we land by the road and the kayak takes us easily across the river. I check the terrain with the day/night sights. Nothing.

Forward under a small moon through the scrubland and the cactus. Not a nice way to travel, but the most direct. At least I'm moving easily on my leg.

All the time we're looking for signs of activity. Nothing so far. GPS is a godsend as we proceed directly towards the caves. Two and a half hours and we're there. It's difficult to see the outline of the smaller cave in the darkness, but the big one shows up well.

The cave I'm looking for is about a hundred metres west of the main one where we sheltered the cars. I leave Maria to provide cover, and crawl forward. If they have found him, this is where they might be waiting.

The last kilometre seems to take an age, but I'm operating a policy of extreme caution. No signs of disturbance around the cave mouth. It's very difficult to see in the dark, though. I turn on my head torch and look within. Can't see anything suspicious. I'm guessing that if the cave has been discovered, it might have been booby-trapped. Can't see any tripwires or signs that the floor has been disturbed. I crawl in. The ropes are exactly as I left them. No indication that anyone's moved them or placed anything underneath them.

I take out the climbing rope I've brought with me, fit the Jumar ascender, fix the rope into the rock and go down. There are a whole heap of methods for hauling someone up, but this is the quickest and the easiest in such a confined space.

Below me I can just see Soto's body, still upright on the rope. It's been two days, and though I expect him to be severely messed up, he should be alive. I come in alongside him and I can hear him breathing very faintly.

Now I can see the bottom of the cave, about ten feet below us. I decide not to bother shifting Soto down there to check on him, but to make a quick assessment here on the rope, then ratchet him back up to the surface. We'll move him at least a kilometre from here before having a good look at him. It's then that I realise something is very wrong.

Soto is five foot six tall and built like a prop forward. The person on the rope is about the same height but slim. More than that, she's female.

I take out my knife and cut the tape from her face. This isn't Soto here in the dark. The face that looks back at me – taut, agonised, fearful in the harsh light of the torch – is Liana.

A burst of carbine fire rings out from outside the cave, and I hear voices speaking Spanish echoing from above me as Liana kicks and bucks on the rope.

I grab Liana, cut her rope and release the tension on the rope beneath me. As we rush towards the floor, I use the rope as a brake. Still, it's all I can do to hold her. I kill the light on my head torch, click out the folding stock on the carbine and point it up. There's a series of explosions from outside. Sounds like Maria's getting busy with her grenade launcher.

I can see nothing up above me at all, but I'm certain that one grenade down here will pretty much be the end of me and Liana. But if I turn on the torch, they'll see exactly where I am. There's no good option here.

Lights above me, scanning the dark. Who is it? A shot zinging past my ear lets me know. I return with a burst of carbine fire, and the torches drop through the darkness to the floor.

I can see by their light that we're on a sort of platform of rock, and then the cave fades into darkness. I grab hold of Liana and slide on down.

Just in time. There's a thump above me, and then a tremendous ear-splitting explosion, bits of rock and God knows what else sailing over our heads. Grenade, as I thought.

I keep absolutely quiet and have no need to tell Liana to do the same. She's utterly silent next to me, and I should guess she's fainted. Another grenade, then another.

Then there's a tug on the rope I'm attached to. Jesus – they're trying to pull me up. I slide up the slope to see more torchlight in the dark above me. I squeeze the trigger on my rifle's UGL, and shoot an M406 High Explosive round directly at the torch, throwing myself to the ground the instant I've fired.

There's a huge explosion and pieces of the ceiling come crashing to the floor. My rope goes slack. Then there's silence, long silence. I click on the head torch. Dust everywhere. I can't see a thing. I wait and wait, and finally the dust begins to clear.

As soon as there's anything resembling visibility I slide down the slope to find Liana, before clicking the torch off again. I sit beside her and wait, giving her sips of water from my bottle.

After ten minutes, I start to cut the tape from Liana's legs, by feel not sight. Then I risk the light to free her hands. She's in a really bad way – beaten up

– and God knows how long she's been down here.

I crawl up the slope and use the torch on the gun to scan the top of the cave. The whole roof seems to have come down; there's no sign of the lip of the climb at all.

This is bad news in the extreme.

OK, think straight. The cave above seems to have collapsed. The entrance wasn't all that far below the surface and there is a chance I could dig it out. The second option is a bit of free-form cave exploration. No guarantees there. The cave we kept the car in did drop away at the rear, but there's nothing to say that it links with this cave system here. I can't take Liana with me if I do try to make my way out like that anyway.

I sit in the darkness wondering what to do. I put the line in to Liana. She's hardly responsive, but she is breathing. I search around the cave with the head torch. There are ways out, but do any of them lead to the surface? I make a foray into a couple of them, but I'm loath to leave Liana. She still hasn't managed to stand up. I wonder what has happened to Maria up top. I'm assuming the worst, and that she'll therefore be no use to us in our current predicament.

My nose is clogged with dust and I blow it to get rid of it. It's then that I realise that from somewhere away to my left I can smell a fire, and something else too – cooking bacon.

Chapter 30

I put my arm around Liana and help her up. She's a tough cookie and almost manages to stand. That's not necessary for long, as we come to a much lower passage. I crawl forward down a tunnel towards the bizarre smell of the bacon. With my hands in the condition they are in, it would be tempting to leave my weapon behind to make progress easier, but there's no way I'm going to do that.

Then the tunnel suddenly opens up a bit, and for most of its length now it looks like it might just be possible to walk. I ditch my body armour and put the helmet on Liana. She can hardly walk, let alone crouch, so as I help her along, the helmet spares her head from the worst of the ceiling.

But then the passage narrows once again, and the roof drops towards us, forcing me to crawl forward for thirty or forty metres, almost dragging Liana behind me. I have to say, this isn't my idea of fun. You get stuck down here and you can't fight it, you can't reason with it, you can't trick your way out. I'm exhausted, but by attaching a length of rope to the climbing harness Liana is still wearing and securing it to my own harness, I can at least alternate which parts of my battered hands take the strain. The going is pitifully slow.

Onward and onward, the passage tighter and tighter. Ten metres, twenty metres. Each little increment seems like a mile. Eventually Liana cries out, '*No más, no más!*' No more! No more!

We rest for a while, and she finds the strength to go on again. I'm finding it hard enough; God knows what it's like for her.

I'm just wriggling forward, my arms above my head, the gun out before me. If the enemy comes the other way now, we're spectacularly shafted – literally.

I caterpillar forward, whispering to Liana so she can co-ordinate her efforts with mine. '*Ahora! Ahora!*' Now! Now! That's the best I can do for 'Come on!' I notice the passage is becoming ever wetter. Great. We're near the Rio Grande, and if there's standing water here, that will be us done for – I have so little energy left.

Twenty metres further on, it's as I feared. The roof dips and the passage is sunk underwater. There's perhaps two inches of air above it. The bacon smell is stronger here, so at the very least air is actually still getting through.

It's nearly impossible to explain my plan to Liana, and I can barely believe I have any strength left for it, but we have no choice and that knowledge spurs me on for one last push.

I'm going to go through the passage as far as the rope will allow me – I'm guessing only another twenty metres. If that's long enough, she should then grab the rope and I will pull her through. Plan B? There is no plan B.

I try my best to explain, but I'm not sure she'd understand even if I were fluent. She seems glad of the rest, though.

I tie on the rope and shove into the water. It's freezing, dark, and tight, but I'm just too tired to panic. With my head tilted up, sucking in on the precious air, I inch forward, trying desperately not to disturb the surface of the water too greatly.

If anyone's on the other side of this, then I may as well have sent them a written invitation telling them exactly when to expect me.

On and on. It seems I've been going for miles, but I can't have been because the rope hasn't gone tight yet. Then I'm stuck, my pack wedged in the long coffin of rock. I jam my mouth into the ceiling, searching for the air. Three breaths and I have my knife out, sawing at the straps, cutting the pack away. I can only use my left hand for this; the right just won't hold the blade steady enough. Thank God there's a serrated edge to this one, and I feel the straps give. I can't afford to lose that pack – there's too much good stuff in it. I hold it in my left hand and kick forward. Finally, a head's space of air. My eyes clear the water and I look about me. There's a dry passage, and my heart sings. It's only about crouching height, but from where I am it looks the size of Wembley Stadium. As I suck in a lungful of air, the smell of bacon hits me again, almost overwhelming me. When my vision clears, I see something; a flickering light, like a fire. It doesn't seem close, though. I kill my head torch.

I give two sharp tugs on the rope and then start to pull. It comes easily at first; Liana's obviously trying to help me. Then the rope snags. I pull hard, and then hard again. Finally it comes free, and Liana emerges spluttering and shivering into the cave. I'm amazed at how short the tunnel actually is; it felt like an eternity in there for me.

I take the emergency blanket out of the pack and wrap it around her.

'*Fuerte*,' I say. Strong.

She looks up at me and says in a clear, steady voice, '*Quiero vivir*.' I want to live.

'You will live,' I say. 'We'll get you out of here and I'll take Soto and you'll see your brother again. You will live.' I almost surprise myself with the strength of my own emotion. It's just that everything I've encountered here is so sick and unpleasant – the whole murderous, stinking drugs trade – that Liana seems like a beacon of hope to me. If I can get her through this, I'll help her settle in the US or the UK. If Maria's still alive, she must be able to help with that.

We appear to be standing in a hollow just above the valley floor, no bigger than six feet wide. I creep forward and peer over the edge. The smell of burning is suddenly explained. A 4x4 is streaming flame out in front of it, black smoke gushing into the sky. There are *sicarios* running around everywhere. Three other SUVs are close by. Maria's been busy here.

Hard choices loom. Do I stay with Liana, or go and help Maria?

I'm going to need to take these guys out before I can move from here anyway. It's terrible to think of what will happen if I die or am captured. Liana will have no one to protect her. But I have to think of this operationally. Maria is still out there by the look of it – armed, fighting, causing the enemy a problem – but for how long?

I strip the M4 and quickly clean it – they don't like dust and there has been plenty of that in the cave. Then I flick on the night sight, more in hope than expectation. It surprises me that it flickers into life. When I was in the army, these things used to pack up at the first hint of moisture, but the DEA ones are clearly more robust. I hope all the clattering and thumping through the caves hasn't knocked the alignment out. No time to worry about that; it's literally hit and hope. In my favour, I have to admit that this is an ideal sniper hide, providing excellent cover. It's got no IR profile – particularly with the blazing 4x4 in front of me – and anyone wanting to storm it is going to have a great deal of difficulty doing so. It's like a natural pillbox. All I have to do is duck down.

I rest the rifle on the lip of the cave and pick my target – a guy who's firing an AK aimlessly into the surrounding scrub in a clearing arc – dead centre of the chest. The sights are clearly out of whack, because the shot blows the back of his head off and he drops where he is.

The suppressor on the M4 doesn't have the effect of silencing the weapon entirely. It's still a noisy gun, but the silencer makes it much more difficult to pinpoint exactly where it's firing from.

My shot causes chaos – some people throwing themselves flat to the floor, others firing wildly. I adjust my aim to take account of the dodgy sights and drop two more, before ducking back into the cave. There's a lot of shouting, and it's clear that one of them hasn't been killed outright, because I can hear some rather pitiful screaming from down below.

I hear the pop of a grenade, more shouting, more gunfire, though not at me.

I look out of the hole using the night sight. I can see the flash of AKs about seventy metres from me. Three of them are quite close together. I fit an HE grenade to the UGL and fire. Then there's a flash somewhere off in the darkness, facing me. It must be Maria laying down fire at these guys. She can't be more than a hundred metres away, though it's difficult to tell in the dark.

No one gets up to charge her. A hundred metres might not sound like a long way, but it is when you're facing an M4 carbine.

I crack a couple more shots into the *sicarios*. An engine starts, more shouting. Whoever is left is now piling into the SUVs. In the cars they're sitting ducks, but I'm going to let them go. They won't be going for help – this is the age of mobile communication. They very likely *are* the help.

Out in the darkness, people are still calling out in pain.

Two cars screech off the hill and no more fire comes from Maria's direction. I phone her.

'Yeah.'

'I'm just up above the burning car.'

'Do you have him?'

'No. I'll deal with the wounded guys and then you come up to the car.'

I look out through the night sight but can see no movement. I crawl forwards out of the cave. One SUV remaining. The groaning and coughing wounded are up ahead. I check around me but can see no one else. I approach them carefully.

One guy has a smashed leg; the other guy next to him is also alive. Neither of them are going anywhere in a hurry, but I kick the nearby guns away with my boot.

Squatting down next to them, I check around with the night sight and catch some movement up ahead. It's most likely to be Maria, but I keep her in my sights all the way just in case it's not. It is.

'Soto?'

'They found him. We were lucky not to encounter a bomb. They'd caught Liana and put her on the rope.'

'Dead?'

'No. In the cave. The roof collapsed on the entrance.'

'How did you get out?'

'I found an exit. Liana came with me, God knows how, but she's going to need a doctor very soon.'

'Let's get her to one, then.'

I cable-tie the wounded men. Then I rush back into the cave while Maria makes a phone call. I help Liana out and into the SUV, which, thank God, still has its keys in it.

It's only when we're driving back down towards the river with the heater on in the car that I realise how cold I am. A fit of the shivers overtakes me and I'm glad it's Maria who's behind the wheel.

The GPS helps us find the kayaks. There are lights

on the US side of the border, which Maria says is the DEA.

She keeps guard by the SUV as I load Liana into one of the kayaks and paddle her across.

I'm half expecting to see the sheriff on the other side, but sure enough, it's a couple of big DEA trucks with a reassuring number of armed agents aboard. There's also an ambulance. Mystery Man is there, looking exactly like all the other agents in their blue uniforms. Maria has explained everything on the phone, so there's no need for talk.

'Now what?' she says to Mr Mystery. 'Do you think Soto will go to his place in the west?'

'Not a chance. It's too well known,' he replies.

'Soto's going to need treatment somewhere and from someone if he spent any time at all on that rope,' I add.

'That's one way,' says Maria, 'but it's going to take a long time.'

'Have you analysed his phone records yet?' I say, turning to Mystery Man.

'They're still looking at them.'

'Just take the three most used numbers and see whose they are.'

'They're really careful like that, it won't work. They change mobiles all the time.'

'Not all their mobiles. Have you identified the numbers on the handset I gave you?' I ask.

'No good for tracing, all disconnected the minute they knew he'd been abducted.'

'Satellite? You could trace if anyone drives from this place to anywhere else.'

'Costs too much.'

'Drones?'

'Likewise, and I can't give that sort of direct support to an operation of this nature.'

'So what then?'

Mystery Man shrugs his shoulders. 'We all say "close but no cigar" and go home. There are other drug dealers, other criminals.'

'Other criminals didn't kill my friend.'

'Not my problem. There's no way to get to him. He could be anywhere and even his closest supporters aren't going to know for a while – it'll be hand-picked guys, hunkered down, no mobiles. Have you any idea how easy it is to go missing in that country if you've got the money and the influence? Guys have been on the run for ten years or more – they send written messages, they pay off officials, they build a couple of schools and a hospital and the local community supports them.'

He thinks for a second.

'There's one way you could get to him, of course.

You could give yourself up to him.' He smirks. 'If you use yourself as bait, then he'll come running,' he adds.

Maria takes me by the arm.

'He's not serious, Nick; in your condition it would be suicide.'

I look into her eyes.

'Can you think of a better idea?' I say.

The plan isn't quite as mad as it sounds. DEA contacts are, by and large, murky. Juan, the guy who got my guns in the first place, doesn't only make his money by selling guns to people doing US agencies' dirty work in Mexico. He wouldn't make much of a living doing that.

He also sells them to anyone who has the money. He's a criminal and a gangster himself. A second sense told me that as soon as he found out who I was after, he'd sell me to the highest bidder. And it's this that makes him useful.

We can arrange to meet him to buy some guns. Given the right information, he will sell me to Soto. Who will either turn up to collect me, or send his boys.

Maria will get a visual on them and try to follow them. That's not going to be easily done on her own. There will also be drone support – Mystery Man says he can't sanction it for general surveillance, but he is willing to spend the money on my protection in this specific case, even given the fact that the drone will very likely have to enter Mexican airspace. He's fairly sure he can get clearance for that.

When we find out where Soto is, we can take it from there. It may be that he presents a target of opportunity if he comes to pick me up.

Again the idea of a team comes up. It's one thing getting a hostage out of a secret location on my own – and that proved hard enough. Abducting a cartel boss from his chosen hideout, or from a Juarez street, might prove a little bit more tricky.

'Do you have anyone who is experienced in surveillance?' I say.

Mystery Man looks at me and raises his eyebrows. 'We're the DEA,' he says.

Turns out that he intends to use a Mexican street gang.

'Are you mad?' I stammer.

'It's a market economy down there. These guys are freelancers. They'll work for us if we give them something they value.'

'And what might that be?' I reply.

'Same old same old. Better prison conditions for certain friends.'

'Will Perez be paying for this?'

'Someone like that.'

'All very neat. But this operation needs more than a few street kids with guns.'

'And that's what we'll get you. A lot of these guys have been army trained, or even special forces. They come out and it's a choice between scratching a living and working for the cartels.'

'So you're going to use people who have worked for the cartels?' I can hardly believe what I'm hearing.

'Sure. But they'll think they're working for a cartel this time too, if they bother to think at all.'

'A cartel that can get their friends better conditions in prison.'

'Yeah. The cartels have links with the DEA. If you want to take down an enemy, why not get the US taxpayer to do it for you and just call in the Feds?'

This is far from ideal. I'm still not sure I won't be double-crossed by anyone we employ. On the other hand, I'm relying on being double-crossed to get to Soto. I need insurance, though.

'What happens if the boys you're using turn out to be using you?'

'Then their uncles or cousins go up to ultramax with Perez.'

'Will the threat be enough?'

'It's a risk. But . . .'

I get his meaning. We've taken a few so far.

'Let's do it,' I say. I've shed a lot of blood and come through too much to turn back now. I'm going to get Soto if it kills me.

Chapter 31

We board the trucks and begin to roll towards El Paso. It's much easier to make the journey this side of the border. Liana will be taken to hospital and, as a potential witness, treated at the expense of the DEA. That sets my mind at rest.

I want to get to a DEA safe house and contact Juan as soon as possible to set up the sting. As soon as we arrive I call him, telling him I need some more guns, that I can pay well. He says OK. So far, so straightforward; the rendezvous is planned for the day after tomorrow.

As soon as I'm done, Maria calls him to say that they've been monitoring my calls. She tells him I've been trampling all over their investigations and he's not, under any circumstances, to sell me any guns. She asks him if he's aware of what's been going on to the east. He says he's heard things, that a Yanqui has been causing Soto a lot of problems. Maria tells him that I'm that Yanqui, and I've killed a lot of Soto's men, including an informant.

She puts down the phone.

'Do you think he bought it?'

'He's a businessman, he'll see the angle.'

'When do I meet my team?'

'Tomorrow.'

'OK, I should get some sleep.'

'You could do that,' she says.

'Or?'

'Or.'

She comes over to me and kisses me on the lips. I suddenly feel massively self-conscious. I'm filthy, and I stink.

'I should take a shower,' I say.

'So should I.'

So we do, together, and it's wonderful. When you spend your days dealing in violence and hate, it makes any good stuff you find along the way all the more precious. It's only when we're lying naked on the bed an hour or more later that she sees me looking at the scars on her back.

'Cigarette burns,' she says. 'A few of the local boys decided to have their fun with me. It was my seventeenth birthday.'

'I see.'

'They're dead now,' she says.

'You killed them?'

She shrugs. 'Boys in my neighbourhood didn't like it. I only had to say who they were.'

'You got your revenge.'

'I didn't want revenge. I wanted justice. But that wasn't going to happen.'

'So that's why you applied to the DEA?'

'Yes. I don't want to live where the gangster is king. I want to make them pay for what they do.'

'And do you succeed?'

'Sometimes I think we do. Other times I think we're just part of the market ourselves. Another factor that the gangs need to take into consideration. Some people say we do good, some not. We seized two billion dollars' worth of drugs last year. The market value's over sixty billion. Things get murky.'

'It seems everything's like that down here.'

'Yes, it's difficult to understand what's right and wrong. It could be that we are the problem.'

'Why?'

'If you legalise the drugs you kill the gangsters' income. You take the murderers and torturers out of it and give production over to some guy in a suit in a drug company. All the misery you see in Juarez and everywhere else from Peru to Pakistan disappears. In some ways the DEA is the cartels' best friend. Besides, who is the government to tell you what you can do with your own body?'

'So why do you do a job you think is so harmful?'

'Because Soto killed my husband. He let him starve to death, and when he died, he dumped the body at the side of the road for everyone to see. It's personal with me. When my grief is gone, perhaps then I can indulge in looking at the bigger picture. Not until then.'

I don't know if she's right. I lie smoking, watching the smoke curl up through the dusk light. People will always kill each other. They'll always find a reason. And if they can't find a reason, they'll do it anyway. If drugs were legalised, would the killing stop? Or would the gangs move into something else, some other form of profitable murder? I stub out the cigarette.

Maria kisses me again and we forget about all this until the morning. Then it's time to go.

Mystery Man has sent someone across already and briefed the Mexican team. I have to trust that he knows what he's doing. I'd like to run my eye over them, but doing so would jeopardise the mission.

I arrange to meet Juan outside the church on the central square. I'm armed with very little – just a Glock 9mm that Maria has come up with. I have only one other weapon – a tiny shim, a piece of metal, that will go into my mouth, between my lip and my upper teeth. If I'm caught, handcuffed or tied, that will be important.

Maria drives us over the border in an unmarked pick-up. We're waved through without stopping.

'Did you arrange that?'

'No, most people go straight through. You'd be unlucky to be stopped going this way.'

'But there was a big screening procedure for foot traffic.'

'The poor are the most likely to smuggle things in to Mexico. They're not white like you and they don't have cars.'

It's been agreed that I'll walk to the RV. Maria will park the car and watch from across the street. The team – all five of them – will be located in two cars on the main roads out. There's one spotter who will phone on directions once I'm picked up.

I'm wearing a hoodie with a pocket, and I put the Glock in there. If I have to use it, I won't draw it, I'll just fire straight through the front of the pocket. I've decided to stop arsing around with the cast and a medic has cut it off for me. It afforded some pro -

tection to my fingers but it identified me too much, and slowed me down.

The medic offers to shoot me up with a painkiller, but I tell her that it's not been hurting as bad as it was.

'You've got used to the pain,' she says. 'After a couple of weeks the body just gives up on signalling.'

'That and masses of ibuprofen,' I say.

'That'll be helping.'

My hand is quite deformed, but I haven't got time to sort it. I'll have the operation when I get back to the UK, anyway. At least there it's free.

I sit out the front of the cathedral until our appointed meeting time – 1 p.m. There's no immediate sign of Juan, no car with flashing lights. I pretend to study the architecture and see if I can clock my support team. No one immediately apparent, which is a good thing.

At 1.15, a Toyota pulls up and flashes its lights. This time I'm a bit more careful and wait for a while to see if anyone gets out like they did last time. Then I wander over casually, hand on the pistol inside my hoodie.

A man winds down the window. It's Juan.

He has a big grin on his face.

'You're looking good, dude,' he says. 'Messed up enough to be a local boy. Get in.'

'You don't have the stuff here?'

'Change of plan. Police interest too hot. Gotta go to a friend's house.'

'Are you going to fuck me over, Juan?'

'No way, man, don't be so paranoid. Get in.'

I climb in next to him and we swing out into the traffic. I make no attempt to check if Maria or any of the others are following. That would be giving the game away.

We motor out of central Juarez and towards the factory slums. Things are going to get more difficult here. Maria can't follow me as easily without drawing attention to herself. The back-up team may be even more conspicuous – outsiders in the area who'd attract the interest of the locals. If they assume my team is there to make a hit, then they could be attacked. Hope the drone's up there.

I also have my smartphone enabled for tracking, but that won't last long if it's found – they'll bin it as a matter of course. Still, until they do, it will let Maria know where I am.

If Soto is there, the plan is to hit him hard and fast. Maria assures me we've got ten guys, all ex-army, to do the job. I hope they know they're not meant to shoot me, particularly now I look so much more like a local.

We start to drive into a slum. I don't recognise it because they all look the same – the badly rigged electricity cables overhead, some so low you could almost jump up and touch them, the kids with no shoes on their feet, the stink of the place.

'This is where you live?'

'No. It's a good place to keep the guns.'

'No chance of them getting stolen?'

'I pay protection.'

'You look like you're your own protection.'

'Yeah, but this is Juarez, everyone pays protection. Even Soto.'

'Who does he pay?'

'Me.'

He jams on the brakes and the car skids to a halt. From nowhere, five other vehicles have arrived – two SUVs and three older saloon cars. One of the SUVs hammers into my side of Juan's car, the other fencing him in. It's a classic box manoeuvre; our car has nowhere to go.

Juan's grinning his face off as *sicarios* swarm all over his car. He has his hands in the air. There's a bloke on the bonnet with an AK, pointing it straight through the window. Another is pulling at the door handle on my side, but there's not enough room to open it. If I wanted to shoot him, he'd be dead. Someone is screaming at them, trying to make them act as a unit, but it's not doing any good. He's shouting in English for a start. Blondie. I should kill him now I have the chance.

But I don't take out the Glock yet, I don't want to give these guys a reason to shoot me. I sit with my hands in the air too.

They finally shift the car on my side and drag me out. I guess the hard stop was so there was no risk of me having any opportunity at all to take control of the situation.

It's here that the inevitable kicking begins. I've immediately got my hands up, my arms covering my head and the ballistic vest providing some protection to my back and chest, but it's still a fair old battering. I do fight back, catching one guy's leg and turning him to dislocate the knee, but there are too many of them. I'm quickly pulled to my feet, cable-tied behind my back, searched, stripped of all belongings and shoved head first into the back seat of the SUV.

Before I've had time to sit up, the SUV takes off, its wheels spinning on the dry mud road, the car slewing from side to side as it picks up pace. We're driving at a crazy speed, weaving through the winding main drag, foot to the floor. Blondie's in the seat next to me, and he punches me hard in the face, breaking my nose.

He looks at me as if he's going to ask me a question. I return his gaze and he hits me again.

'Want the bad news?'

'Looks like I'm going to get it.'

'There is no team supporting you. Your little girl is all who's following you, and she's going to be joining us soon.'

I say nothing.

'The DEA are not incorruptible. Your man who set up the operation. He's ours.'

I don't want to believe that, but it has the ring of truth. No wonder he was so relaxed about me coming in here. And how did they know that Soto was suspended in the cave? I told Mystery Man at the DEA. He told them.

'I was sent to die down in that cave.'

'Yes. And you've been sent to die here. Only this time you will.'

'Mystery Man's the inside man.' I say this to myself as much as anyone else.

'Your girlfriend's boss. You're naïve. You still think in terms of plants, of corrupt officers. The whole system is corrupt. Even you, if only you knew it. Everyone buys and sells, everyone's bought and sold. The DEA give you up and Soto helps them out – pays a little tax, allows a shipment or two to be

264

found. Maybe he gives them money, maybe he gives up a few of his men. Now you might think he's an informant. But he's also running people in law enforcement. They might not see it that way, but it's how it is.'

No point saying anything. He seems to want his fifteen minutes, so I'll let him have it. If there is no team coming to get me, if Soto really has struck a bargain with the DEA, then I can't see a way out. I'm manacled, I have no weapon, I'm ridiculously outnumbered. I've been a fool.

'Everyone knows the rules down here. You don't play by them. That's why you're sitting here next to me with a busted face. That's why you're going to die a long and excruciating death. But first you're going to tell me who you've been working for.'

I look at him. I believe what he's been telling me. Things will only get worse from here. I head-butt him, right on the side of the temple. He goes flat out and I try to kick the driver in the head over the seat. No good, though, can't get a clean shot at him. The passenger turns round towards me and levels his pistol. I use my other foot to kick his hand, just as the car swerves violently to the right. It knocks the gun aside. I don't know if he intended to shoot, but the gun goes off, splattering the driver's brains all over the window. I expect the car to accelerate, or tip over, or something dramatic. It doesn't. All it does is grind to a halt. I try to twist the ties off, but I don't have time.

The *sicario* in the passenger seat leaps out, and now I'm trying to get the cuffs under my arse so my hands are in front of me. Not enough time. I'm dragged from the car again and this time treated to a proper beating – six or seven guys laying into me. Even as they kick me, I can tell they're not trying to kill me. The kicks are going into my legs, my belly, my nuts and my back. If they wanted to kill me, they'd have stamped on my head. Still, they're none too accurate and I do take a couple of good clouts to the face.

Then I feel myself lifted into the air and I'm slammed into the boot of a car. The lid shuts and I'm in darkness. I'm coughing up blood. I need to think clearly but I'm out of ideas. Nothing I can do here.

I'm in a lot of pain and it's all I can do not to retch. Should I try to get the ties off now? Not going to be possible. The shim's still wedged under my lip – probably not doing me much good up there; I can feel it embedded in my mashed gums. But the ties are behind my back. There's no room for manoeuvre. The car goes over bump after bump. We have been going for so long. My body is screaming. I think I've broken a rib at least and my eyes are closing up. Every jolt sends new agonies through me. Eventually it all gets too much and I black out.

Chapter 32

Time doesn't flow right in the dark and in pain. You can't tell if you've been somewhere an hour or a week. I'm crammed in so tightly that I can hardly breathe and I have to fight to stay conscious. It's not a fight I always win and I drift in and out of wakefulness. But wherever I am – awake or in my dreams – there's no let-up from the pain.

I begin to hallucinate. I'm in Canada with Chloe, my daughter. It's a sunny day and we're cycling in the woods. I'm on a boat on a sparkling ocean. I'm lying on the sea bed, held down by a huge stone. But always I'm in pain. This is torture, for the purposes of extracting information, I have no doubt. Blondie said as much in the car. That at least gives me hope that it will end.

You'd think training would help here. And it's true, we did go through a lot of torture resistance training in the Det and SRR. People always get the wrong idea about it, though. There aren't any techniques to allow you to resist torture. I've read the IRA's Green Book – the terrorist manual. It has a whole section on torture resistance which amounts to 'remember you're fighting for a just cause and tough it out'. Lots of revolutionary movements have written on torture – they have to face it regularly – but none of them have come up with any magic yoga practice or disassociation technique that will make the whole thing a cakewalk.

Facts about torture seem to tumble through my mind, snippets of interrogation classes. The Gestapo, in World War II – despite the best efforts of their fingernail rippers and electric shockers – got most of their information from straightforward public co-operation and paid informers. Even the Japanese in Burma said that torture was a poor way of gathering intelligence. The Japanese army did it because they held prisoners in contempt, rather than to gain information. Funnily enough, spies during the war were issued with a guaranteed torture resistance method – a cyanide pill.

I start to have fantasies. There *was* a support team. Maria has found me. The tracker in my phone has led her here. A whole division of US Marines is just about to come storming through the doors to rescue me.

There's a voice in my head. I recognise it as one of my instructors from my first spell in training, back in the day, when I was in the Det.

'You're the torturer's nightmare. You're your own nightmare. A man without any information to give that they'll believe.'

That's the problem with torture – people who have nothing to tell you will tell you things and make them sound convincing just to make the pain stop. My story's a true one, but will the guys who have me in here recognise that? Even professional, trained interrogators have problems working out when someone's telling the truth.

Another snippet of a class comes back to me. It's in a weird form. I see my old instructor, and he's got something tied to a metal bedstead, one of those with a kind of wire net to support the mattress. But there isn't a mattress on it. There's a body. In my hallucination, it's a pig's body. Or it could be me. Or a woman. They're electrocuting this pig. I know what this is – it was a favourite tool of the Pinochet regime in Chile, Mrs Thatcher's chums. It was known as the *parrilla*, the grill. They'd strap the victim naked on to it and then use electrodes to burn them, to violate them.

All this is in my head and I just about get enough clarity to know why. It's anxiety, and it needs fighting. I'm worried that they won't recognise the truth when I tell it to them. Other fears start to loom from the darkness. They're not torturing me and they'll leave me here forever. I'll give them the information and they'll put me back in here. I'm trying to get hold of these thoughts but there's no point. At least they're a distraction from the agony of these cramped conditions.

Light. I'm pulled from the hole. My legs straighten but I can't walk. I'm going down a corridor of some sort – a weird scene – bedrooms either side of me, people stretched out on beds. For a second I think I'm in a hospital. Have I been rescued? No.

I try to force my brain to take in what it can. I'm in some sort of dormitory building. It has rooms of five or six beds, not unlike a military barracks. The light's artificial.

I'm dragged down a flight of stairs and into a basement. My clothes are torn off me and I'm left sitting naked in the middle of the floor. I can't stand, my legs just have no feeling at all. I can't hold my head up either; it's been forced into a bent position by the ceiling of the hole I was put in and I can't look up. I faint again.

I'm slapped awake.

'Not so tough now.'

Blondie's voice.

'Sit him up.' Another voice, Mexican. I recognise it. Soto. There's bright light in the room but I manage to focus on him. He looks bad; ten years older since I last saw him.

I'm pulled roughly upright but I can't maintain a sitting posture and I slump to the floor.

'You weakling piece of shit, look at you. You stink. Aren't you ashamed of yourself?' It's Blondie talking.

'Sit him up.'

They pull me upright again, and this time I manage to sit.

I try to order my thoughts. Blondie's belittling me, he's stripped me. This is a classic hard interrogation technique. He wants some information, clearly. That means they need me in a fit state to talk to.

'We do what we like with you here,' says Blondie. 'You're a piece of meat to us.'

This is standard stuff, make the victim feel powerless. The knowledge of their technique doesn't make it any easier to bear, though, particularly as I *am* powerless. The fact that you know how someone is trying to fuck you up isn't much of a consolation.

A kick comes in to my side but I'm too numb to feel the pain. It makes it difficult to breathe, though.

'Stand up.'

My body is suddenly racked by a great convulsion of cramp and I lie writhing on the floor.

Blondie leans in towards Soto.

'He's not as tough as I thought. You won't get any sense out of him for a while. He's in too much pain, crying like a little girl.'

Soto whispers something to someone. I can't see who. I'm grabbed by two people from behind. Where did they come from? Someone ties a tourniquet around my arm. I try to struggle. I feel an injection into my arm and an enormous rush goes up and across behind my forehead. It's intensely pleasurable for a few seconds, but then I'm retching on to the floor. I haven't eaten enough to vomit. I find myself giggling, and a warm glow spreads all over my body.

Suddenly the pain is gone. I'm woozy, pleasant, drunk. They take the tourniquet off and sit me up on the floor. After a couple of minutes my head clears.

'That's better, isn't it?' says Soto. 'Let us begin: what are you doing here and who are you working for?'

'I'm on my own. You killed my friend.'

'I don't believe that,' says Soto.

My head's spinning now but the pain is gone, and that alone makes me feel fantastic.

'It's the truth. My friend was Andy Lyons. He was a good guy, someone with kids who wanted to do right. Just making his way. You killed him. I came for you.'

271

Soto takes out a knife.

'If you were in the hands of the Araña cartel, they would cut the skin off your face while you were still alive. But, you know I might do the same. I've killed a lot of good fathers. A lot of good mothers, sons and daughters too. No one ever came after me like you have. I know you're ex special forces. So I ask you again, who do you work for?'

'I sail a yacht. A little boat. I teach people to sail.' My voice sounds different. Is it the drug, or my strangely alien-feeling teeth? I can't feel any pain, but I know that they've been smashed in at the front, I can feel them rough on my tongue.

'We can put you back in the box if you don't co-operate.'

'You're going to kill me anyway.'

'Yes. But not in the box. I must avoid that. It would kill you too quick. You will die alone in the dark, starved, mad, in pain, yes. But, the box is too kind. I may suspend you from a rope, as you suspended me. That is in my mind.'

'I can only tell you the truth, what I told you in the car.'

'So why did you leave me in the cave?'

'You had captured someone who helped me. I went back to free him.'

'Out of the goodness of your heart?'

'I put him into that mess. I had to get him out of it.'

'Don't bullshit us, you piece of crap!' Blondie's in my face, not an inch away. I think he's realised I'm past head-butting anyone.

'You took some information off my computer.'

'Yes. It will be used to incriminate you.'

'I doubt it. It went through our man at the DEA.'

'Your man?' I thought Blondie said I wasn't thinking about it the right way if I thought in terms of people being bought.

'He may as well be. That's incriminating information, but it incriminates him too. We have made certain payments. Why did you take that information if you just want revenge? Why aren't I dead?'

'I don't want revenge. I want justice.'

'Well you'll get that. But *my* justice. Not yours. And you're still not telling me the truth. That's a very weak dose of opium. It will wear off in an hour or two. You'll go back into the box until it does. Then we'll talk again.'

I'm dragged back down the corridor, trying again to see where I am. It's some sort of big house, and I'm being taken along a balcony. Down from the balcony are very small windows. They're curious things. They make the place very dark. They remind me more of pillbox slits.

I'm taken to a little cupboard built into the wall, like an airing cupboard or something like that. I get a good look at the locking mechanism as they stuff me in. It's just a bar, two metal brackets holding it shut. You could knock it up with a stick. Except I don't have a stick.

The drug they've given me has a curious effect. I feel quite clear-headed but there's a sense of unreality – I realise as I drift off into sleep that I don't really care that they're putting me in this place.

I'm awoken by terrible cramp and the familiar agony. I can't tell how long I've been back in the box this time. It opens up and I'm dragged out again, glad of the relief as my legs come free.

It doesn't last long. My feet scrape on the concrete as I'm pulled down the corridor and back down to the basement. A stupid urge to fight these bastards comes into my mind, but I can hardly stand, let alone hit anyone. My legs are still completely numb.

There's a chair in the room now and some small jugs of water. Blondie has a cloth in his hands and Soto is sitting at the side of the room. It doesn't take Einstein to work out what they're going to do to me.

'Waterboarding,' says Blondie, 'but Mexican style.'

I'm sat down on the chair and it's tipped right back, so I'm lying practically flat on my back with my feet and knees above my head. The blood's been returning to my legs and it feels as though someone has set them on fire. I try not to panic as a towel is placed right across my face and I'm held down by both shoulders.

Already I'm finding it difficult to breathe, with just the cloth on my face. On the other hand, being upside down is forcing blood back into my neck and shoulders, and the terrible cramp I can feel there begins to lessen. The respite is short. My feet are pulled upwards so my body is at a twenty-degree angle, my head lower than my heart. Water is poured on to my face. I try to hold my breath, not to breathe in, but it's no good. Water is going up my nose, over my eyes. I've experienced waterboarding in training, but this is something else. The water's burning, not hot, but with pepper or something in it.

I choke, cough and try to breathe, but it's like there's a jellyfish on my face. The breath pulls the wet towel tight against my nose and mouth and I struggle against the people who are holding me. My eyes, my nose, my throat are burning and I can't breathe. But it doesn't stop. More water, more burning, still no breath. Waves of panic go through me, anger, but then nothing. All there is is the desire to breathe, that's all. There's no more at all.

The towel comes off and still I can't see. I suck in breath but it's agony.

'You ready to tell us where you're from?'

I try to speak but I can't; my whole mouth is burning up.

'Do it again.'

The towel goes back on and a wave of dread sweeps over me. My lips, my tongue are on fire. No breath. My heart is pounding, as if it's screaming for air. Can't breathe, can't breathe, that's all I can think.

Towel off.

'Ready to speak?'

I cough, trying to force out words. They want a story, I'll give them a story. Anything. But I can't speak.

'Again.'

'No!' That word comes out OK.

I'm held back again. It's like I've got a screaming feedback noise in my head. It obliterates all thought, everything. I'm not me any more, I'm just an overwhelming need for air.

They take their time this time. How long? It could be two seconds, it could be two minutes. I black out, and when I recover, I'm sitting upright in the chair.

I still can't see.

'You don't like the chilli?' It's Blondie's voice.

'That's all we got on the menu for the next three weeks.'

Again I try to vomit but just retch.

Someone gives me a glass of water. I gulp it down. Water's thrown into my face.

'OK,' says Blondie. 'Soto's taking a leak. So you can talk now or I'm going to blow your brains out and I'll tell Soto you tried to escape.'

My streaming eyes blur into vision. There's a pistol pointed at my head.

Chapter 33

'I'm employed by the UK Serious Organised Crime Agency,' I say, 'in a deniable role.'

Soto comes back into the room. My eyes are clearing a little, though still painful, but I can speak. Maybe Maria wasn't caught. Maybe she'll get someone here to help me. I cling to that because it's all I've got.

'The Feds?' says Soto.

I take a long time with my answer. The longer I'm here talking to him, the longer I'm not in that box or upside down having chilli water poured up my nose.

'Sort of.'

'And your mission?'

'The UK wants you back on its soil for trial.'

He laughs.

'So they send one man?'

'I was only meant to scout the mission. One man is less noticeable than twenty.'

'Not when that one man kills so many of my soldiers.'

'You brought it to me. I just defended myself.'

Soto laughs again.

'So there will be others?'

'If I go missing, people will look for me.'

'Your government doesn't mind operating without permission on foreign soil.'

'No. Not if it has to.'

He shakes his head and lights a cigarette. He seems to find this idea outrageous.

'This is a country we are proud of. You can't walk in here and do what you like.'

I say nothing.

'Write down the name of your controller.' He hands me a pen and pad of paper.

I can barely write John Fardy's name. I don't want to endanger him, but this might be a weird way of getting a message to him. OK, I can't say 'I've been caught, sort something out to rescue me', but anything at all that might lead him to conclude I'm in trouble is worth trying.

'We can check this out.'

'Do. He'll pay for my release.'

Soto, who so far has remained quite calm, suddenly explodes. He leaps to his feet and starts screaming an inch from my face.

'Do you imagine you have enough money to buy off a principal of La Frontera? Do you think the cops could pay me? I pay cops, not the other way around.'

He's red in the face, spitting as he speaks. It's the first time I've seen a glimpse of his famous temper.

'That's not what I meant.'

'What?'

'You're looking for a way into the UK. A contact in SOCA has got to be useful. You put pressure on him, use me as a hostage to get what you want. It would give you some leverage.' I'm busking furiously, anything to buy me some time.

He ponders for a minute.

'Maybe, but that misses the point.'

'I don't understand.'

'The point is, and the reason that we are all here – I want to watch you die.'

I can't say anything to that. We sit in silence for a minute or two. The room swims around me.

Then he goes on: 'We already have leverage in the UK. We made an example, things got easier for our men on the ground. We have the ability to fly what we want in. And we can get what we want out. I don't need your man.'

'Is money so hard to shift?'

'Not money.'

'Then what?'

He looks at me hard. 'Fuck you,' he says slowly. 'Now you can stay here to die. Don't worry, I have a doctor here. We'll give you enough fluid to survive for a very long time. Until then, it's you, your piss, your shit, here in the dark. Occasionally, when it amuses me, I'll come down here and beat you. Most of the time you'll be on your own. This is my safe house. I always have someone here. It could take you five years to die if we plan it right. And look.'

He points to the ceiling. There's a camera there. 'It's infrared. I get to watch you dying down here any time I like, without even having to get out of my seat.'

He stands up, punches me in the face. I fall backwards off the chair and I'm lucky not to be knocked out cold. Blondie drags me across the floor and puts another cable tie around my existing bonds. He secures that to a smooth ring that's been drilled into the floor. Then he gives me a farewell boot up the arse and he and Soto leave, turning off the light and locking the door. It's pitch black.

This, unbelievably, is the position of maximum opportunity. My physical and mental state is not going to improve from here. I calm myself, putting all fear aside. Fear is perfectly reasonable and anyone who says he doesn't feel it is lying. It's how you manage it that is important in situations like this. It can only cloud my thinking. I reduce my focus to the here and now – never mind about what might come tomorrow. I have to work fast. He can't be watching me all the time. It was just dusk when he dragged me out of the hole, and he's been down here with me for maybe an hour.

My options are plain. I could wait, bide my time and hope Maria rescues me. It's vaguely realistic, but I don't know if Maria has been captured or not. I have to try to do something right now. I have resigned myself to the fact that I'm probably going to die, but I've decided that if I do, it's going to be quickly and in a fight, not rotting to death here in the darkness.

Then I remember the shim. My teeth and gums are so mashed that I can't feel whether it's still up there. Tentatively, I slide my tongue carefully over my broken front teeth, but I can't work out what is tooth and what might be the shim. Then I feel it, an alien edge that can only be one thing, and my heart races, spurred on by a tiny glimmer of hope.

My hands are tied behind my back. Take your time, relax; try to recover. I try to count out the minutes and hours but it's impossible in my beaten-up state.

When I estimate that a few hours have gone, I start to move. There's music playing upstairs but it's no guarantee that Soto's not at his desk. Carefully I bring my legs through my arms to get the cuffs in front of me. In case Soto is looking I try to move in increments, so that he'll assume nothing is untoward. This is harder than it might appear with the cuffs secured to the floor. It takes forever, and, for a while I'm stuck in a ridiculous position, my right leg refusing to bend enough to pull through. Finally, desperation gives me the strength to do it.

I'm exhausted and really need to recover, but there's no time. I've practised the next bit too many times to make a mistake, though I'm normally used to having good teeth to hold the shim in.

Using my tongue at first, I work the blade out of the bloody rut it's been forced into during my numerous beatings, until finally it's free. My eyes streaming tears, I then move it around in my mouth until I find two teeth I can bear to bite down on. It's excruciating, the pain shooting like electricity up through my gums and across the front of my skull, but it's all I have, so I persevere, biting hard on the shim and holding my face up against the mechanism of the ties.

After a surprisingly short amount of time, the pain subsides and there's a glorious, reassuring hiss as the cable tie comes free. Carefully, so carefully, I move my arms apart and wait momentarily for the pain that must surely come as blood flows back into my wrists. When it arrives, my whole body constricts with the effort not to scream out loud. I can feel my head rolling back in agony – the pain is almost the worst I have felt in this whole appalling time, and inside I wail. If Soto is watching, he'll have no doubt whatsoever about exactly what's going on.

As the pain finally begins to loosen its hold on me, I lie flat out, exhausted, and wait; wait for the inevitable harsh scrape of boot on concrete, a sound that will surely herald their arrival.

But it never comes, and soon I am feeling around my vicinity, and then the larger interior of the cellar. Steps. I haul myself up them, fall, then haul myself up once more on legs that buckle and waver underneath me like those of a toddler. I listen. Can't hear anything but the music, though a tiny crack of light runs down the edge of the door. I feel for the light switch. It's an enormous risk, but I need to turn it on; and there's no way they are just watching all this unfold without doing anything to stop me.

I click on the light. I can't see anything for a few minutes as my eyes readjust. I lock my knees to stop myself from falling down as the feeling begins to creep back into my legs There's not much to help me here. There's the chairs they used to interrogate me, a bizarre set of folded clean towels for the waterboarding, and not a lot else.

I stumble back down the stairs and examine the ceiling. Solid concrete, as are all the walls. All the walls, that is, except for one. The wall by the stairs, right next to where I started and conversely the last to be examined, is a stud wall. It looks like all the others, but it isn't; it's plasterboard.

I hobble over to one of the steel chairs. It has shaped metal legs with plastic cups on the bottom. I can't get them off – my teeth aren't up to the job and neither are my hands. I have to work with what I've got. I break off the two front legs by kneeling on them. They don't come free easily and it takes me a good five minutes of waggling and pulling before the brackets holding them give way. I'm left with the piece of metal that forms the two legs. I'm praying that the music upstairs, which I can hear quite clearly now, will cover what I'm about to do.

It occurs to me to smash the video camera, but there's no point. It will just make more noise than is necessary, and I'm convinced now that he's not anywhere near it, for the time being at least.

Bracing myself and using all I have left – my full body weight – I thump the bottom of one of the legs squarely into the board. I hit it at the perfect angle, first time lucky, and it crunches right through up to my knuckles. That should be the noisiest bit. I rake at the wall and the board comes away in chunks. There are a couple of down beams I hit straight away, but I work around them. The plastic cup on the bottom of the foot quickly degrades, leaving a nice sharp metal edge. It doesn't take me long to get a hole dug between two timber supports wide enough for my shoulders. Adrenalin is driving me. I scrape away the rubble and crawl through the hole. I'm still naked, so it hurts like crazy, my ribs stabbing shots of pain through me as I raise my hands to wriggle in. There's just enough light coming through the hole to see by.

I'm in a wine cellar. There are racks and racks of

it. There's also an ancient pack of bottles of mineral water. I grab one and drink it down in long gulps, before vomiting the whole lot up again in great agonising coughes and retches. With the next bottle I take it carefully, sipping cautiously until a good amount has flowed down my battered throat. This time it stays where it's supposed to, and as I reach for another bottle, I see ahead of me a set of narrow stairs going up to a wooden door. A door I see as I edge closer that's only secured by a Yale-style latch. The music's still pounding outside. I turn on the light and have a good look around. There's very little I can use here. Just two useful items. One is a door – still in its plastic wrapping. I move that against the hole in the wall, disguising it. The other is a large old-fashioned fuse box. I grab a dusty bottle of wine from one of the racks next to me and carefully and repeatedly knock it against the brick floor with increasing force until it quietly shatters. Now I have at least the broken neck of the bottle as a weapon; it's pretty pathetic but it makes me feel better.

Right, here goes. If I was a religious man, this is when I'd be praying. As I'm not, I'll just concentrate on the task at hand. My legs feel better than they were, but still shaky. I'm convinced I've broken some ribs and I'm bruised from head to foot. Can I lift my arm enough to use the bottle? No. Can't worry about that. I know from experience that when it comes to a life-and-death situation, you hardly notice injuries that would keep you in bed for a week in other circumstances.

I pick my hiding spot carefully. I have to assume that when I kill the lights, whoever comes to fix the fuse will come down with a torch. So if I'm in front of him, he'll see me. I need to hide at the side of the stairs, advance and take him in one go.

They may get nervous if the lights go. They may check the camera too, so I'd better throw every switch just in case. What if there's more than one of them, and one covers from the top of the stairs? God knows. No, not good enough. I need a plan. OK, I have one. A change of hiding place, low behind the racks.

I plot out my steps. Five from the light switch to the trip switches, two forward to the wall, down the wall six paces, a 180-degree turn, three paces forward and lie on the floor. I do it twice and then I'm ready to go.

I turn off the light switch and feel my way to the fuse box. I find the trip switches and flick them all off with both hands. The music above dies, as does the sliver of light coming through the door. Then I'm scrabbling back to my hiding place, lying flat on the floor, the sharp bottle neck in my hand.

I control my breathing; I'm panting. I hear voices from above. The door opens and a torch beam scans the darkness. Down it comes, down the stairs. As I predicted, there is another one at the top. I can hear him speaking to his mate.

The first man goes to the switch and trips it. The lights down here don't come on, but the music starts again. He goes to leave and then he sniffs. He turns around. He's caught the whiff of the wine that spilled when I broke the bottle. He speaks to the guy at the top of the stairs, who turns the light on.

I hold my breath, keeping absolutely still.

The first man says something to the guy at the top of the stairs, and I hear the word '*botella*', which has to be 'bottle'. The other guy replies and the only word that stands out is '*nada*'. Nothing.

The guy at the bottom of the stairs is clearly keen to rejoin whatever party is going on upstairs and decides the smashed bottle isn't his problem. He goes back up, turns off the light and closes the door.

I retrace my steps to the fuse box. I give it five minutes and flick the switches again. The music dies once more and I hear shouts of annoyance from above.

I go back to my hiding place. The man comes down again. This time, as I thought, he's alone. These guys live as long as they're suspicious. When the electricity goes, they're bound to have a nagging idea of foul play, no matter how far into the desert they are.

So they send two guys to check it out. The second time it's just the sodding electricity arsing about again and they send one.

He comes down the stairs quickly, his torch shining directly on the fuse box. He knows what to do. He puts his fingers to the switch and I take him, bad right hand over the mouth, the left stabbing the broken bottle into his neck, two, three, four times. He kicks and struggles, but I've clearly severed something major and in seconds he's dead. There's blood everywhere, on him, on me, on the floor. I flick the switch, turning the lights and music back on. He has a snub-nose Smith and Wesson in a hip holster. It's a good one. I check it. It takes five rounds, and it has five rounds. He's wearing jeans and a T-shirt and he's about my size. I quickly strip him and put the clothes on. They're soaked in blood, but in the

286

darkness – and it will be dark – who cares; it's better than being in the buff. His shoes are far too small, so I put his socks on so my feet won't show up.

Feeling immeasurably better, I climb the stairs and peek around the open door. Directly opposite me is a laundry room. It's very strange to see something as domestic and unthreatening as a couple of washing machines and a dryer in a place like this. It'll suit my purposes, though.

Back to the cellar. The fuse box has a whole row of circuit breakers in it. I pick the torch up from the floor, level it at the box and start pulling the circuits out, one by one. When the main lights upstairs go, I pocket that circuit breaker and quickly rip out all the rest, throwing them behind the door that's covering the hole in the wall.

Voices from above – angry and complaining. I use the torch to go back up the stairs and into the laundry room. I have to wait until they find the body. I have five shots and a whole heap of guys against me. I need to face armed opponents and at very close range, because I can't afford to miss and I've got to get their guns. Five shots might not put down five men, even in the darkness. And even if they do, after that I'd be quickly overwhelmed.

It's really dark in here. The little windows I saw earlier out on the corridor admit hardly any light, and in the laundry room, crouched behind a washing machine, I can't see my hand in front of my face.

They're calling a name from somewhere in the building. Presumably they want the guy who did the trip switch to go back and do it again. Well that's not going to happen.

There are baskets of clothes next to me. The clean smell has an oddly emotional effect on me. It makes me think of home, of all those precious things you take for granted in your day-to-day life – clean clothes, fresh air, showers, baths. The thought comes and goes in a flash. I need to concentrate here.

After about five minutes, someone comes along the corridor. I hear a name. Eduardo. From the tone, he is asking what Eduardo is arsing about at. There's a weak light. I guess it's the torch setting on a mobile. Then a shout goes up and I know – it's game on.

Suddenly there are *sicarios* all over the place. Orders are barked through the darkness, I even hear a couple of cars set off. A big search is going on, and from the anger of a voice that sounds like Soto's, I guess they've discovered I've turned down their hospitality in the basement.

The door of the laundry room flies open, a torch beam cuts the darkness, but whoever it is doesn't notice me behind the washing machine. As he turns, I see he has an AK with a bayonet fitted. In one movement I slip out from my hiding place and blow the back of his head off, catching his gun as he falls. Instantly, torchlight fills the room, revealing the position of the *sicarios*. Instinct takes over and I pop two bullets in one direction, two in another, dropping to the floor as AK fire rakes over the top of me. I fire from a prone position, four shots one way, three the other. In the flash of the gun I see two bodies to my left, people diving out of the way to my right.

It's almost completely dark as the weak light of a mobile phone lying on the floor flicks off. A torch

288

from the basement. Someone's coming up the stairs. If I fire, I'll give away my position to whoever it is. Adrenalin gives me the strength to leap forward and drive the bayonet through the *sicario* coming up the stairs of the torture room. I feel his weight on the end of the bayonet, hear him shout out as he falls. The torch drops and goes out. Pitch black. Two enormous bangs, two flashes. There are men in the basement, firing pistols wildly, the bullets zinging around the walls, but I'm down low. I send the corpse of the guy I've bayoneted down the stairs, and the shooters hear the noise and start firing at him. I can't see anyone down there between the flashes, it's so dark. I click the AK to full auto and give a burst into the basement. Bullets flash everywhere, it's like the Fourth of July and I'm lucky not to be hit. There are two thumps and both of the men in the basement are down, but the AK's empty. It still has the bayonet, though, so I'm not letting it go. In the pitch black I feel my way to the bottom of the stairs. I click on my torch for an instant to locate the pistol of the man I've bayoneted. It's a Glock 18 auto, which means that it's likely to have a big magazine.

I go down to the hole I made earlier and peer up. There's a torch at the top of the wine cellar stairs but it's pointing at the floor. He's hiding in the frame of the door, afraid of what's around the corner.

I thump my head looking through the hole, and he makes a noise, shouting something into the darkness, a request for identification I should guess.

They have a problem here – they have to look before they shoot. I know there's only me in here and I can fire without hesitation. I take aim at the torch and double-tap. He collapses down the stairs. More shouting and a hail of fire down the hall.

I crawl back through the hole in the wall, AK first. Another hail of fire and a thump at the top of the stairs. A torch is flicked on and scans the cellar. There are two more *sicarios* at the top of the stairs. Four shots from the Glock and they both go down.

Now there really is chaos. Screaming, shouting, cursing, random firing. The air is thick with the smell of cordite. I can't rely on them not realising I'm in the wine cellar for long. I go forward up the stairs. One of the dead guys has an M4A1. I discard my AK, put my pistol in my belt and pick it up. Put it on to fully automatic and give a burst round the corner straight down the hall. In the gun's flash I see the long hallway, stairs going up halfway down, the dorm rooms coming off it.

There were at least four dorm rooms. Six bunks in each. Twenty-four men here. The same again on the top floor. How many have I killed? Eight, nine so far? Forty to go, if they're all here.

I'm commanding the hall now; anyone who steps into it will be dead. Or they would be if I could see them. It's a stalemate. No one knows who's down here. No one knows who's alive and who's dead. They may not even have worked out that it's me. Or if they have, the news might not have got back to Soto. I still haven't given up hope of getting him.

I'm lying absolutely still when someone treads on my leg. With all the noise of the gunshots I haven't heard him coming up behind me. I keep still and he just walks over me, assuming I'm a corpse.

'Argh!' My leg is so painful I can't help myself

crying out. There's a flash of gunfire and the man above me falls dead. They've shot their own guy thinking it was me. In the sudden light I see a chilling sight. The reflection of the IR goggles that went with that advanced rifle. They've got night vision.

Chapter 34

I crack a full auto burst towards the person in front of me and I hear a slump. The M4's out of ammunition, so I reach for my pistol. This time I do turn on the torch. I've got command of the corridor, and if the night-vision guy is still alive, any advantage I had from being a lone man in the dark is severely reduced. He knows I've shot at him now, so he has his target. My man is down, but I'm just in time to see another gun come around the corner, and I dive for the shelter of the cellar as the corridor erupts around me.

The gun fires and keeps firing. Then it stops. I'm out of the doorway at the sprint, a double-handed grip on the pistol, holding the torch at the same time. I put two rounds into the guy with the automatic rifle, but he's wearing a ballistic vest and all my shots do is drop him to the floor. He hasn't managed to reload, and I put two shots into the back of his head. The torchlight swims with gun smoke. I quickly take up his rifle and reload. It's one of the mystery models I found in Soto's briefcase. He has four more magazines in an ammo belt, as well as the night-vision goggles. I put them on and kill the torch. The world pops into lurid green. There's one staircase to the top floor, but I'm not taking that. I have to assume that there may be other people with night vision about. Otherwise I'd just exit through one of the dorm windows and light the place up with the HE rounds from the assault rifle. I move to the dorms, but there's no one in there alive. There must be twenty men dead down here by now.

My window plan quickly becomes academic, because there are no windows, just slits in the concrete at about firing level.

I scroll to remote view on the rifle's little thumb wheel. Now the goggles are projecting the view from the rifle's sights. I put it around the corner. Two guys in night-vision goggles are creeping forward. I fire a burst, as do they, but all I have exposed is my hand. The gun jumps, and shots go clattering down the corridor as they run backwards to the stairwell for cover. It's then that I notice an icon in the bottom of the goggles' HUD. *Manual delay*. I rotate the little wheel and, in combination with pressing a button on the other side of the gun, get down to an icon that allows me to dial in delays of up to two seconds. I choose that. I mark the target on the doorway and fire an airburst shell into the ceiling just above the stairwell. As it smacks into the plasterwork, I duck behind the door. In two seconds there's an enormous explosion.

I dial back to standard night-vision view and make my way down the corridor very carefully, remembering that I'm still in my socks. It's like the gateway to hell, bodies everywhere, the ceiling burning, clothes burning. There's no way out on this level.

I'll have to take the stairs. I fit another magazine, click the shells to another two-second delay. Round the bend of the stairs, a burst from the rifle and I fire a shell, ducking back round.

Another almighty bang, sounds of screaming. I can't mess around here. I don't want to kill Soto, but I can't risk myself. Another two delayed HE rounds go up the stairs. I duck back round and feel the heat sweep over me. Then I'm running up the stairs. It's a big living room, again with no clear windows, just what amount to firing slits. There's total confusion, people lying around the floor, some screaming, some choking. There are three big sofas in there and they've all gone up like matchsticks. I can't stay in here. I shove forward through the smoke, holding my breath, the goggles saving my eyes.

There's a door, a big solid metal number with a slide bolt. Everyone's going for that. In the panic, no one pays me any attention – I look completely indistinguishable from the rest of the *sicarios*. Someone blunders through the door and I'm out into the desert. There's a whole group of women about two or three hundred yards off. These must be the party girls. I guess they exited when the shooting started, but have nowhere to go. The night is full of stars, but it's far from light. I can see the house clearly now – it's got a natural rock roof and would be almost invisible from the air or from satellites. There's even a mobile phone mast disguised as a water tower feeding an animal trough.

I can see the lights of three SUVs coming towards

us. They're intense in the night-vision glow. I guess they suspected I'd got out into the desert somehow when they noticed I was missing and have been driving around looking for me. Now the house has got a bit warmer they've worked out I must be here and come back.

There's enough confusion and screaming to let me get away, which is just what I plan to do. The burning house will give me a direction to enable me to walk away in a straight line in the dark. I don't mess around, I just head off away from the SUVs, striking out into the desert scrub as quickly as I can manage.

There's a lot talked about escape and evasion, but the key thing is to put as much distance between you and the enemy as possible. If they have night vision I will show up clearly on that. However, if I go behind the house and just head off with the burning building between me and the pursuers, then I might stand a chance.

On the other hand, this is the moment of maximum confusion. There are three cars coming to a halt. I'm wearing the night-vision goggles, carrying one of their guns. They're not going to suspect it's me.

Then suddenly I'm up in the air and just as suddenly I'm down again, smack on my back. My hearing's gone. Dirt covers my face and fills my mouth. It takes me a second to realise what's happened. There's been a gigantic explosion in the house. Tongues of flame come bursting through the slit windows, shattered glass and sand are still pattering down all around me. Change of plan.

People are out of the cars, pointing at the house, running towards it. I'll give these guys one thing, they don't lack for bravery. They go towards the doors, trying to get in to help their mates.

I pull down the goggles. In the light of the burning house I can see one figure standing with his hands on his hips, shaking his head. Is that Soto? I can't miss such a chance.

I walk nearer to him, around the back of the cars. One of them, a big Mercedes M-Class SUV, has its key left in it. I don't even bother drawing a weapon on Soto. I've got the assault rifle at my side and he'll realise he won't be able to get his gun out nearly as quickly as I can shoot him.

He's now twenty feet from me, all on his own. He seems genuinely stunned by what's gone on and can't stop shaking his head.

I walk up to him.

'Get in the car.'

His eyes widen as he looks down at my gun. There are screams from the house. Men are pouring out, some on fire, some carrying others who are unconscious.

'I think I prefer to die here,' he says.

'OK.' I raise the rifle slightly.

He stares into my eyes and I can see he doesn't want to die. He's not afraid, not at all. I think he's a bloke who doesn't do fear. But he is a pragmatist. He's working out his best way of survival. He moves towards the car. As he walks, I lift the pistol out of his belt – it's an H&K .45. I have no time to pat him down, so I'm just going to have to keep an eye on him.

I collapse the stock on the assault rifle, which allows me to put it on my knee when I get into the car.

Then I tell him to get in the driver's side and wriggle across. I can't risk him going around the blindside. He does as he's told, and so far no one's noticed anything. I get in, closing the door and winding down the window on my side. I wedge the pistol between my leg and the door. There's a mobile phone in a holder near the dashboard.

'Any moves at all and I'll kill you,' I say.

I click the dial on the grenade launcher to a four-second delay and hammer the car into a J-turn reverse, bringing me alongside the line of cars. I put the Merc into drive, then take the pistol with my right hand and point it at Soto while shooting the grenade launcher as best I can left-handed. I stick the remaining four grenades into the cars and then floor it, dropping the assault rifle down the side of my seat while still keeping the pistol trained on Soto. I steer with my left hand, thanking God for automatics so I don't have to change gear. There are four big explosions behind me. No idea if I destroyed any of the cars, but it can't have done any harm.

Soto is looking at me in disbelief.

I turn off the lights as we speed forward over the desert. We're hurtling forwards as fast as I dare – which isn't as fast as you'd think. Out here, the important thing is to keep going, not to break speed records. I don't want a puncture or, worse, to hit a boulder or flip the car.

'Put El Paso into the sat nav,' I tell Soto.

'Fuck yourself,' he says. He knows I'm not going to

shoot him for that. We're travelling blind then, not knowing where we're going. I could locate the Pole Star – in theory. As far as I know, it's visible down here, but what with subduing a hostage and driving flat out through an unfamiliar and rough terrain, I think I've got enough on my plate at the moment.

So we just scream on into the desert. Cars are sparking up behind us now, their lights visible in the mirror.

Can't worry too much about that – I just have to keep going forwards.

'How far do you think you'll get?' says Soto.

I ignore him, concentrate on winding through the desert shrubs. I need to make a call, see if Maria made it out of there. I'll have to think of that if I get time to stop.

An explosion goes off behind us. Soto's boys are shooting at me.

'You might want to call them and let them know you're in the car. Tell them to back off while they're at it.'

He reaches forward and dials, says something in Spanish. I can't tell what, but the cars behind are still coming.

'What?'

'I told them I was here and I told them not to fire. But they are coming and they are going to get you. You won't shoot me unless you really have to. You've had plenty of chance to do that.'

'Whoa!' The car lurches sideways as the ground suddenly falls away. I feel us go light on my side as the wheels rise up. They come back down again with a bang. We've been driving for three minutes now at about forty miles an hour. That's about two miles by my reckoning. I can see them gaining in the mirror, lights blazing. I'm a trained pursuit driver, but I'm wounded, driving one-handed and keeping half an eye on Soto. They know the ground and are not injured.

Only one thing for it. I bring the car around in an arc to face the oncoming cars. I can see three with their lights on.

'What are you doing?' says Soto.

'You might want to put your seat belt on.'

He looks at me as though I'm mad as I put the headlights on full and slam my foot down on the accelerator. They can't shoot at me – or at least they shouldn't shoot at me. I've got their boss in the car next to me.

I head directly towards the oncoming lights, now steering with my right hand. I'm not going to shoot until I'm right on top of them. If I try to change the magazine on the assault rifle, Soto will attack me. I'm already worried he'll go for me as soon as I put the gun out of the window. It has one fresh magazine in it. Will that be enough?

We're thundering towards them. I'm hoping to get in close, deliver a burst while we're on the move and then come back and do the same again, hoping they won't return fire. Headlights in front of me, suddenly swerving away. I stop, J-turning it, to see the lights of a car barrel-rolling one over the other. We've made one pass and already someone's flipped his SUV trying to get out of my way. The remaining two cars have stopped, men spilling out. I put my foot to the floor again and hammer towards them, rifle resting on the wing mirror, ready to shoot.

I see ground, black sky, ground, black sky; there's an incredible bang, a huge scraping. I see a face at the window and then it's gone. What's happened? Soto has just grabbed the wheel and turned it hard, flipping the car and ploughing it sideways into the ground.

Chapter 35

The car comes to rest on Soto's side, my side up. The windows have all blown out. There's a dead man staring at me from under the bonnet. We've run someone down. Our headlights reflect back off the ground, giving his face and the interior of the car a ghostly glow. Soto looks flat unconscious. A guy comes around the front of the car, peering in. I give him two from the assault rifle and he drops. There's shouting from outside. I click off the seat belt and stand up out of the window of the car, using Soto as a firing step, looking around me.

Three cars – all SUVs. We've rammed one and another's flipped. There are about six guys with AKs and pistols – no more than silhouettes – all to my front. I take the AKs first, three of them in quick succession. Then I drop back in behind the underside of the car, grab the pistol and crawl out through the shattered window, using the front of the car for cover.

Rounds shake the vehicle as I crawl around to the back. I use the night sight to pick off one of the guys with an AK, then another. I squeeze the trigger again. Nothing happens. Lost track of the number of rounds fired. Bad mistake.

Suddenly three of them are rushing me, firing wildly. But the guy at the front has a pistol, and he gets in the way of the two behind with AKs. Four shots go past me as he comes round blasting. But he doesn't know exactly where I am, and each one misses.

I take him out with the pistol, dead centre of the chest, and he goes down. The others dive to the other side of the car.

I hear them calling out to Soto, but he doesn't reply.

There's two of them left. It's then that I smell something from the other side of the car. Petrol. I take out the Zippo I got from the guy whose clothes I took, spark it up and throw it over the car, then jump backwards. It's as if the arc is in slow motion, a fireball going up into the sky before falling to earth again with devastating consequences.

There's a loud bang, screaming, shouting, a feeling of heat, and I emerge from behind the car to stick the remaining rounds of the pistol into the guys on the other side. Then I'm rushing for the front, dragging Soto clear.

The explosion wasn't as big as I'd hoped, but it provided enough of a distraction to allow me to come around and kill the men.

I pick up a pistol and tour the smashed-up cars. No one left alive. Some ugly sights too. Not good. Still, them or me.

I check Soto's pulse. He's alive. I put him in the

recovery position and try to right the car. No chance.

I take out the phone from the dashboard holder and start up the navigation app. These things are unbelievable to an old dog like me; they certainly would have saved a lot of bother back in the regiment. I'm near a place called Los Jugettes, which isn't too far from a place called Puerto Palomas – about forty kilometres. I look around me. One flipped car, one torched, one rammed. I've got a car, some weapons, sod me, even a can of drink and a tortilla wrap in the remaining SUV. Things are looking up if I can keep Soto alive. I call Maria. She answers.

'I'm here, with Soto. I've got him alive.'

'Where?'

'Can't say. Near a border town. I've got a car.'

'You can't come across. My intelligence says they're all looking for you.'

'Your boss too. He's corrupt.'

'Not exactly.'

'What do you mean?'

'Look, there are deals to be made. He made one and he made sure I got out. When you didn't have Soto and were a loose cannon, you were there to be traded. Now you have him, I'll see what I can do.'

'Don't go to him.'

'He's a good guy. As far as there are any good guys.'

'He nearly had me killed.'

'So he could save a few more. He gives you to Soto, Soto's got to give him something.'

'What?'

'I don't know. Not money. Names, addresses. Guys he wants.'

I find this incredible. I gulp down the water.

'He's incriminated by the evidence I found for you.'

'I'm sure he never did anything for personal gain.'

'He's still broken the law. I need to come in. Can you get me across?'

'No, but you can try yourself.'

'How?'

'The fence. There are holes. Find one, get through. Call me and we'll pick you up as quick as we can. I'll have a chopper down there.'

'That puts me in DEA jurisdiction, under your boss.'

'There's no other way.'

'Yes there is. I'll need your help with a car. After that I'll do it on my own.'

'You need US law enforcement on your side.'

'No I don't. And if you use anyone else now, make sure you can trust them.'

I call John at SOCA.

'Can you get me a list of Frontera cartel assets in the US?'

'What are you looking for?'

'A boat,' I say.

Chapter 36

Soto's groggy but he's not too badly hurt by the car crash. I find some jump leads in the back of the car and use them to tie him up. Then he goes in the boot – or what passes for a boot in these SUVs: under the parcel shelf, basically.

I've got an AK with five magazines and a bayonet, a Glock with three magazines, a pepper spray and – just as importantly – some soft drinks and a bite to eat. My teeth are agony but I don't let that stop me wolfing down the tortilla. I've also got the now empty assault rifle. I want someone to ID that. There's a fair bit of money in the narcos' wallets – dollars and pesos. There's also – as you'd expect – a good few bags of coke and other drug paraphernalia, along with a whole blister pack of Valium. I guess being a *sicario* isn't all that good for the nerves. I ditch most of the drugs but keep the Valium.

I drive towards the border. Have to be careful here – there's more surveillance on the US side than your average prison camp. However, there are ways of getting across.

It begins to get dark about eight miles from the border. I travel without turning the lights on. No point making it too easy for the patrols. I need to find a place where people are crossing. I know there are often scores of them out here, some using guides, some chancing it alone on hearsay, some just chancing it. Those that haven't got any money have to walk across the desert. Those who have – Ernesto told me – can take a cab almost to the border. Then they cross on foot while the cab – unbelievably – enters the States legally, saying it's going to pick someone up. It collects them the other side of the border and drives them to the town. It's a numbers game – people flood across and a percentage, sometimes a big percentage, get through.

I'm driving for quite a while before I catch movement on the horizon. Just a ripple against the sunset. I head towards it. Soon, I start to spot people. They're scared of the car, lying low as I pass, but some of them aren't very good at it, or are in barer areas, and I can see them.

I need to make contact. I can't get Soto across the border on my own. It's not going to be easy for a gringo, but there's no other way of doing this. I need some way of earning their trust. It doesn't arrive on day one, and I just sit in the desert, which, it being November, isn't too hot. I'm very hungry, but there were enough soft drinks in the car to keep me hydrated. Soto? I don't really care about him. As long as he's breathing, that's fine by me. I want him in a bad way, because then he's not going to be making a break for it. I don't sleep – that would be unwise.

As the sun sets again, I see people moving once more. I need to approach someone, but how?

I sit in the dark of the desert for a while, lights off, scanning with the night sight. Then I see a car approaching. It's going quickly and weaving drunkenly about the place.

Suddenly it stops.

I peer through the sights. Yup, two guys have found someone in the bush about half a mile away. It's dark enough, so I'm going to have to leave Soto. I don't like that, but it's the only way. I take out four of the Valium. Then I take the pistol and open the boot. Soto's wide-eyed. To his credit, he doesn't flinch or move away from the gun. He is a hard bastard, but I guess I knew that.

I put the pistol to his head, then I take the pills and shove them into his mouth. He can't swallow them, or won't. I go back to the front of the car and get the last of a can of warm Coke. I put that to his lips and force in the pills. He swallows them. I shut the boot.

I take the AK and limp forward across the bush, keeping low.

These guys aren't paying any attention to me. It's the normal pounding music and insults, waving weapons. In their headlights I can see they've got a family, or two couples – two men, two women – and they're basically bullying them, shoving them around, menacing them with weapons. They're so inattentive I can all but walk up behind the car. I fix the bayonet – no point making this a noisy job.

One of them has just got his trousers down and is gesturing to the women. The other is pointing a pistol at one of the men – a kid of around seventeen. I come out from behind their car and stick him with the bayonet.

Only the kid's cry of surprise alerts the wannabe rapist, and not soon enough. I close the distance quickly, and in three stabs he's down.

The people look like a family group – darker-skinned and smaller than most Mexicans I've seen.

'*Amigo*,' I say, '*amigo*,' gesturing to myself.

They look understandably terrified. I put down the gun.

'*Amigo. Necesito socorro*.' I need help.

They just stand there nonplussed.

'*Por favor. Venga conmigo*.' Please, come with me. Amazing how being in situations of terrible danger improves my Spanish. I take out some money in dollars. This makes their eyes light up. I pick up the gun and they follow me back to the car.

Thank God Soto's still there. They look even more nonplussed when they see how he's trussed up.

'*Señor no buen*,' I say, which I think is 'man not good'. I gesture for them to carry him. '*Frontera, no más. El* . . .' I've said 'as far as the border, no more', and I'm trying to make fence gestures, whatever a fence gesture looks like.

They nod, and the two blokes pick up Soto, one by his legs, the other by his body. He's bound too tightly and too messed up from the crash and being transported in a boot to offer much resistance. We carry him forward into the dark.

It's remarkable how many people are here. You think there's no one about and then the desert suddenly moves, like a huge bunch of commandos all crawling forward for the kill.

My two blokes haven't questioned me. I suppose they've seen I'm armed, I've got money and I've protected them. They're also fit as you like, clearly guys who are used to working on the land. All I care about is that they're tough, have their minds on the job and do as I ask.

We follow the mass of people. This is one of the few places on earth, I think, where you could be carrying a trussed-up hostage and no one would even raise an eyebrow. My guys are running well here, the women beside them. I wonder about them, where they've come from, how they're related. Then the fear comes back and I don't wonder anything.

We reach the fence, and I'm surprised. I've seen it before as a solid metal wall. Here it's a chain-link thing, endlessly cut and ragged at the bottom. In the distance a chopper patrols, its lights sweeping the floor, and I can see headlights on the highway in front of us.

Who are they? Border patrol, vigilantes? It's time to get rid of the AK.

We shove Soto under the fence. I am actually a bit concerned about him. He's lolling around like he's been slugged. I've some experience of Valium – I had to take it for a while to get to sleep after I got blown up in Iraq – and I thought four pills would be fine. Can't worry about that. Got to get going.

'*Más dinero?*' I ask the blokes with me. More money?

'*Sí.*'

'*El camino.*' The road.

We run forward through the desert. It's hard to pick how far away from us the road is. Beside us are about twenty other people, all spreading out.

We keep running and I can't believe these guys' endurance. Then a car peels away from the highway and its headlights come towards us. The guys and their women just split, going four separate directions into the desert, dropping Soto. I can't leave him, and I'm too messed up to carry him.

The car slowly approaches me. Nothing to do, I just wait.

Someone's shouting at me.

'Get on the floor, *el piso, el piso*!'

I do as I'm told, sitting straight down. Someone comes walking up to me. He's got a pistol out, levelled at me. It's got a torch attachment that's right in my eyes.

'You're going back where you came from, boy. Cory, call the cops in.'

The gun's lowered slightly. I see it's not a cop but a fat bastard in a camouflage jacket.

'I'm not Mexican, I'm English.'

'You ain't American, that's all I care about. What the fuck is that?'

'That's Alberto Soto, number two in the Frontera cartel.'

'Like fuck. You're just running wetbacks.' He crouches down, the gun pointing lazily at the ground.

'So why is he tied up?' I ask.

'I don't know, but . . .'

Suddenly I feel stupidly angry. These people are nothing but hillbilly vigilantes. I jump at him, taking the gun in a big sweep, knocking him backwards off his haunches and lying on top of him. I've got his gun, and now it's at his head. His two mates raise their weapons.

310

'Shoot me and you'll shoot him. Now you drop your guns and we'll all get out of here alive.'

There's a voice from behind the car. A man has shouted out in Spanish.

'You trapped us,' says one of the vigilantes. He's about seventeen, carrying a pump-action shotgun and an attempted moustache.

'Right. Now put your gun on the ground.'

They both do as they're told. From behind them the shape of one of my helpers appears. He takes up the guns.

'*Gracias*,' I say, stepping off fat boy, but keeping him under the gun.

'*Dinero*,' says the bloke. Money. I hadn't paid him, so he came back when he saw it was safe. Fair play.

The others come forward now, both women and the other guy.

'You're about to make a donation to the South American migrant protection fund,' I say to the vigilantes. 'Take off all your clothes.'

I make them strip, and the clothes are loaded into the back of the car.

It's a big pick-up – four seats and a covered back. We shove Soto into the back seat, putting him on the floor, and the two women and one of the blokes manage to pile on top of him. I have to make them realise they can't all travel in there. We'll stand out too much. It takes a bit of explaining, but eventually the bloke gets in the back, still counting the money in fat boy's wallet, while his mate sits up front next to me.

We drive out of the desert. I've now got a fair bit of cash, some mobile phones and more guns than I need – in fact more guns than I want. We've also got more snacks and drinks than you'd get at the average English wedding reception. Boy, these vigilante guys can eat. There are five packs of doughnuts, three big bottles of Coke, crisps, sandwiches. It's as if they've stocked up for a crack at the South Pole.

I stop quickly to get some shoes on. My feet are killing me, but there's a pair of cowboy boots that are two sizes too big – that's fine, though, because my feet are so swollen. We're about six miles from the road and make it quickly. This will become a marked car in about an hour. Never mind: by then I'll be a long way away.

We drive on through El Paso, where I let my passengers out. They seem pretty happy – they've got a fair bit of cash, some cigarettes, even some new clothes and a mobile phone. I gesture to it. '*Cuidadoso*.' Careful.

Then I'm out of El Paso, heading east on Highway 90. I've used the map on the phone to discover that Interstate 10 would be quickest, but I think I'll have less chance of getting nicked on a more minor road. I call John.

'How's it going?'

'OK,' I say. 'Do they own any boats in the US?'

'Can't find any.'

'Right, well I'm going to get one and I'm going to be leaving off the east coast of the US. Can you get the navy to pick me up?'

'What?'

'I'll have someone who is wanted in the UK on board. This is important; there must be a frigate or something about the place.'

'Do you think they'd do it?' he says.

'Of course, why not? If I can get him into international waters, we're laughing.'

'I'll try.'

I could just go to a marina and steal a boat. But that's fraught with difficulties. I have no idea what security is like at US marinas, and I'm hampered by having to take care of Soto. He's not in all that good a way and he needs care soon. Only one course of action.

I call Maria.

'I need a boat.'

'What sort of boat?'

'One I can safely steal so you can deny it.'

'Where are you headed?'

'Disneyland.'

'Where?'

'Florida.'

'Let me see what I can do.'

'Do not go through your boss under any circumstances.'

It's been about an hour now since I stole the car. I have to assume fat boy and friends have made the road. When the cops stop laughing, they'll put out an APB or whatever they use nowadays. No guarantee they'll find me, or even, given the human tide sweeping towards them over the border, care too much.

It's 1,400 miles to the east coast. I could go to the Texas coast, at 600 miles, but then I'd have to travel another thousand miles by sea across the Gulf of Mexico. You can't do sixty miles an hour in a ship. At this rate it'll take me a day exactly. I'll need to sleep, which might be possible if I drug Soto up. I could keep

313

going for a day, but that's a recipe for disaster. It's one thing running on foot and forgoing sleep. Do that on the highway and you could pass out.

There's a great chance of getting pulled – US highways are thick with cops. Still, it might not happen. You could drive all day in the UK in a stolen car and, despite CCTV and number-plate recognition, you'd be unlucky to be stopped by the police. Here, I don't know. I'll also have to stop for petrol at least twice. These pick-ups have bad fuel consumption. I have enough money for petrol, but I have the problem of Soto to contend with when I'm at the pump.

All it will take is for someone to look into the cab and they'll call the cops. I can't trust them and I can't trust the DEA. And that's presuming I can even find a gas station – it's midnight and the roads are deserted. I need to change cars.

It's also going to be tricky getting Soto on to the boat. My hands are in a bad way and it'll be immensely difficult – if not impossible – to get him aboard at the same time as stealing it.

Maria calls.

'Little Talbot Island State Park. There'll be a boat for you there and I've got authorisation for you to take it.'

'From who?'

'Don't worry about that. It's in everyone's interests for Soto to leave the country now.'

'Everyone?'

'Everyone but his. There isn't enough evidence to tie him to anything conclusively here.'

314

'OK, I . . .'

Oh dear. There's a flashing light in the mirror. I've picked up a cop.

'I think I'm about to be arrested,' I say.

'Who by?'

'The local police.'

'Don't stop for them. Soto will go back to Sheriff Macmillan and he'll find a reason to let him go.'

'So what do I do?'

'Where are you?'

'Just coming up to a turn for a place called Alpine.'

'Lose them and then call me.'

'OK.'

There's no way I can outrun a cop car in a pick-up, so I slow down. All around us the terrain is hilly, covered in scrubby little trees and dirt trails. I pull over next to a farm track. I want a way out if this goes wrong.

The cop pulls up behind me, and a giant voice booms out into the night from the car's loudspeaker.

'Put your hands on the steering wheel.'

I do as I'm bid. I don't really know what else to do here.

'Kill the engine and turn on the interior light.'

I do.

He comes out of his car. In the mirror I can see him walking towards me.

There's only one of him, thank God. He has his gun drawn. I have the pepper spray under my leg.

He comes up to the car, weapon pointed at me.

'Get out of the truck.'

I open the door. He's following procedure very well. I've had no opportunity at all to close on him.

Soto sits up in the back like Freddy Krueger at the window.

The cop sees him and trains his gun on him, and in the instant he's not looking at me, I hit him with the pepper spray. He goes down, loosing off shots. They spark off the road, hit the truck, go into the air, but nowhere near me. He falls on to his front, crawling on all fours.

I go straight for him, taking him in a stranglehold. Seven seconds and he's out. I cuff him and take his weapon and Taser. As he comes round, he goes into the boot of his car.

I leave his radio where it is and just swipe his food – half a lukewarm hamburger, but it'll do. There's also a spare pair of cuffs. No keys, but that's going to be Soto's problem, not mine. I cuff Soto, though I leave the cables on. The cuffs are just insurance really. As soon as he comes round properly, he'll be able to make a better effort at breaking free.

Then I'm in the truck again, driving off and obeying the speed limit. I guess that the cop probably radioed in that he'd pulled me over. Other cars will be on their way. If I meet one coming towards me, he won't be able to read my plates because of my headlights. He will, however, notice if I'm speeding. The longest I've got is about fifteen minutes, but I can't rely on that. It would be great to get fifteen miles away, but I don't have that luxury. One thing's for sure – the cops won't be using the back roads to get here. As soon as I can, I pull off down a minor road. After a while, farm tracks start appearing. I turn off the lights and drive up one. At the top of a ridge there's a big house – lights on. Can't go there.

I back down it again. The next lane, however, is quite a big tarmacked road, if full of potholes. It leads to a big building, all boarded up, and I quickly drive around the back of it. It's better than I expected. There's a large loading bay in the back, and I put the car in there. Now we won't be visible from the air, which is just as well, because in the far distance I can see a chopper's lights starting to quarter the ground.

I consider giving Soto some more Valium, but I want to preserve my supply for when I really need it. Besides, he's cuffed, gagged and physically in bad shape. He's not going anywhere. He's pissed himself quite badly in the back, which isn't pleasant to drive in, but there's not a lot I can do about that.

I call Maria.

'I need a car.'

'Where are you?'

I hit the sat nav app on the smartphone and give her the GPS readings.

'Don't send anyone you don't trust. And don't come yourself. You could be followed.'

'I got that. Stay safe.'

'I'll try.'

Soto's dozing again. I check his bonds. His hands aren't in a good way because I tied him tightly and they've been getting a restricted blood supply. I loosen the cables. There's no point overdoing it now. I'm crazed by exhaustion, my judgement is off and I suddenly feel very alone and very exposed sitting here and not moving. I fire up the engine and head off again, anywhere. I don't know where I'm going any more; I just have to keep moving. My vision is

317

blurring, and there's an irritating whirring and whooshing noise in my ears. Suddenly I'm weightless and we're up, up in the air, and then there's a crack and all is quiet.

Chapter 37

'Don't worry,' says a soft voice. 'I'm here to help you.'

'I wasn't followed. You need help.' I hear myself mumble.

I can hear a man's voice, then the woman's voice again. Maria?

Where am I? My eyes flicker open. For a moment I'm confused. I'm lying on a blanket in the dust – my SUV is on its side with its whole front end ground into the dirt, bent and warped. What the hell happened?

Maria is next to me.

'You're awake,' she says, smiling. 'Lucky we found you. I guess your body finally had enough eh?'

'I must have passed out.' I try to sit up, but instantly regret it as I collapse back down on to my back, my head thumping fit to split.

'Slow down, you've had a big bump.'

'Soto!'

'Don't worry, he's here, Miguel is with him.'

I look across just in time to see Miguel lifting Soto into the back of a car.

'Stolen?' I say.

'No. Borrowed.'

'Good.'

Maria wants to look at my wound, but we've no time for that. No matter how bad it is, the course of action's the same – get out of here. Instead she satisfies herself with helping me up and into the car.

As the Toyota labours down the farm track, I knock back a couple of ibuprofen to try to do something about the top-class headache I've got, but I'm not too hopeful. I need a doctor soon. At the moment the running tally is four broken teeth, a furrow in the middle of my forehead, a broken right hand and a snapped little finger on my left hand.

There's no way I can travel in the front of the car looking like I do. There are wet wipes, but it's a bit like trying to get rid of an oil spill using a J Cloth.

'You need to go to hospital,' says Maria.

'No, don't bother. Let's get to the boat.'

There's a blanket on the back seat and it's good to just kip for a bit. As I lie down, it's as if my whole body is shaking. In minutes I'm fast asleep. When I wake, we're still driving, but it's Maria at the wheel.

'How long have I been out?'

'Eight hours.'

'How many to go?'

'Another sixteen maybe.'

This is good, though. We have three drivers and can be confident. Fuelling isn't easy, but we use automated stations where we can, come in with music blaring and park at the far end of the pumps, get in, get out. Soto makes no noise anyway. Periodic checks on him show he's not dead.

One question comes into my mind. How is Soto still unconscious? 'What did you say to make him take the pills?'

Miguel says nothing for a while. Then: 'They hit my mother's addiction centre.'

'Is she all right?'

'Everyone dead,' says Miguel.

'Ernesto?'

'Him too.'

'I'm sorry to hear that,' I say. Not much more you can add there really. This is a brutal war – and war is the right word.

America rolls by – a big country. We survive on stuff eaten from 7/11s, which suits me, as I'm not much of a fine-dining man even when I have got all my teeth.

I bang down a cocktail of painkillers and I'm almost tempted to neck the Valium for an extra kip. Can't do it, though. I need to be awake if anything kicks off.

On the way I have my first real chance to talk to Maria in a while. It seems the information I got from Soto's laptop has disappeared into a black hole. It was kicked upstairs to the bosses and nothing's been heard since. Mystery Man's doing? 'His name's Bryant,' says Maria, 'and yeah, maybe. Maybe politics I don't know about.'

'By politics, do you mean corruption?'

'Isn't that what people normally mean by politics?'

There's still nothing to incriminate Soto in the US – only suspicions. It turns out that I'm more of a wanted man than he is for all that I've done since I've been down here. They also fill me in on Liana. She's been granted temporary asylum in the US and is recovering from her ordeal in the mine – slowly.

Miguel came along because Maria thought we might need an extra pair of hands to handle Soto. She's right. You don't tend to dwell on your injuries when it's all kicking off around you. Now that I've got ten minutes to spare, I can see my right hand is going to need some major work. My head, which still hurts like hell despite the fact that I've swallowed my own weight in painkillers, will need something doing to it too.

Every time we change driver – a job I'm yet to do – Maria looks at my forehead. She purses her lips and shakes her head, but seems to find it mildly funny too.

'What's the joke?'

'I don't know what I see in you,' she says, 'but it sure ain't your looks.'

She gives me a hug. I can't tell you how good that feels. It makes a change to have someone touch me who isn't trying to strangle me or stab me.

The road winds on, night into day, the endless American freeway, the Texan scrub giving way to Florida greenery – the towns all looking the same to me as I drift in and out of sleep. We go past Houston, New Orleans, Tallahassee, through forests, past lakes. The countryside's stunning, the towns and villages almost as beautiful. As I hover between waking and sleeping, my body seems to be reliving all the violence of the past few weeks. I jolt awake to what I think is gunfire, only to find that I've imagined it. I see burned faces, bodies. At one point I imagine that the whole car is filling up with blood; another time that we're like a submarine in a sea of blood, drowned faces looming at the windows. Then I wake up to pain, pills, another little town or empty expanse of country.

Alabama is incredible – in its scenery at least. Palm trees start to appear; we go over an enormous bridge spanning the ocean, with another running beside it. It's beautiful and terrifying in equal measure.

These thoughts are bad signs I've learned to recognise. I'm on the edge, not good. It's like I think my luck's about to run out. Still, could be worse, I could be Soto. I've heard nothing from him for a while, but he's alive. We stop to check when we get a quiet minute, and slip another couple of Valium between his damp lips. Doesn't look so tough now.

Then we're into Florida, going through forests of what looks like pine, but I guess can't be. I fall asleep again, and then it's night. We're at a petrol station.

I don't get out. We've been turning off the interstate every time I want a leak and finding somewhere quiet. I can't get out in the state I'm in, it would attract too much attention.

'A hundred kilometres to destination,' says Maria as we pull out.

'Good. And your contact has this boat, for sure?'

'Yeah. I called in a favour.'

'From who?'

'Our friend in ultramax.'

'Does the DEA regularly use drug dealers as an alternative source of funding?'

'Can't see nothin' wrong with it,' says Maria.

I suppose she's got a point, but I think it's a bit murkier than the British police would be comfortable with.

'Is the boat equipped with food?'

'Yes. And water. Three good big tanks.'

We hit Jacksonville and I take no notice of it, just concentrating on planning an RV if things go wrong. It has to be on the coast too. I pick somewhere called the American Beach – not too far away.

We head up north-east by night and arrive at the park. There's a ticket office there but no one at it, so we drive straight on through. Maria uses her phone to find the exact location. We go down a tarmac road and turn off up a dirt track between scrubby sand dunes. And there on a wonderful white sand beach is the boat, anchored about fifty metres out in the water. A rowboat is pulled up on the shore. The yacht's a decent size – forty-plus feet, a sloop. Not a bad little boat at all. It's much bigger and more luxurious than the yacht I work down in Southampton – about £100,000 worth of boat. Weirdly, I find myself getting excited. I don't usually get too worked up about possessions, which is just as well, as I haven't got any, but I get the same feeling when I see a boat like that that a lot of blokes get when they see a Ferrari. I have another feeling, though. Other than the headlights, it's pitch black. There were big storm clouds around at sunset. I'm going to be going out into unknown waters in uncertain weather. Can't be helped. Got to be done.

We pull up in the dunes and I get out. Even though I guess it must still be November, the night isn't cold, though there's a fair offshore breeze. I look all around me using the night sight. Nothing about the place looks suspicious. Everything's quiet.

I take Miguel's mobile and walk down on to the

beach. I feel so dirty, I just want to jump into the sea and swim for the yacht. In my state, though, I may as well issue every shark within ten miles with a personal invitation to a banquet.

Miguel walks past me carrying Soto with surprising ease, and dumps him in the rowboat. Maria is suddenly beside me, her hand in mine, and I know it's time to go. I turn, but her arms are round me and we embrace, and then I'm in the boat and pulling hard for the yacht. Each stroke is agony – my hands, my ribs just don't want to let me row. I have to, though.

When I reach the yacht, I tie up and climb aboard, leaving Soto in the rowboat. I use the torch to look around. Nothing suspicious, but I'm taking no chances. I check out the cabin – looking at the fridge, the doors, the head even, for signs of a booby trap or bomb.

It takes me about an hour, and I get a nervous call from Maria. I tell her it's OK, I'm just being careful. There's a pause, and I promise to call her with my progress. It's only then that I haul Soto aboard, stow him down below and finally slip out into the open sea – free of Mexico, free of the United States, free of Andy's memory, free of everything and homeward bound.

Chapter 38

Eight months down the road, my teeth are mended, my hands are reset and healing and they've even made a fair job of fixing the wound on my forehead – though I still have to put up with John calling me 'Harry Potter' and 'the boy wizard' every time we meet for a drink. We were picked up by HMS *Diamond*, who have a first-class medical facility on board, and they patched me up very well.

Soto, it turns out, was not old school. He sang like Maria Callas as soon as he got back to the UK – giving up the passwords on all the information I'd downloaded when at his house. It sent a few people down, both sides of the border, and helped prove Maria's case.

It also pointed in a very interesting direction. The arms he was getting were supplied by the UK conglomerate Bulwark – headed up by my old mate Sir John Carlyle, who I crossed swords with in Afghanistan.

Turns out the UK gangs and the attack on my mate Andy was because Soto needed to open an entirely new source of income to fund a hugely ambitious project, and the UK, with its enormous appetite for drugs and relatively unorganised groups of criminals, was seen as ripe for a takeover.

Bulwark would fly arms out from their UK factories on executive jets. Drugs would come the other way. As usual, Sir John would never be touched by this; if it ever came out, it would be put down to the work of corrupt flight crew or ground crew. Anyone but him would take the blame.

But this wasn't the extent of their ambition.

Bulwark were going to arm Soto's boys with top-grade military weapons. Furthermore, they were going to supply a breakaway faction of the army. They were looking to take over a country – or a large part of it. They would then run contracts for everything in Mexico – arms, hospitals, bridges, mines, you name it. The drugs part of the business would be handled by Soto in complete safety, in return for selling the government of his country to a multinational company.

Of course, Bulwark pulled their normal defence – this was the work of a rogue cell of managers, the guilty parties should be brought to justice. But questions were asked and a public inquiry into the firm's affairs will launch next year.

I never did call Maria. I guess you could call it a holiday romance, but without the holiday or indeed any significant romance.

So here I am. I've got no woman, no job now, as my sailing boat business sort of wound itself up while I was away, and nowhere to live.

But I have got something. It's a letter from a

solicitor who's been engaged by someone he can't name at the DEA to establish ownership of the yacht. It seems that, as it was taken in international waters and no one has claimed it, they have a problem – and you can't just leave yachts lying around.

However, he tells me that if I would care to call him and put a claim on the yacht, then I might get it just because no one else has. It's currently in the naval dockyard in Portsmouth.

I think that's one call I am going to make.

Devil to Pay

Ross Kemp

**Nick Kane is a man with nothing to lose,
and everything to prove.**

A model soldier fighting for queen and country, it seemed nothing could stop him becoming one of the very top officers. But that was then.

And this is now.

Injured in a bomb blast on reconnaissance in Iraq he's forced out of the army and into the quiet life. But after a year in civvies rebuilding his life and his relationship with his family, things for Nick are looking up. That is until he finds out that his old army buddy Ben is dead.

Word is that he took his own life, but Nick knows that Ben had everything to live for, and when he starts to question the circumstances of his friend's death, he discovers that there are people who will stop at nothing to cover up the terrifying truth.

Explosive and gripping, *Devil to pay* is the electrifying new action thriller from bestselling author Ross Kemp.

arrow books